# A WOMAN'S TOUCH

# BERNADETTE CARR

LOVE SPELL BOOKS  NEW YORK CITY

LOVE SPELL®

May 1998

Published by

Dorchester Publishing Co., Inc.
276 Fifth Avenue
New York, NY 10001

ISBN 0-505-52261-6

The name "Love Spell" and its logo are trademarks of Dorchester Publishing Co., Inc.

Printed in the United States of America.

## DEDICATED WITH LOVE

*To my husband, Brian, my most vocal supporter. Yes, you are the inspiration for all the love scenes.*

*To my daughter, Tori, who I consider perfect though I may be prejudiced by a mother's love and pride.*

*And to my best friend, Sharry, who wouldn't let me quit and who offered immeasurable encouragement.*

*Thank you all for being there for me.*

# A Woman's Touch

# Chapter One

*Montana, 1896*

Matthew Ward reined his sorrel to a halt near the log railing of the corral and looked out across the rolling acres of the ranch toward the looming mountain range in the west. A patchwork of shadows from the billowing cumulous clouds moved over the untamed landscape, but his brother, Travis, was nowhere in sight.

The saddle leather creaked as he gripped the saddle horn, swung his leg over the horse's rump and lowered himself to the ground. As he looped the horse's reins around the top rail of the corral fence, he patted Red's neck and rubbed the animal's velvety nose.

"Extra oats tonight," Matt promised, though Red always got extra oats. The animal regarded Matt with trusting brown eyes.

# BERNADETTE CARR

A few chickens scratched over by the barn, but otherwise the place had an unexpected air of desertion. Peter usually came running, and in the past month, Matt had grown accustomed to his young stepbrother's presence. Today, he'd even made an effort to get back early on account of the boy's birthday.

As he crossed the yard to the well, the April breeze lifted curls of dust from around his boots and swirled them across the hard-packed ground. The annoying squeak of the windlass was the only sound in the quiet barnyard. Matt frowned at the unsplit wood still piled by the chopping block, evidence that Peter had neglected his chores.

As he carried water to the horse trough, Matt contemplated the issue of raising his half brother. What had his stepmother, Grace, been thinking when she had sent Peter from back East? Discipline, responsibility. Those were the words she'd used in her letter. Well, Matt didn't profess to know anything about teaching a twelve-year-old discipline or responsibility. He had liked things just as they were, himself and Travis running the ranch, working the cattle, trading off on the cooking duties and getting by with the odd trip to town.

While Red lowered his head to drink, Matt pushed up the brim of the gray felt cowboy hat that shaded his eyes. Things always changed just when you got used to them. Just when running the ranch had become second nature, he'd found himself saddled with a half-grown kid who had yet to learn responsibility. Zach, his father, would never have let either him or Travis get away with not chopping the wood.

Finished drinking, Red got Matt's attention with a gentle nudge of his nose.

"Yeah, okay, boy," Matt said, pulling his attention

back to the moment at hand and leading the horse to the barn.

Light from the loft window slanted down through the cracks in the boards overhead, illuminating the barn's interior in dusty yellow strips. The aroma of fresh hay greeted him. At least the kid had remembered to clean out the stalls.

"Peter?" Matt called up into the hayloft, but there was no answer. He unsaddled Red, made sure he had fresh feed and his oats and rubbed him down before eventually heading up to the house.

The heels of his boots thudded on the plank steps of the veranda, echoing hollowly as he crossed the narrow stoop. At the door, he paused to remove his hat. He slapped it against his thigh to rid it of the day's dust before stepping inside the log ranch house.

Matt hung his hat on one of the pegs beside the door and ran a hand through his hair, combing the thick chestnut waves with his fingers. Pulling his gloves from his back pocket, he dropped them onto the bench underneath the hat pegs. As he crossed to the kitchen, each step stirred a puff of dust from the wood floor.

Washing up by the back door, Matt thought he heard Butch barking beyond the square garden plot, down by the creek. The budding tree branches and the incline prevented him from seeing the dog or Peter, who was probably with him.

Stopping in front of the stove, Matt cursed softly under his breath as he realized the wood bin was completely empty. No use in calling Peter; the stream was too far away. Might as well save his breath. It was just as easy to chop the wood himself. He crossed the living room, slapped his hat back on his head, grabbed his gloves and went outside.

# BERNADETTE CARR

Matt had chopped a substantial pile of wood, enough for both the night's cooking and the evening fire, when Butch bounded into the yard. Barking, the wet collie leapt around Matt, his plumed tail slapping Matt's legs, his patchy black and tan fur leaving muddy streaks on the dusty denim. Matt ran a hand over the thick fur on Butch's head and scratched behind the dog's ears before Butch was off again, galloping across the yard, scattering chickens in a frantic race toward the back meadow where Matt could make out the red of Peter's plaid shirt.

Matt scooped up an armful of wood and carried it inside. As he came back out, Peter sprinted into the yard with a fishing pole over one shoulder and a string of trout banging against his leg. The floppy brim of one of Matt's old hats shaded the boy's freckled face.

As he spotted the pile of wood, Peter grimaced slightly and looked guiltily at Matt before quickly filling his free arm with wood and hurrying to the house. Matt knew he should have scolded him, but he couldn't manage to be angry. He'd been young once, too, though it seemed more years ago than he cared to remember.

Discipline. Grace's word rose from the back of his mind. Tomorrow, he thought. He just didn't have the inclination right now to worry about such things. He picked up another armful of wood, and almost bumped into Peter as the boy raced back out through the front door.

"I'll get the rest, Matt," he said breathlessly. "Sorry I forgot." He rushed past him and down the steps, pulling off his hat as he went, using it to tease the dog. The sun glinted on his tousled blond curls, a feature inherited from Grace. Matt's and Travis's mother, Kathleen, had died in childbirth on the wagon train to Montana when Matt was only six. Matt had his mother's auburn hair and her dark eyes, while Travis resembled Zach, stouter, more solidly built, with straight golden brown hair and pale blue eyes.

When Matt was eleven, his father had married Grace. Six years after the marriage, Grace's first pregnancy and her poor health had forced her to return East. Matt wondered if she knew, when she boarded the train in the fall of 1883, that she would never again return to Montana or see her husband. Caught in a blizzard, Zach had died the following winter.

Now, Grace had sent Peter to the ranch, where, as she had written, she hoped the ruggedness of the countryside would lend maturity to a growing boy. Matt suspected that it was Grace's failing health that had compelled her to send the boy back to the ranch. Secretly, he dreaded receiving news from Boston. How was he, a plain down-to-earth rancher, to console Peter if Grace passed on?

Butch's toenails clicked across the floor, and wood clattered as Peter dumped another armful into the bin in the kitchen. Matt forced his thoughts back to the present. Though Peter had neglected his chores, at least the boy had spared Matt the decision of what to make for supper. He set Peter to cleaning the fish while he lit the stove and sliced potatoes into a heavy cast-iron skillet.

Twenty minutes later, as the fish began to sizzle golden brown in the pan, footsteps on the porch caught Matt's attention. Travis, finally. Matt heard his brother shake the dust from his hat before the door swung open.

"I could eat a horse," Travis declared as he hung up his hat and coat and pushed a lock of ginger hair off his forehead. He crossed the room and peered into the frying pan.

"Well, lucky for us, Peter caught some trout instead," Matt said.

Travis grinned and tousled Peter's hair on his way to the washbasin, while Peter set battered enamel dishes on the stained surface of the wooden table. Bent forks followed from a drawer in the homemade china cabinet. Peter's fingers left prints on the dusty countertop.

Matt flipped the fish fillets. "How are the fence lines? Corbey's sheep haven't run through them again, have they?"

"No," Travis said as he finished washing up and wandered over to pluck a potato slice from the pan. Popping it into his mouth, he spoke around the hot chunk of food. "They're still in one piece." He licked the butter from his fingers. "Did you get that north line mended?"

Matt nodded. "Lost a calf, though." He glanced sideways at Peter, who had taken a seat. Did the boy think they'd forgotten that today was his birthday? Neither of the brothers had mentioned it this morning before they rode out. "Mountain lion, I think," Matt continued, turning back to Travis, but the jerk of Peter's head told him that he'd gotten the boy's attention.

"You sure?" Travis asked, his brows drawing together in concern.

Matt nodded. "Saw a couple of prints. Looks like a big one."

"Do you think we'll have to go after him?"

"Let's leave him be for a while. As long as the cattle stay together, the cat shouldn't cause us too many problems. That calf must have strayed through the fence break. I think it's the sheep ranchers who have cause to be concerned. Next time I see Corbey, I'll let him know about it."

He set the blackened frying pan on the table and divided the potatoes and fish onto all their plates as Travis settled into a chair.

"Going to have to start thinking about branding pretty soon," Matt said as he sat down. He reached for a cold, slightly charred biscuit, split it and slathered both halves with butter using the handle of his fork.

"I could get you a knife," Peter volunteered as he frowned at the way Matt applied the butter.

"No need," Matt said as he finished with the biscuit and licked the fork handle clean before spinning the utensil around and stabbing up a piece of fish.

"Going to have to bring that last herd in from the north pasture before we can brand," Travis added.

"I'll have to go over and see if I can get George Thompson's crew for the branding. Say three weeks from now?" Matt bit down on a slice of potato. Half-cooked, it crunched between his teeth. Undeterred, he stabbed up another forkful.

When Peter turned his attention to his own plate, Matt raised questioning brows at Travis, who grinned and nodded, affirming that he had indeed gotten Peter's present.

Matt finished eating before pushing his plate away and leaning back in his chair. The subsequent squeak, as the chair tipped on its back legs, drew a startled look from Peter.

Dropping the chair back down, Matt dumped the last biscuit out of the pail and reached into his pocket for the candle stub he had tucked there earlier. "I almost forgot," he said as he pushed the candle into the biscuit's crust. "Today's your birthday, isn't it?"

Peter's face lit up. A wide smile deepened the dimples in his cheeks and lent a sparkle to his blue eyes.

Shoving his chair back, Travis went to get a match and the small package wrapped in brown paper and hidden on top of the wall-mounted match container. "It probably ain't like all those fancy gifts you'd have got back in Boston," he said as he handed Peter the parcel.

Peter ducked his head as he fumbled with the string. The paper fell away.

"This is great," he said with enthusiasm as he turned the ivory-handled pocketknife over in his hand. He opened the blade and tested the sharpness with the pad of his thumb. "Thanks." He gave each of them an appreciative smile as he ran his fingers over the smooth handle.

"Well, make a wish and let's eat the cake," Matt said with a smile. He leaned back knowing there was yet another gift. Travis struck the match upon the table surface and, when it flared to life, lit the candle.

Peter stared into the flame for an instant. "What I really wish is that my mother could be here," he said solemnly. Sadness flickered for an instant in his eyes. "But since that isn't going to happen, I'll wish for something that we all need." Matt noted the way the boy looked at the top of the counter and the scarred tabletop and finally the legs of Matt's tilted chair. "I wish we had a woman to look after us."

Matt's chair legs hit the floor with a bang. "Cripes! A woman! That's the last thing we need!"

Peter raised his brows over eyes that suddenly seemed too wise for a twelve-year-old. "We need someone who can cook and clean and sew." He looked pointedly at the piece of twine that was strung through the top buttonhole of Matt's shirt.

"You let a woman in here and the next thing you

know, you have to take your boots off to come into your own home," Matt protested. "Women are more trouble than they're worth." He crossed his arms firmly over his chest.

Peter stared down at his plate. "I don't care," he said quietly. "I miss having one around."

"Are you going to divide up that biscuit or do I have to?" Travis said, interrupting in an obvious attempt to change the subject.

As Peter reached for the biscuit, he blinked quickly, but not before Matt saw the telltale sheen of moisture in his eyes. Matt cursed himself silently. He should have kept his big mouth shut. The poor kid must be missing Grace something awful. At this age birthdays were special, and this was the first one the kid had spent without his mother. Matt let out a sigh.

"Sorry, Pete," he said as he reached across the table and patted the boy on the shoulder. "It's your birthday. I guess you can wish for a woman if you want." Matt eyed the piece of biscuit that Peter broke off and handed him. "Do we have any of Mrs. Willoughby's peach preserves left?"

Peter shook his head. "No, I think we finished them last week."

Matt frowned. "I've got a powerful hankering for something sweet to put on this birthday cake. Are you sure they're gone?"

"Pretty sure."

"Well, go out and check, will you?" Matt suggested.

The root cellar entrance was in back of the house. Peter rose and went out the door. As soon as the door slammed shut behind him, Matt and Travis leapt to their feet and followed.

Peter stood completely still, staring at the pinto that, despite being hampered by its reins, which were wrapped around a shrub at the corner of the house, was trying to reach a tuft of grass at the side of the back steps. Standing in the open doorway, Matt grinned at Travis and nudged him with an elbow. "You'd think the boy never saw a horse before," he whispered, speaking just loudly enough for Peter to hear him.

Peter didn't turn around at the sound of Matt's voice. It seemed he couldn't tear his eyes from the animal. "What's he doing here?"

"Well, I think it's somebody's birthday," Matt said quietly.

Peter spun around, his pale blue eyes wide with hope. "You mean . . . ? Is he . . . ?" he stammered. "It's my birthday," he finally stuttered.

"It sure is," Matt agreed.

"He's really mine?" Peter reached out to stroke the smooth brown patch on the animal's neck. The horse's skin twitched beneath his fingers.

Travis crossed the porch, pulled the reins loose and handed them to the boy. "Better try him out and see if you like him," he suggested.

Peter didn't give them a chance to say anything else. Quick as a jackrabbit, he was in the saddle and urging the horse into a gallop with a poke of his heels.

"Don't run him too hard, and rub him down when you get back," Matt yelled after Peter as he thundered out of the yard.

"You sure he's old enough to help with the roundup?" Travis asked as they went back into the house.

"He's got to grow up sometime." Matt gathered the plates from the table and stacked them in the basin. The fingerprints on the counter suddenly annoyed him. He swiped them away with his hand. A woman! What a thing for a twelve-year-old to wish for. The boy wouldn't know trouble if it jumped up and bit him.

While Travis got a fire going in the hearth, Matt settled down on the couch. "Humph. Can you believe that? A twelve-year-old wishing for a woman."

"Now I could understand if it was *my* birthday," Travis said as he grinned at Matt. "It's only three months away. Do you think I'd get a woman if I wished for one?"

"No. And Pete isn't going to get one either."

"From the look on his face, I think the sight of that pinto drove any thought of a female out of his head."

"I hope so." Matt ran a hand over his stubbly chin.

"Quite a birthday present, his own horse," Travis mused.

"He needed a mount and we could use the help," Matt said firmly.

Travis snorted. "He could have rode ol' Blue and you know it. I swear, you're as bad as Grace, spoilin' the kid."

*Wanuskewin Heritage Park, Central Canada, 1996*

Courtney James returned to the park building after getting the last of the senior citizens settled on the bus and finally agreeing to accept Bill and Eileen's dinner invitation. She found it impossible to refuse with Bill hinting at how disappointed they would be if she didn't come. For some reason, she never seemed to be able to say no to them. Perhaps it was because the people at the seniors' home had become a surrogate family of sorts after her grandmother passed away. Whatever the reason, she'd promised that she would stop by later, as soon as she had finished setting up a few games on the used computer that had been donated to the children's ward of St. Peter's Hospital. But now, while the seniors were headed home, she intended to explore the park trails before returning to the city.

She moved quickly through the exhibit building, past buffalo replicas and statues of Native Americans. She stopped for a moment at the glass wall that backed the structure, and stared out across the flat prairies, letting her eyes trace the broad valley carved by the North Saskatchewan River, above which the Heritage Center was perched.

Absently, she began to twist a strand of her long, ebony hair, a characteristic, besides her five-foot-nine height, that she had inherited from her grandmother's Cree ancestors. From her French ancestors came her pale complexion and the hint of curls that softened her thick, black tresses. From the glass windowpane, her reflection looked back at her. Stormy gray eyes the blue-silver of polished steel contrasted with the dark color of her hair.

She sighed. She could fix computers, debug programs and analyze long strings of binary code, but she couldn't seem to find a way to eradicate her deep sense of solitude. Despite surrounding herself with people in her volunteer work and at her job, Courtney always felt that she stood just a bit apart, that she was different, out of place. All of her life she had struggled to feel that she belonged somewhere, that she was making a difference in someone's life.

A flicker of movement to Courtney's right drew her attention. A costumed Indian approached on silent moccasin-clad feet. Age had chiseled deep wrinkles in his dark skin, but he moved easily despite his apparent years. A full-feathered headdress covered the majority of his white hair and flowed down the back of his beaded rawhide outfit. He wore a knee-length fringed tunic, laced at the neck, and rawhide pants that tucked into fur-trimmed moccasins. Around his waist, an intricately beaded leather bag hung from a strip of rawhide. A small woven pouch dangled from another strip around his neck.

Courtney assumed he was a member of one of the groups that reenacted authentic dances and customs at the park, or perhaps one of the interpretive staff hired to assist visitors.

"You have come to seek the past," the Indian stated as he stopped beside her. "Come, I will show you the way." Before Courtney could protest, he moved toward the doors that led to the walking trails and beckoned for her to follow.

Courtney hurried after him. "I really don't need a guide."

He turned back with a surprised look on his face. "I must show you the way," he insisted quietly, "or they will send me back now."

Courtney looked around for "they," but the building was deserted, unnaturally silent, as if awaiting her reply. It obviously meant a lot to this old man, and she had no desire to be the cause of his unhappiness. She could humor him for now, she supposed.

"You will come?" he asked as he held open the door for her.

Stepping outside, Courtney halted at the edge of the concrete patio. A cool April breeze swept up the valley sides and caught the heavy strands of her hair, lifting it in a dance that sent it swirling around her face. Capturing the errant locks in her fingers, she looked across the valley to where snow still lined the riverbanks and chunks of ice bobbed atop the blue-gray water.

"See the ice? It is a sign of encouragement."

Courtney started at the Indian's unexpected closeness. Regaining her composure, she looked to where he pointed. In a crook in the river, a single block of ice defied nature and flowed upstream against the water's relentless current.

"Not all things are meant to follow the natural progression of life. Not all life circles go such," the costumed Indian said, motioning clockwise.

The circle of life. Courtney had heard her grandmother speak of such things. The native peoples' beliefs stressed the importance of the circle, especially relating to life, from birth to adolescence to maturity to old age, before returning to the earth, which brought forth a new birth.

"Sometimes the spirit is lost," the guide said as he turned and looked into her eyes. "You must rediscover your spirit to find peace." His dark pupils were like bottomless black pits.

Her spirit lost? He'd hit too close to home. That was exactly how she felt. "Are you a volunteer here?" she asked, hoping he wouldn't recognize her subtle attempt to change the direction of the conversation.

He smiled, a stretching of the lips that turned up the corners of his wrinkled mouth but did not expose his teeth. "I am a shaman. I have been sent to show you the way."

He seemed a little eccentric, but not the least bit threatening. Courtney reminded herself again about the park's interpretive program. Heritage Park wasn't a commercial exhibition with outlandish rides and loud spoon-fed excitement, but a gentle test of the imagination where nature called the senses to relive history.

"You may call me Opimihaw."

"Opimihaw," she repeated, liking the feel of the word on her tongue.

"One who flies," he translated as she followed him to the head of the walking trails. The eastern path wound past the university's archaeological dig sites, but the shaman turned to the west, where Courtney had intended to go. With several of the senior citizens confined to wheelchairs, the group had been unable to explore this far, but Courtney's curiosity had been piqued by the mention of a mystical medicine wheel. She wanted to see it before she returned to the city. But the shaman could not have known that. Nevertheless, he led her down the appropriate path, through stands of bare-branched poplars and whispering chokecherry trees, to the valley floor and the buffalo jump at the base of the hill.

He paused, and with a sweep of his arm that encompassed the entire clearing, began what Courtney presumed must be the standard narration. "Speak and the trees will hear you. Whisper and the winds will carry your voice to the heavens. Shout and the very rocks will tremble and echo your words to the caverns of the earth. This is sacred ground. The white man speaks of great Egyptian pyramids, but before those pyramids existed our people gathered here. For twelve thousand years, this valley has echoed with the voices of the People and those of our brothers, the buffalo. Look to the cliff." He motioned through the trees to the slope rising above them. "That is the buffalo jump. Close your eyes and hear the thunder of hooves. Feel the ground tremble. Smell the dust and the trampled grass. Know that the People's spirits are strong in this place."

Respectful of the reverence in his tone, Courtney complied. In the hushed silence, with her eyes closed, she *could* almost imagine the thunder of the stampede, feel the ground reverberating with the pounding of driving hooves, smell the dust-thickened air. She could imagine the shrill cries of the braves as they drove the buffalo toward the cliff edge. Her heartbeat quickened. The echo of her pulse pounded loudly in her ears. Any second now the great beasts would tumble over the precipice, crashing and falling down the steep incline. Discomfited by the sensations induced by her imagination, Courtney quickly opened her eyes.

The shaman lifted his face to the sky and whispered, with closed eyes, *"Mi taku ya pi owasin."*

Courtney's heart quickened at the eerie stillness that compacted the air around her. The words didn't sound like her grandmother's native language. "Is that Cree?" she asked, breaking the strange silence.

The man lowered his head. "No, it is the traditional greeting of the Dakota people. Many tribes came here: the Cree, the Dakota, the Assiniboin and others. It was a great gathering place, a tree with many different nests."

He shivered visibly, though Courtney could detect no change in the temperature. "Come, we must begin the smudge," he said.

Courtney's steps crunched on the gravel path, but his were silent as he led her up the incline. The medicine wheel was on the hill's crest. According to the park brochure, its significance had been lost over the years, but the Indians still revered it, crediting it with special powers.

Despite a sign asking that visitors stay on the path, the shaman crossed the open ground, his steps silent in the flattened mat of post-winter vegetation that was just beginning to sprout with spring growth. As he stopped in the middle of a ring of smooth white stones barely visible amidst the scattered lavender blooms of crocuses, he looked expectantly at Courtney.

"Shouldn't we keep on the path?" she asked. "The sign says to keep on the path."

"Sign?"

She motioned toward the wooden placard, only to find it gone. She blinked twice, but no sign appeared. "It was just there," she muttered, frowning at the vacant spot beside the path.

"This land has survived for thousands of years. Another set of footprints will not be harmful," her guide assured her.

Perhaps she'd seen the sign in another place on the trail and had confused the location in her mind. One last glance confirmed that no sign existed where she thought it had been. Hesitantly, she picked her way through the grass until she stood beside the Indian and the patterned circle of stones.

"We must cleanse our bodies and spirits of all negative energy," the shaman informed her. He sat down cross-legged by a scraped-out fire pit that Courtney had not noticed before. "Sit," he ordered, patting the grass beside him.

From the leather bag at his waist, the Indian withdrew a bound stalk of grayish-green leaves. The musky aroma of the plant wafted to her. Courtney breathed deeply as she lowered herself to the ground. "Sage?"

He nodded as he spread the fragrant herb in the dirt recess of the pit. A braided stalk of what appeared to be grass followed from the depths of the pouch.

"Sweetgrass," he said reverently as he laid it beside him.

"Really?" Courtney leaned forward and studied the almost hairlike braid. Prairie sweetgrass was practically extinct, what with the expanding numbers of tilled and cattle-grazed acres. She remembered a newspaper article about an Indian group trying to save some of the last of the natural grass fields.

"First we will cleanse with the sage," Opimihaw was saying. "Then we will send our prayers to the skies, borne on the smoke of the sweetgrass."

Courtney had not expected such an extensive interpretive tour. She would have to remember to recommend Heritage Park to her friends when she got back to the city. She tucked a stray lock of hair behind her ear and intently watched the old man's actions.

As the shaman bent over the pit, there was a snap of combustion, a flicker of reddish flame and then a puff of heady smoke. He cupped his hands around the blue-gray cloud and swept it toward him, running his hands over his face and back over the headdress and his white hair. He repeated the procedure as he issued instructions to her. "This is the smudging ceremony. Wash away the bad spirits and negative thoughts with the smoke of the sage."

Feeling a bit self-conscious, but unwilling to refuse since he had apparently gone to such great lengths to reenact this ceremony, Courtney reached, cupped her hands, captured the wisp of fragrant smoke and drew it over her face and hair. In the distance, drums rolled and took up a steady rhythm. For a second, the sound disoriented her, and then she recalled that native dances constituted part of the daily park demonstrations. The chants drifted from the direction of the Heritage Center. Looking that way, Courtney froze. The building was gone, the hillside bare except for rocks and grass. Smoke from the sage drifted into her face, burning her eyes and blurring her sight. Leaning away from the fire, she blinked rapidly to clear her vision. The building was there just where it had been before. She shook her head at her own foolishness and, after another quick look to assure herself of the building's existence, turned her attention back to the shaman, who had begun to chant softly, in unison with the voices drifting from the dances.

As her eyelids drooped, Courtney knew she could close her eyes and believe it was hundreds of years ago on the wide-open plains. Just the People, one large family camped on the edge of a life-giving river. She could hear the flap of tepee hides catching the wind, smell bannock cooking on an open fire, hear the barking of dogs and the shouts of children. The image reminded her of her grandmother, and she shivered as loneliness and a deep sense of loss shadowed her thoughts.

Slowly, she opened her eyes and silently issued the prayer that she had often heard her grandmother recite. *Be well, be happy,* she thought. *I hope you find your spirit guide and are reunited with your life mate.* The old man touched the braid of sweetgrass to the flame. The smoke from the burning tip drifted upward, and Courtney watched it disappear into the blue vault of sky overhead.

The shaman touched the grass to the fire again, but this time when he withdrew it, the smoke drifted toward Courtney and the aromatic tendril wrapped around her head like a halo.

"That is also your grandmother's prayer for you," the shaman stated mysteriously. Courtney's heart thudded in her chest. How could he have known that she had issued a prayer when she had not spoken aloud?

Hypnotized, she watched his weathered hands as he set the braid of sweetgrass aside and spread his fingers over the burning sage. The smoke vanished. When he lifted his hands from the fire pit, nothing remained but ashes. Awed, Courtney forced her attention back to him as he started to speak again.

"In this medicine wheel you will find your spirit guide and a future that is buried in the past." Raising his hands, he took the pouch from around his neck and slipped the leather thong over her head. The small rawhide bag was surprisingly heavy, the weight of its contents resting soothingly in the valley between her breasts. Courtney touched the pouch's smooth decorated surface. It wasn't embossed with beads, but rather colorful woven sections of a long, flat material that was stiff to the touch.

"Porcupine quills," the shaman said in reply to her unasked question. "A talisman, for luck on your journey."

The sound of the distant chanting had grown fainter, and here on this plateau, where the wind swept up off the river below, the stronger gusts caught the sound, carrying it away, so it faded in and out like the dramatic sound track of a suspense film. The aroma of burned sweetgrass clung to Courtney's hair and clothes like a heady perfume that left her slightly light-headed.

She felt powerless to resist as the shaman helped her stand and centered her within the circle of stones. She tottered slightly until she got her balance on the mound of rocks beneath her feet. She struggled to concentrate on the words that Opimihaw whispered.

"This is not a medicine wheel with the traditional spokes that mark the summer solstice. This is a special wheel with links to the spirit world. You need to find your spirit, Courtney. I sense that your circle runs in an unusual direction. I have been sent to show you the way."

Courtney felt dizzy. The realization that he had addressed her personally seeped slowly into her thoughts, but she felt too numb to question how he knew her name. He began to walk in a circle around her, around the mound of stones, moving counterclockwise. There must have been something in the smoke, she thought as her limbs refused to cooperate when her mind urged them to move. His chanting merged with that in the background, growing louder, building in volume and tempo and urgency. The shaman walked faster. The earth began to spin. Courtney felt overwhelmed by an urge to look up. In slow motion, she raised her face to the heavens.

Clouds scurried across the clear sky. Gathering overhead, they boiled and tossed and then gradually shifted until a face began to take shape. Courtney was sure she gasped, but the air seemed to barely trickle into her lungs. The face above her was that of her grandmother, her eyes closed in perpetual sleep.

A breath of warm air washed over her, bringing with it a strange feeling, a combination of encouragement and comfort, like a firm hand guiding her.

From the turbulent white froth of clouds, Courtney thought she heard the sound of her grandmother's voice. "Come, Courtney," it urged, and she felt oddly reassured.

And then everything around her began to fade to darkness. Courtney thought she screamed, but there was no sound, only an infinite black void and the sensation of being propelled through space at an exorbitant speed.

On the crest of Anderson's Ridge, Peter slid from the saddle and rested his cheek against the pinto's neck. A horse of his own. He could scarcely believe it. It was the best birthday present ever. He wished his mother could have been here to share his happiness. His heart ached every time he thought about her. He knew why she had sent him away. He'd overheard the doctor. He blinked twice and hastily turned his thoughts back to the animal at his side.

"I'm going to call you Patch," he said as he wrapped the pinto's reins around a branch of the lone twisted poplar on the hill's crest and tangled his fingers in the black-and-white mane.

From this ridge, he could see the ranch house to the west and for miles in every direction. Patting the horse as it lowered its head to graze, he moved off a few paces until he stood in the middle of a circle of stones that he had discovered atop the hill. He watched the smoke curl from the house's stone chimney. It was too bad Matt and Travis couldn't see how much they needed a woman. Matt would never admit that his cooking wasn't that great, and his meager attempts at cleaning would have appalled any female Peter had known back East. But it was more than just cooking and cleaning. It was an emptiness inside of him, a hollow feeling that Peter couldn't quite explain. Something he couldn't see or touch; something he just felt.

The boy lifted his face to the sky. "Thank you for Patch, God. He's a great horse and I really appreciate him. But I still wish you would send a woman to look after us." He thought about his mother and closed his eyes against the surge of loneliness and longing. "We really need one," he whispered.

Peter's eyes snapped open at the howl of the suddenly rising wind. The violent gusts whipped at his hair and beat against his body. Overhead, clouds rolled across the sky, an eerie black mass gathering, spinning into a vortex that centered over the crest of the hill. Bits of grass and dry twigs swirled into his face, and he shielded his eyes with his arm as he stumbled over the ridge of worn stones toward his frightened horse. A shrill whistling sound made Peter clamp his hands over his ears. Behind him, light shimmered in a thick beam that bolted out of the sky. Patch reared. The reins jerked loose as the horse's hooves flailed the air and landed with a thud on the ground. Freed, the pinto ran. Peter leaned into the wind, his gaze torn between the unbelievable light and the fleeing horse.

"Patch!" The wind snatched the word away.

Behind Peter, there was a sharp crack like a whip being snapped right next to his ear, and then a soft whoosh. Warm air ruffled his tangled blond curls. The light pulsed, blindingly bright, then faded. And suddenly, the wind was gone, dying abruptly, leaving an eerie silence. The boy slowly turned. For several seconds he could only stare at the motionless shape on the ground. Finally, he forced himself to approach. He stepped forward cautiously, convinced that his eyes were playing tricks on him.

A tumble of long dark hair spilled over the woman's shoulder. Peter reached out and touched her. She was solid, warm beneath his fingers.

"Hello." He gently pushed on her shoulder. No response.

"Ma'am." He shook her slightly, then jumped back as her limp body fell sideways. Her eyelids fluttered open and he found himself staring into eyes the color of quicksilver.

"Help me," she whispered. Then her eyes drifted closed again.

Peter bent close. "I'll get help." Turning, he broke into a run, slipping and sliding down the hill, racing the half mile across the meadow toward the ranch. At last, he stumbled into the yard, where Matt stood with his hands on his hips. Travis held Patch's reins. They must not have seen the disturbance in the sky, for they seemed unaware that anything had happened.

"Are you okay? Did he throw you?" Matt asked.

"No." Breathless from his race down the hill, Peter bent over, hands on his knees. A tangle of blond hair fell across his forehead as he struggled for breath. "A woman. Hurt. Needs help." Peter pointed to the top of Anderson's Ridge.

As he stared toward the top of the hill, a sense of impending doom settled in the pit of Matt's stomach. Ragged gray strips of clouds marred the blue expanse of the sky. He swallowed against the bitter memories that threatened to wash over him. He hadn't been up there once in the last six years, not since his sister, Katie, had died.

"Hurry, Matt." Peter's insistent tugging on his sleeve jerked Matt's thoughts back to the present. He focused on Peter's urgency and the fact that a woman might be in trouble and in need of help, anything to keep the old memories at bay, anything to garner the courage to go up that hill.

# Chapter Two

Courtney let out a moan as she pushed herself into a sitting position. She felt bruised and battered; every muscle protested her slightest movement. She gulped in a deep breath of cool fresh air and shook her head, trying to clear it of the dizzying effect of the old Indian's smoke. She must have blacked out for a second. She wondered if there'd been some sort of drug in the twisted braid of sweetgrass. She still felt disoriented, but at least the sense of suffocation had disappeared. Lifting her head, she pushed her heavy hair back off her forehead, letting her fingers comb through its length as she looked around. Her hand froze, and then slowly dropped to the ground as Courtney's breath caught in her throat.

A dark blue ridge of snowcapped mountains topped the horizon beyond the gentle roll of grassy hills. She closed her eyes and shook her head in an attempt to clear her mind of the hallucination. She was nowhere near the mountains. What could have induced such a sight if not some sort of drug? What was going on?

She opened her eyes. A shiver evoked a trail of goose bumps along her arms. The mountains were still there. Growing frantic now, she stumbled to her feet and glanced around. The Heritage Center building was gone, Opimihaw was gone and the graveled paths were gone. The landscape consisted of sloping foothills and rangeland rather than the banks of the North Saskatchewan River. In stunned disbelief, she turned slowly in a circle. All traces of civilization had vanished. Except . . . a ranch house. Her gaze fixed on the wooden structure. She took a cautious step toward it, almost afraid that it might evaporate like the colors of a rainbow. She stumbled on a ridge of rock, looked down to get her footing, then quickly jerked her head back up, half expecting the building to have disappeared or moved away, elusive like a phantom wisp of smoke. But it was still there.

She wanted to close her eyes, to try again to shake off what surely was just an illusion. If she did, would the Heritage Center be back when she opened her eyes? She was afraid that if she looked away now, the ranch house would also vanish. Oddly, she didn't feel drugged. Even the dizziness had passed. She felt completely lucid and sane. Yet how could she be and still see what she was seeing? And hear what she was hearing?

Yes. She tilted her head to listen. The breeze rustled the leaves of the tree behind her, and from somewhere beyond her line of vision, she could hear the lowing of cattle and a dog barking. She tuned her attention to the dog. The sound grew louder as a dark collie bounded from around the side of the house. A boy riding a pinto followed close behind. The wind carried snatches of his words to her, not enough to comprehend but enough to convince her that what she saw and heard must be real. Then two mounted men rounded the corner, ranchers judging by their jeans, boots and cowboy hats.

Another possibility surfaced in her mind. Perhaps she'd been kidnapped, drugged, taken from the park and was being held here. Maybe she had escaped and in her drugged state had wandered away and up this hill. For an instant she thought about running. Her mind struggled, torn between fear with its urge to flee and the desire to grab onto something real and concrete like the house and the people. Frantically she glanced around, but there was no sign of civilization other than the ranch, just fields and hills as far as she could see in any direction. There was nowhere to run to. Besides, she thought, trying to calm herself, why would anyone be interested in kidnapping her? It wasn't as though she had tons of money or the plans to some secret government weapon. She sniffed at the thought. Too much television, she reasoned, quelling her rampant imagination with a quick shake of her head. There had to be some logical explanation for all of this.

The boy was pointing at her now, saying something she couldn't hear. The tallest man pulled up short, his horse edging sideways. Then he leaned forward and the horse burst into motion. The boy and the other rancher followed suit. The lead horse moved with a rhythmic bunching of great muscles, eating up the ground, charging up the hill, approaching Courtney at an alarming speed, leaving the other riders in the dust. Only the collie kept pace. Courtney stared spellbound at the horse's flying hooves and streaming mane. Wind resistance plastered the man's shirt to his solidly muscled chest and stomach.

Strong thighs gripped the sides of the saddleless horse as the beast pounded up the ridge toward her. Courtney gasped. Did he mean to run right over her? She took a faltering step backward just as the man sawed on the reins and brought the animal to a jerky, stiff-legged halt right in front of her.

Barking, the collie dodged around the horse's legs.

The man slid from the sorrel's back and stilled the dog with a jerk of his hand and a curt "Sit," which the animal instantly obeyed. The stranger drew a sharp breath through his teeth and shifted sideways, turning so that his back was to the lone tree. He hesitated as though all his adrenaline had been spent in the race to reach her and now he was at a loss as to what to do. Then he took a step toward her. His hat brim was pulled low, shading his eyes, effectively hiding them from her. All she could see was the bridge of his straight slender nose, a tight-lipped mouth and a square jaw darkened by a shadow of whiskers. Long dark hair swept his collar. Uncertain of his intentions, Courtney stepped back.

As if sensing her fear, he halted. The second man arrived in a cloud of dust and slid from his mount, distracting Courtney's attention momentarily before it was drawn unerringly back to the taller man.

"Are you hurt?" His voice was low and husky, washing over her like a warm summer wind. Her heart gave a startled thud at the rich baritone.

"No." Her reply emerged shaky and hoarse as though she hadn't spoken in a long time and wasn't really sure whether she was all right or not.

"Pete said you needed help."

Pete. That must be the boy's name. He had been here when she first came to, she remembered now. He must have gone for help. She rubbed her head and grimaced as her fingers touched a sensitive spot over and slightly behind her right temple.

"Where am I?"

The shorter man stepped forward and pushed his Stetson back on his head. A thick lock of tawny hair protruded from beneath the hat brim and dangled before his pale blue eyes, eyes that were full of such concern that Courtney felt sure it couldn't be contrived. "She must have fallen and hit her head," he suggested to the other man.

"Did your horse throw you?" the dark-haired rider asked as he scanned the area.

Courtney frowned, feeling disoriented again. "Horse?" she mumbled.

"Didn't you have a horse?"

"No."

"Okay," he said slowly. "No horse." She could feel his scrutiny even though she couldn't see his eyes. "Just how did you get here then?"

Courtney's sigh came from the very bottom of her lungs. "That's the sixty-four-thousand-dollar question, isn't it?" she quipped, trying to make light of her confusion.

"Huh?"

"Never mind." She waved away his not-so-eloquent response with a flutter of her hand. When he continued to regard her silently from beneath his hat brim, she attempted to explain. "One minute I was listening to the Indian's chanting and the next, I ended up here."

"Indians?" The shorter man snapped to attention. "We haven't had a problem with Indians here for almost twenty years," he protested as his eyes flicked nervously across the hills around them.

Now it was Courtney's turn to be puzzled. "Where exactly am I?" she asked pointedly. This conversation was quickly turning bizarre.

"We're forgetting our manners," the dark-haired man said as he tipped his hat. "I'm Matthew Ward and this is my brother, Travis."

The new angle of the hat brim allowed Courtney a glimpse of his eyes. Jet-black, they scrutinized her warily from beneath exquisitely long lashes.

"And you are standing on our land. This is Anderson's Ridge."

"And exactly where is your land situated?" Courtney asked slowly as she glanced toward the distant mountains.

"Lawson County."

Lawson County? She frowned. She'd never heard of it. "What's the nearest city?"

The dark-haired man planted his hands on his hips and studied her for a moment. Matt, she reminded herself. He'd said his name was Matthew. It was Travis who answered her question.

"I guess that would be Great Falls."

"Great Falls? Great Falls, Montana?" That was at least six hundred miles from Heritage Park. Her shock must have shown in her face.

"Are you okay? You look mighty pale, ma'am."

"Montana," she muttered as she stared at the mountains on the western horizon.

Just then, Peter arrived, still panting from his race down the hill and weary from struggling with the pinto, who kept shying away from the top of the hill. "I told you so, didn't I, Matt? I told you there was a woman." As he dismounted, his excitement transmitted itself to the collie. The dog jumped to its feet and leapt around the boy with an eruption of barking that made all the horses skittish.

Courtney backed away from the commotion. Montana! The idea refused to sit in her mind. It couldn't be! And yet, the sight before her eyes attested the fact. There definitely weren't any mountain ranges in central Saskatchewan.

"How did I get here?" Courtney wondered aloud.

"I know," Peter said.

Three heads turned toward him in unison.

The boy grinned. "I wished for a woman," he announced happily; then his expression grew serious. "We need one," he explained earnestly to Courtney. "Then you just appeared."

"Just appeared?" Matt's tone held no amusement.

"Well," Peter clarified, "there was a lot of wind and noise first. That's what scared Patch."

"Patch?" Matt frowned, and it appeared to Courtney that she wasn't the only person having trouble following this explanation.

"My horse," Peter told Matt before he turned his attention back to Courtney. "I just got him today," he informed her before continuing. "Anyway, there was this really bright light and then there you were."

Matt stepped forward and placed a hand solidly on Peter's shoulder. "I think we need to have a little talk about fibbing," he said. "Maybe a trip to the woodshed. That's where Zach used to take Travis and me until we learned not to stretch the truth."

Peter's eyes narrowed rebelliously. "I'm not lying," he maintained adamantly as he ducked out from under Matt's hand, stepped forward and planted himself at Courtney's side. He turned his freckled face up to look at her. "Am I?"

He seemed so sincere that Courtney didn't have the heart to disagree. Besides, she didn't want to be responsible for a trip to the woodshed. She wasn't about to have that on her conscience. "I'm sorry, Peter. But I really don't remember what happened before I woke up and saw you."

"Well, I guess you wouldn't know about the wind

or the light since you weren't here yet," the boy reasoned. His attention flicked back to Matt. "Shouldn't we invite her back to the house?"

Travis stepped forward and volunteered his horse, holding the reins out to her. "You can ride Dusty back, Miss . . ." His voice trailed off and Courtney realized that they didn't know her name.

"Courtney," she supplied as she decided that, whatever had happened to her, it didn't seem that these men knew any more about it than she did. Considering her situation, it wouldn't be sensible to turn down an offer of assistance. "Courtney James."

"Miss James." Travis's blue eyes were warm and admiring as he chivalrously offered her his mount.

Courtney eyed the horse dubiously. The buckskin looked gentle enough, but she'd only ridden a horse once, and that was on a trail ride that some of her high school friends had arranged. Even back then she'd insisted on a mild-mannered animal, and had been given a swaybacked mare that docilely followed the other horses down the myriad of trails, only quickening her steps when the barn finally came back into view at the end of the three-hour trip. This animal wasn't even saddled. "I'm afraid I'm not that comfortable around horses," Courtney explained. "I'd rather walk if you don't mind."

Peripherally, she noticed a quick jerk of movement as Matt Ward's head snapped up and he stared at her. From underneath her lashes, she watched as he scrutinized her face before letting his gaze wander downward. His eyes narrowed perceptively. Courtney looked down, assessing her attire. She brushed at the bit of dirt that dusted one side of her jeans and one sleeve of her suede jacket, but other than that she could find no reason for the man's disapproval. "Is something wrong, Mr. Ward?"

"No, nothing's wrong," he assured her smoothly. Too smoothly, Courtney thought as he dipped his head and used the hat's brim to conceal the upper half of his face.

"Come on," Peter called as he started down the incline. His voice seemed to shatter the uneasiness that Matt Ward's stark assessment had instilled in Courtney. She hesitated for a minute while she sorted out her thoughts and tried to find some options to resolve her current situation. She only had a few dollars with her. But if she could persuade one of these men to give her a lift into town, she could get some money wired down to the local bank and take a bus home.

"I was born in Boston," Peter said as he led the way down the hill.

Leading his horse, Travis took up a position on Courtney's left as she followed Peter. Partway down the hill, the boy seemed to realize that they were missing someone.

"Matt, aren't you coming?" he shouted back up the hill.

Courtney turned. Sure enough, Matt Ward was still on top the hill. He hadn't budged a step since the one he'd taken after his hasty dismount.

Thoughtfully rubbing his chin, he looked up only when Peter called out again.

"You go ahead." Matthew Ward pulled his Stetson down more securely before grabbing a handful of his horse's mane and swinging effortlessly up onto its back. "I think I'll take a look around first. I'll be down in a while."

Matt carefully kept his back to the tree, and refused to allow the memories into his thoughts as he waited until the trio made their way down the hill and started across the meadow. Despite his reluctance to linger in this spot, he had to admit that there was something mighty strange about Miss Courtney James. Why, even her name was odd. What kind of name was Courtney for a girl anyway?

And those clothes! It just didn't add up. She wore a sweater that was a couple of sizes too big and all stretched out at the neck. And her pants! That a woman would be caught wearing pants at all was shocking enough. Might be all right for Jane Caldwell, the old widow over in Morrison County; after all, she was trying to run a spread all by herself and pants made for easier riding than a dress did. But Miss Courtney James? No, he just didn't think she belonged in pants. Oh, they fit all right! She was wedged in there like a . . . like a. . . . Surprising those pants didn't just split a seam! He frowned at his recollection of the long limbs that shaped the denim material with softly rounded curves. He shifted slightly as his own Levis seemed to get tighter all of a sudden. Damn women anyway! Always distracting a man from where his thoughts should be.

Why would a woman wear pants like that? Did she come from a poor farm family? Was that why the sweater was too big and the Levi's too small? Were her clothes hand-me-downs?

Matt shook his head. Her boots were a new fashion. He hadn't seen a pair quite like that before, but ignoring the style, there was still the matter of quality, and if there was one thing Matt Ward recognized it was a good pair of boots. He could almost feel the buttery softness of the leather just by looking at it, and it had been finely tooled, too, with a distinct pattern etched in the smooth black leather. The boot top had been turned over into a cuff of sorts, and the tanned rawhide fringe intrigued him. If it was some new Eastern fashion, it was the first he'd seen of it. New boots, yet hand-me-down clothes? And a coat styled like a man's shirt? On top of it all, she claimed to be uncomfortable around horses. Could you beat that? Uncomfortable around horses? Matt shook his head. There was definitely something more to Miss James than met the eye.

A fresh smell lingered in the air, a distinct portent of rain from the strips of gray cloud that seemed to have gathered overhead. Matt nudged Red into a slow walk. He leaned forward and studied the ground intently as he guided the sorrel gelding over the area where Courtney had stood. Peter's tracks and those of his horse were plain as day, as were Travis's and his own, but no matter how hard Matt looked, he couldn't find a trace of wagon tracks or hoofprints of any strange horses. Nor could he even find the footprints of another person, other than those of Miss James headed back to the house.

He took off his hat and ran his fingers through his hair as he reined Red to a halt. From the top of the ridge, he could survey the countryside for miles in either direction. Where had the woman come from? Maybe she *had* dropped out of the sky as Peter claimed. Matt huffed at his own absurdity. He was a pretty good tracker, but not flawless. Someone had obviously gone to great lengths to cover their tracks. Wondering why was going to bother him.

He turned Red back toward the ranch, then stopped. The light was fading. In the west, the sky was a fiery glow, streaked with deep purple slashes of cloud as the sun sank toward the jagged horizon. The slanted rays gilded the rocks that topped the hill. Wind whispered through the branches of the poplars that lined the creek below. As a boy, Matt had come here to be awed by the view and mystified by the strange rock circle, a circle with a central mound and spokes all carefully aligned with smooth white stones. He'd always fantasized that it was a magical place. But that was years ago, before Katie's death. Now he was a man, and grown men knew better than to believe in fairy tales. But now Miss James had appeared near the circle. A woman, he thought as he squeezed the bridge of his nose. This was the last thing he needed.

Keeping the horse between himself and the sight of the lone tree on the hilltop, he dismounted and studied the ground around the pile of rocks. His eyes lit briefly on a clump of twisted grass as he bent forward and picked up a small leather pouch. Turning it over, he noted intricate embroidery. The pouch itself was suspended from a rawhide throng. With the ends of the broken strap dangling between his fingers, Matt stretched the top of the bag open and dumped the contents into his hand. The glossy black stone that fell out was a flat oval, its surface carved in a circular pattern with a deep cross cut into it. He smoothed his thumb over the indentations a couple of times before finally dropping it back into the pouch and shoving the whole works in his back pocket.

"Let's go home, Red," he said as he remounted and tightened his legs on the horse's sides, suddenly anxious to be away from this place. Besides, he had to deal with the issue of Miss James. Might as well get it over with. Maybe it would distract his thoughts from other directions, from things that he didn't want to remember.

Courtney hadn't been able to get a word in edgewise in the past twenty minutes. She'd already learned that Peter was a stepbrother to Matt and

Travis, that he used to live back East until his mother had sent him out to the ranch so he could learn responsibility. She thought she saw something in the boy's eyes, a flicker of sadness, but it vanished as the lad launched into a description of his new expertise at fishing.

She was bustled into the house and fussed over as she settled onto the couch, a piece of furniture that was as uncomfortable as it was outdated. Stiff horsehair covered an unyielding pad of hard cushion that rustled like straw as she shifted positions, unsuccessfully trying to get comfortable. From the kitchen on the other side of the fireplace, Peter brought her a mug of water.

She noted the old-fashioned blue enamel mug as she sipped the cool water. Mugs instead of glasses, a man's preference, practical and functional instead of decorative. They must have their own well. The water tasted metallic like well-water. It reminded her of when she was growing up on the farm. Her grandmother's kitchen pump had been hand-operated and the water had had this same taste and the faint smell of damp earth.

Travis watched her with interest as Peter talked away at a mile a minute. Self-conscious, Courtney avoided Travis's stare by pretending interest in her surroundings. She didn't have to pretend for very long. Her host's home suddenly had her full attention. The single-story house was constructed of rough-hewn log walls. The rustic decor was like something right out of *Bonanza*. The embers of a recent fire glowed in a massive stone fireplace that divided the kitchen from the living room. Travis, noticing the object of her attention, rose and added another log from the stack near the hearth.

"Are you warm enough?" he asked.

Courtney nodded absently as her gaze strayed around the room. The place was a museum. An authentic coal-oil lantern sat on the mantle beside a gilt-framed, beautifully restored picture of a woman in a hoop skirt. A wooden rack above the fireplace held three rifles and a shotgun. Courtney didn't know much about guns. The sight of so many in the open had a tendency to make her nervous, so she quickly turned her attention elsewhere. At her feet a tattered, braided rug covered a plain plank floor. Apparently, the ranch wasn't too prosperous. Would someone this poor resort to kidnapping? And would they go out of the country to do so? That didn't seem likely.

"Have you been ranching here long?" she asked, hoping her question passed as merely polite conversation.

"Matt and Travis came out here on the wagon train," Peter told her with a perfectly straight face.

Courtney laughed politely at his joke. "That long, huh?"

Travis just nodded as he rubbed his palms on the dusty legs of his jeans. Courtney sipped the water and had another flash of intuition. Maybe this really was pumped well-water. She felt a twinge of sympathy as she began to pay attention to the little details around her. She realized what Peter had meant with his comment about needing a woman. The place could use a thorough cleaning. There seemed to be a layer of dust on everything. She looked toward the window, taking in the dirt-streaked glass and the curtains made of frayed flour-sacking material.

Outside, dusk was beginning to shadow the yard. Courtney checked her watch. Eight-ten. The date showed as April fourteenth. That couldn't be right. The seniors' bus had left the Heritage Park at five-thirty. She'd been there at least an hour after that before she blacked out. That would make it six-thirty. It had to have been almost an hour since she had come to on the hill; seven-ten. Was it possible to get from Wanuskewin to Montana in a little over half an hour? Six hundred miles? After a fifteen-minute drive to the nearest airport? Maybe they had reset her watch to throw her off. But who would go to that extent and why?

Footsteps echoed on the porch outside, and Courtney stiffened. Was she about to meet her abductor? She heard a slapping sound, and the door swung open. Courtney slowly let out the breath she hadn't realized she'd been holding. It was only Matt.

"Couldn't find your horse," Matt said as he flipped his hat over one of the empty pegs by the door.

"I don't have a horse." Courtney got a good look at him now that his face wasn't hidden by his hat. He had a rugged look, his face tanned dark by the sun, weathered by a lot of time spent outdoors, cut in stark lines, from a high forehead and prominent cheekbones to a solid, whisker-shadowed jaw. His dark hair, combed back off his forehead, had a slight wave on the top and a persistent curl at his frayed collar.

"No horse?" He regarded her with dark unblinking eyes.

For a second, Courtney got the impression that he was baiting her to see if she would change her story. Well, she thought, maybe he was as mystified by this whole incident as she was.

She rose from the couch. "Do you think I could use your phone? I'll call collect."

The three males looked at each other as if they expected someone to explain or translate her words.

"Our what?" Matt finally asked.

"Your phone." Her reply was met with three similar blank looks. "Telephone. You know, the modern method of communication." Surely they weren't so backward that they didn't even have a phone. Lord. It was probably one of those ancient phones with the button you had to pull up before you could dial. She'd never been able to figure those out. She'd probably look like an idiot when she had to ask how to work it.

All three males were still staring at her as if she'd lost her mind.

Travis finally managed to find his voice. "Haven't got a . . . phone as you called it."

Not likely! Courtney wasn't falling for this. Everybody had a phone. This was the nineties, for heaven's sake! "Please. I don't know what you want but you must have the wrong person." Perhaps she could appeal to their sense of honor. Surely even poor Montana ranchers had some code of ethics, even nowadays.

Matt had tipped his head back and was studying her from beneath those long lashes. "What we want? Lady, you're the one who showed up here. I think we should be asking you what it is that *you* want."

Courtney felt the first spark of anger beginning to flicker to life. She'd been drugged by some Indian pretending to be with the park staff, and probably kidnapped and dragged halfway across the country— hell, into another country altogether. Now she was confronted with three strange men—no, two men and a boy—who refused her the use of a phone. She'd be better off out of here. "I think maybe I should leave."

"Fine with me."

Courtney relaxed slightly. At least Matt seemed agreeable to that request. He even headed for the door and held it open for her. Now they were getting somewhere. If he'd give her a ride to town, she'd be able to get this whole mess straightened out in a matter of minutes. She gave him an appreciative smile as she swept past him.

As she stepped outside, the door slammed forcefully behind her. Courtney froze. She was alone on the veranda. No good-bye, no offer to drive her to town—wherever that was—no directions, nothing! She couldn't believe it. She planted her fists on her hips and glared at the closed door. So much for common courtesy. She had a good notion to go back in there and give Matthew Ward a piece of her mind.

Unfortunately, after what had already happened to her today, and with the lingering confusion she still felt, she wasn't sure she had a piece to spare. She should probably just be glad to get out of there. After all, she was a modern, liberated woman. She could find her way to town on her own. All she needed to do was follow the road. Surely, the people at the next farmhouse would be more helpful. She didn't much like the idea of walking alone at night, but there was always the chance that someone would come along and give her a lift. Her imagination quickly provided a barrage of images of what could happen to a lone woman hitchhiking. She stamped one booted foot on the porch. She didn't have a lot of choices here.

"You threw out my woman!" It was Peter's angry voice.

God, Courtney thought as she combed her hair away from her forehead, was this whole family deranged?

"Matt. It's almost dark. She could get hurt out there." That had to be Travis trying to talk some sense into his brother.

Matt's reply was low, but not quite low enough to

escape Courtney's hearing. "This is what happens when you let a woman into a house. Right away brothers turn on each other. I just gave her what she wanted."

Chauvinist! She stomped down the steps and headed across the yard toward the two ruts that led off down the slope of the valley in the twilight. Not much of a road, but right now she wasn't choosy. The way those brothers were acting, she was probably safer on foot anyway.

Courtney was no stranger to walking. She walked regularly. It was a great way to relieve stress after a long workday, and a convenient method of exercise. So it wasn't surprising that she was able, especially in her current mood, to cover a lot of ground by the time it was completely dark.

The sound of hooves behind her didn't come as that much of a surprise either. One of the Ward men had probably come out to rescue her. She didn't even hesitate as the horse came abreast. She just kept putting one foot firmly in front of the other.

"Miss James, please stop for a minute," Travis Ward implored as he dismounted and fell into step beside her.

Not the arrogant one. Well, that didn't surprise her. She halted and turned toward him expectantly. "Make this quick. I'm kind of in a hurry."

Travis removed his hat and twisted the brim nervously with both hands. "I know my brother was rude, but I think you should come back to the house for tonight."

"I'm perfectly capable of looking after myself, Mr. Ward."

"I have no doubt that you are, ma'am," Travis said. His head was bowed, but Courtney didn't think he saw the hat he was mutilating with the nervous twisting of his hands.

"I promise I'll take you to town myself, first thing in the morning. I just wouldn't feel right knowing you were out here by yourself at night."

She couldn't stand what he was doing to that Stetson any longer. "Travis, your hat."

"What?" He looked up at her.

"You're mutilating your hat."

"Oh." He stared down at the rolled brim. "I guess I am." He put his hands behind his back, taking his hat out of her line of sight.

"Listen, Travis. I appreciate your concern. But I'm a big girl. I can take care of myself. It's obvious your brother didn't want me to stay. I can't imagine him begging me to return."

Travis's head jerked up and he stared at her open-mouthed for a second. "I don't think that's gonna happen."

"Me neither," Courtney said. She spun on her heel and started walking again.

Behind her she heard the saddle leather protest as Travis remounted. "Okay," he called over his shoulder as he galloped off.

Good, Courtney thought. That was settled. A few more miles and she'd be out of here. There was a rise ahead. She should be able to see something from there.

A solitary cloud momentarily obscuring the moon made her realize just how dark it was. Overhead, the sky was a carpet of stars. She stared up, mesmerized. You couldn't see stars like that in the city. They cast their own brand of light that was absolutely stunning. There was still a nip in the spring air, and her fingers were beginning to tingle from the cold. She searched her pockets and found one of her leather gloves. The other one was missing, probably lost somewhere between central Canada and the northern United States. She almost laughed at the absurdity of the thought.

From a distant hilltop, a coyote's howl rippled through the air. A shiver of concern left a cold trail up Courtney's spine. Thank goodness she wasn't going to be out here too long. She started up the incline to her proposed vantage point.

At the top of the hill, she stopped dead. Ahead of her, there wasn't any town. There weren't any farmhouses. There wasn't even a single yard light and she could see for miles. She hadn't expected this. Just where the hell was she anyway? Out in the middle of nowhere? How could there be no sign of civilization? There weren't even any power or telephone lines. That observation made her concede that maybe the Ward brothers really didn't have a phone.

She turned and looked back the way she had come. On the side of the road, back about thirty yards, a rider sat quietly on his horse watching her from beneath the wide brim of a Stetson. The moonlight glinted coldly on the steel barrel of the rifle laying across his lap. Her heart leapt right up into her throat. She swallowed it back down as her muscles tensed for flight.

# Chapter Three

"It's just me."

She recognized Matthew Ward's gravely voice instantly, but the recognition did little to calm her erratic heartbeat or reassure her of her safety.

"Is there a town down this road?" she demanded.

"Yep."

"How far?"

He shrugged. "Another twelve miles or so."

Twelve miles! Even at a brisk pace it would take her hours to cover that distance. "Does anyone else live nearby?" She was desperately trying to salvage some measure of pride. Anything other than having to admit defeat to this man.

"Nope."

"Would you tell me if they did?"

His laugh took her completely by surprise, and maybe him, too, she thought, as it was choked off in mid-chuckle. "Lady, you got spunk. I'll give you that," he said in a low murmur that she had to strain to hear.

She wasn't about to thank him for such a dubious compliment.

His gruff tone seemed to slide over her skin like sandpaper, a discordant caress. "Stubborn as a jackass, though. Just like a woman."

She stared at him in silence for a long minute, or rather, she stared at a smudge of shadow that lurked under that hat brim. The coyote howled again, closer this time. Matt lifted the rifle, pointing the barrel skyward while resting the butt on his thigh. "Never thought you'd make it this far. But we'd best get on back now."

Her brows peaked at his audacity. She opened her mouth to tell him exactly what she thought of his suggestion, but the rustle of something in the underbrush stopped her. His horse nickered nervously. Courtney clamped her mouth shut and bit back the retort that had threatened to escape.

"Been a mountain lion on the prowl the last few nights," he stated casually.

Courtney moved closer to the horse and away from the brush. This might just be a ploy to scare her, but with the town still over twelve miles away, she didn't seem to have been left with any recourse other than to accept his help.

He held his arm down to her, and she realized that he expected her to ride on the horse with him.

Abruptly, he cocked his head and looked beyond her. His attention was riveted on a spot in the brush behind Courtney. She could hear nothing other than the faint whisper of leaves in the breeze.

Moonlight glinted on steel as the rifle barrel came down in a flash of movement. A shot rang out and a wedge of dirt leapt from the path as the bullet thudded into the solid-packed soil directly in front of the spot where Matt's attention focused. Courtney's scream lodged in her throat as the echo of the gun's report vibrated inside her skull.

"Give me your hand." It was no longer a request.

Maybe there had been something there, or maybe this was all an elaborate ploy to make her believe she was in danger. Either way, it didn't seem that she was in any position to refuse his order.

He laid the rifle back across his lap as he reached down with his left arm. She held out her right arm, expecting to be hauled up in front of him. "The other hand." She dropped her right arm and lifted the left one. His gloved hand clasped her firmly just above the elbow.

"Step on my foot." He extended his boot to provide a makeshift stirrup. She placed her foot on his. He lifted her as if she was weightless, the muscles of his thigh straining against the denim of his pants. "Swing your other leg over."

She didn't need further instructions, damn it. She knew how to get on a horse. Okay, granted this was a new experience. She'd never ridden behind a saddle before. ·

The horse bucked slightly as her weight settled on his rump. She wrapped her arms around Matt's waist to keep from slipping. As he kicked the horse into a trot, the uneven pace almost unseated her, forcing her to tighten her grip just under his rib cage, her arms pressing against the solid warmth of his flat stomach. For the first few minutes, she concentrated on staying seated with the horse's rough gait. Matt set a deliberately jolting pace, she realized as she bounced uncontrollably against his back. Damn him, if he wasn't purposely making this ride difficult. Her breasts rubbed up and down on the ridges of muscles that lined his back. Just when she was about to protest this as cruel and unjust treatment, he let out a strangled growl and slowed the horse to a sedate walk. He shifted uncomfortably in the saddle, leaning forward so he broke the contact between them.

Courtney's eyes widened with satisfaction as realization dawned. He hadn't slowed the horse out of consideration for her. But Matthew Ward wasn't completely immune to the feel of a woman against him either. If he had intended the horse's uneven pace as a torture for her, it had also proved very bothersome for him.

She smiled secretly, but didn't say a single word on the whole ride back, or even when they finally arrived in the yard and he unfolded her arms from around his waist. Instead of helping her down first, he swung his right leg over the horse's head and slid to the ground. The action left Courtney grabbing for the saddle to maintain her balance.

When she didn't get down, he gave a grunt of disgust, looked up at her accusingly and then lifted his arms to help her down. As she started to lean forward, he spoke. "Now you see, that is how a woman should behave, quietly and obediently."

Courtney set her jaw and narrowed her eyes in indignation. Awkwardly maneuvering herself forward into the saddle, she slid her left foot into the stirrup, gripped the saddle horn and swung her right foot over the horse's rump. Her aim was dead-on; she caught Matt squarely in the chest.

"Oops, sorry," she said in a small fluttery voice accented with her best imitation of a Southern belle as he stumbled backward and cursed under his breath. "I guess a lady just doesn't know her own strength sometimes." She batted her eyelashes at him, then eased to the ground all by herself.

The door to the ranch house swung open and Peter spilled out in the slash of light that came from within.

"You came back," he said as he reached her side. He gave Matt an accusing look for having sent her off in the first place, and then grasped her hand and clung to it. "I'm glad."

"Just for the night, Peter," she announced. "Travis has promised to take me into town tomorrow."

The boy's face fell, but he didn't say anything. Then, as though he had decided to ignore her words, he tugged her toward the house. "Come on in. We worked out all the sleeping arrangements while you were gone." He turned his back pointedly on Matt.

"I'll just rub Red down," Matt said sarcastically as he massaged the spot where Courtney's boot had landed. "You go ahead."

Courtney glanced back over her shoulder and watched him lead the horse away. A twinge of regret nagged at the back of her mind. Just a little twinge. The regret vanished like a feeble spark doused with a pail of cold water as she reminded herself of his words. A woman should be quiet and obedient! She didn't think so.

Inside, Courtney relinquished her jacket at Peter's insistence and moved to stand in front of the hearth, where the fire dispelled the night's chill. She rubbed her arms briskly to warm them.

A single kerosene lantern added to the light provided by the flickering flames before her.

Peter hovered around her like a mother hen. "Can I get you anything, Miss Courtney? Something to drink? Are you hungry?"

"Nothing, thanks, Peter. I'm fine right now." Oddly

enough, she wasn't hungry. The last thing she'd eaten was a burger from the park restaurant just before seeing the senior citizens off. If she'd been drugged and brought here hours ago, she should have been famished. Maybe the drug that had made her forget everything also dulled the appetite.

"We still haven't cleaned out the other bedroom. It's kind of a storage room right now," Peter said, chattering on. "Since you're our guest, you can have Matt's room. It's the nicest."

Courtney grimaced. "What is Matt going to think about that?"

Peter just shrugged and smiled at her as if she was a gift he had just opened and was completely delighted with. "He can sleep in with Travis. I don't mind the couch."

It was only for one night, Courtney reminded herself.

Despite his excitement, Peter yawned. He quickly hid it behind his hand.

"Maybe Miss Courtney is tired, too," Travis suggested. His blue eyes studied her with such longing that Courtney felt her breath catch in her throat. Travis's interest was definitely more than politeness. She glanced quickly away. She didn't need that kind of complication right now, not on top of everything else that was happening to her. She felt compelled to look back, but just then the door burst open and Matt strolled into the room.

Peter hastened to explain the new sleeping arrangements as Matt hung up his hat and coat. For an instant, as Matt turned, Courtney thought he would protest, but he just huffed under his breath and stared at her through narrowed eyes, dark eyes, ebony eyes.

"It's late," he said finally. "We'd all better turn in.

You've got chores first thing in the morning," he said, leveling a stern look at Peter as the boy appeared about to protest.

Late! Courtney checked her watch. It was barely ten o'clock. Talk about early to bed, early to rise.

Travis stood, and all three men seemed to hesitate. With a jolt, Courtney realized they were waiting for her. She smiled at the unexpected politeness. She felt as if she had just been hugged. It was the oddest sensation. Whatever had happened to respect and courtesy to make them seem alien when you were the recipient of them?

Unfortunately, before she could retire, she had another more urgent need, a personal one. "Where is the bathroom?" She looked around but could see no sign of one.

"Bathroom?" Matt repeated. All three brothers looked puzzled.

"The washroom," Courtney clarified.

"There's a basin in the kitchen, if you want to wash up," Peter suggested.

This wasn't working. "No. The toilet."

Peter flushed red to the roots of his hair and Travis gave a startled choke. Only Matt seemed unaffected, though he eyed her with some sort of speculation. Lord, all she wanted was the bathroom. What was such a big deal?

Peter moved toward the kitchen, keeping his head lowered. "This way," he said in a hoarse voice.

Courtney came to a halt when the boy opened the back door and pointed outside. Moonlight glowed on the path that led to a small wooden shack with a lopsided moon cut in the door. "An outhouse?" She couldn't keep the incredulity out of her voice.

"It's brand-new," Peter assured her in a whisper. "Matt just built it this year."

She couldn't believe she was standing here discussing the virtues of an outhouse. First no phone, now no plumbing. She surveyed her surroundings again. There weren't any light fixtures or any appliances or even any electrical outlets. "It's fine Peter. Thank you," she said as she stepped outside, pulling the door closed behind her. She leaned back against the solid wood planking. It was hard to believe people still lived like this. Or maybe it was all an elaborate ruse? But why?

She had no answers. Slowly she pushed away from the door. The moon gave enough light for her to find her way down the path. Far off a coyote howled. The sound, lonely and isolated, suddenly seemed fitting for the surroundings. Courtney quickly used the facilities and hurried back to the house.

As she entered, the three males all jumped up and quickly busied themselves. Travis straightened a faded afghan on the back of the couch. Matt dropped to one knee and began to stoke the fire. Peter fumbled with the lantern. Courtney noticed a basin on the counter and a wooden water barrel. Casually she slid the wooden lid aside and scooped a ladle of water into the basin. She would just act as though this was normal. It wasn't necessary to remind these people of how many of life's luxuries they were missing.

She scrubbed her teeth with her forefinger and some of the cool water. Then she dipped her hands and splashed the liquid over her face. Opening her eyes, she cast around for a towel. One suddenly appeared. Slowly her gaze traveled upward to Matt's face.

"Thank you," she said as she took the towel from his hand. She buried her face in it to conceal her sudden flush of uncertainty. When she had finished, she folded the threadbare cotton cloth carefully beside the basin.

Peter had spread a blanket on the couch. She recognized the cream-colored wool with its blue, red and yellow stripes. Her grandmother had treasured several of the famous Hudson Bay blankets. They were hard to come by nowadays. The boy sat on the edge of the couch, waiting.

She had to leave the room before he could get ready for bed. She looked down at her own attire. She didn't have anything to sleep in, and she knew she wouldn't be comfortable sleeping unclothed in a strange house with three unfamiliar men. "Could I borrow a shirt from someone?"

"What do you need a shirt for?" Peter asked as he shifted on the sofa.

"To sleep in," Courtney replied more casually than she felt.

"Oh." Peter ducked his head again.

The boy certainly was shy around women, or around her at least.

Travis seemed speechless. He fixed an unwavering gaze on her that left her feeling like a piece of prime beef. He had the courtesy to look slightly abashed as he realized she was watching him watch her. There was little doubt in her mind where his thoughts had been. She hoped there was a lock on her door.

"I've got a clean shirt," Matthew finally volunteered as no one else seemed able to answer her request. He disappeared into the front bedroom and reappeared a moment later with a folded white garment.

"You can sleep in there," he said as he pointed to the door he had just come out of. Courtney thanked him, took the shirt on her way past and escaped into the bedroom. Hoping to put a halt to whatever ideas either of the older men might be entertaining, she closed the door firmly. Instantly she was enveloped by darkness. Instinctively her hand sought out a light switch before she gave herself a mental shake and reminded herself that there was no electricity. She wasn't about to go back into the other room for a lamp. Her eyes gradually adjusted to the lack of light, and her sense of panic abated as she realized that the moonlight illuminated the room well enough for her to see.

There was no lock on the door, which didn't really surprise her considering the other things the house was lacking. She made do by wedging the room's spindle-backed chair under the latch before she began to undress. Laying her clothes on the foot of the bed, she inhaled the faint sweet tang of cedar as she slipped into the nubby cotton shirt. Her eyes strayed to the claw-footed dresser. The drawers were probably cedar-lined. The top was cluttered with articles: a wide brush, several coins that gleamed slightly in the pale blue light, a handful of some kind of square nails, a piece of leather that looked like it might have come from a horse's harness, a crumpled red bandanna and a faded picture that she couldn't make out in the darkness.

The log walls were unadorned except for a row of wooden pegs. Courtney's eyes widened at the sight of the gun and holster hanging there so nonchalantly. This was right out of a Western movie, she thought.

In fact, the whole room reminded her of a trip to a museum or one of those old forts that had been reconstructed and done up to resemble the style of the nineteenth century. Right down to the bed. The patchwork quilt couldn't quite disguise the dip in the middle of the mattress.

The place even smelled old, she realized. And male. The scent of dust and leather blended with the faint aroma of kerosene.

Courtney folded back the quilt and lowered herself onto the mattress. The bedsprings creaked. She tucked her cold feet under the blankets and shifted to find a comfortable spot in the too-soft mattress. She lay staring up at the ceiling wondering if she would ever fall asleep. Tomorrow she intended to set things in motion and get home. She tried to reason out the day's events, but to no avail. The effort only made her toss and turn, unable to find sleep.

Matthew listened to the faint sound of bedsprings creaking from the room next door. He tried to suppress the mental image of Courtney tossing in her sleep, and tried not to think about the way his shirt must fit over her body. But he found ignoring that image as difficult as ignoring the memories of the way she had felt pressed against him, firm breasts rubbing up and down his back. His groin tightened painfully at the thought. He shifted on the bed.

"Can't sleep?" Travis's voice arose out of the shadows on the far side of the room.

"Can't you?" Matt shot back.

"It's damn tough," Travis admitted.

There was going to be nothing but trouble until she was gone, Matt acknowledged as he realized he wasn't the only one affected by her presence. Travis had been afflicted, too. Women! All they ever did was get men in a stir and cause trouble. Thank God, she'd be gone tomorrow. He rolled onto his stomach and pounded the pillow into a more obliging shape. Next door the bedsprings creaked again. With a muttered oath, he pulled the pillow from beneath his face and covered his head with it, wrapping it tightly around his ears.

The faint light of dawn tinted the room with a pinkish glow as Courtney peeked out from under half-closed eyelids. It was early yet, plenty of time to get ready for work. She snuggled back down into the mattress and then jerked awake, her heart suddenly accelerating to a point that left her breathless. She scanned the strange room and memory came rushing back. She took a deep breath to still her frantic pulse. This wasn't home. She was stuck in the Montana hills. She took another calming breath, only it didn't calm her.

Coffee! She could smell coffee. That must have been what awakened her.

The sound of someone moving around and the low murmur of voices came from beyond the door. Courtney lay in bed listening to the noises as her heartbeat gradually slowed back to normal. The back door opened and closed and Peter's higher-pitched tones filtered through to her.

She heard Travis's voice. Even if the words were muffled, the inflection indicated he was scolding Peter for something. Matt intervened with a few gravely words. It seemed everyone was up. It must be later than she thought. She pushed her feet out from under the blankets and shivered at the chill air. With a burst of adrenaline she threw the covers aside and grabbed for her clothes. She pulled the jeans over her hips and pushed her feet into her socks before she removed the wrinkled shirt and replaced it with her sweater. It took a minute for the clothes to absorb some of the warmth from her body, but finally she ceased shivering.

She ran Matt's wide brush quickly through her

long hair, then retrieved her watch from the dresser top. She stared in dismay at the hands. It wasn't yet five o'clock. She dislodged the chair and padded out into the living room.

"Do you realize what time it is?" she asked as she crossed into the kitchen.

Peter jumped up from his chair and flashed her a beaming grin. "See, I told you we should have woken her up, Matt. It was just all the excitement from yesterday that made her sleep so late."

Courtney looked toward the men. "Sleep late! Nobody in their right mind gets up this early."

Matt cocked an eyebrow at her. "It's almost sunup. What time do you usually get up?" he asked disdainfully.

Courtney opened her mouth and then closed it. She reminded herself that they were isolated ranchers, which, she supposed, might justify getting up with the sun. And which probably explained the early retirement the night before.

"Later. I usually get up later," she stammered.

"I see." Matt gave her a look that said he suspected she wasn't telling him something, but then he smiled a tight superior smile as if he'd just figured it all out. "How'd you sleep," he inquired smoothly.

"Fine," Courtney replied cautiously. "And you?" She didn't like that gleam in his eye.

A snort of laughter cut off Matt's reply as Travis chuckled. He gave Matt a grin and a knowing look before disappearing out the back door. Matt glared after him.

"Peter," Travis called, "help me bring in some more wood."

"Did I say something funny?" Courtney asked as Peter disappeared out the door.

"No," Matt assured her with an odd expression

that he quickly disguised. "Nothing funny at all."

Courtney headed for the stove, drawn by the smell of food. Her stomach growled in anticipation. She seldom took the time to fix herself a hot breakfast. "I don't usually eat breakfast," she confided as she leaned over the frying pan lined with sizzling bacon.

"Is that due to your profession?"

Her head snapped up. Profession? What did he know about her or her job? "My work keeps me busy," she finally answered suspiciously, carefully refraining from being more specific.

"I bet it does. Coffee?" he offered.

She nodded.

"I suppose you drink a lot of coffee." He filled a metal cup from the pot on the back of the stove and handed it to her.

"It helps me stay awake if I have to work late." Just where was he going with this strange conversation? The questions were innocent enough, but she felt as though she was being interrogated. She took a sip of the hot coffee as she wrapped her fingers around the mug to warm her fingers.

He smiled a knowing smile and let his gaze travel down the front of her sweater, then back up in a lazy manner that warmed her skin in the wake of his perusal.

The back door swung open and Peter and Travis stomped in, each with an armful of wood that they dumped into the bin by the stove. Peter launched into an excited story concerning his new horse. The boy's chatter distracted her from Matt's discerning look. She set her coffee down as Peter handed her plates as though she was part of the family. His actions made her forget Matt's remarks, and filled her with a strange desire to belong to a family where the members were able to take each other for granted so easily.

She carried the plates to the table. Old coffee rings made brown circles on the worn top. Looking around, she spotted a cloth near the washbasin. She retrieved it and wiped the tabletop. It took a little scrubbing, but it finally came clean.

When she straightened, all three males were watching her intently. Matt looked away, but Peter just grinned at Travis. "See, I knew this was a good thing. It's working already."

Travis rubbed his chin but didn't reply. Courtney suspected it hadn't been the table he'd been looking at as she'd leaned over to scrub the spots.

"This is the best birthday present," Peter exclaimed as he brought the silverware and set a fork beside each of the four plates.

"It's your birthday?" Courtney grabbed the chance to try to direct everyone's thoughts to something other than herself. She didn't appreciate the way the two mature, able-bodied, stuck-out-in-the-middle-of-nowhere, probably-hadn't-seen-a-woman-for-days men were looking at her.

Peter nodded. "Yesterday."

"What did you get?"

He grinned from ear to ear. "You."

Courtney almost choked on her own breath. "What?"

Matt carried the frying pan over to the table. "Peter thinks he wished for you and you just appeared."

"Really." She was having a hard time breathing. Surely, she hadn't been kidnapped as a birthday present for a ten- or eleven-year-old boy!

Travis laughed. "I tried to tell him that it was just a coincidence, you being up on that hill, but he doesn't want to believe it."

"The light brought her for me," Peter insisted.

"That's enough of that talk," Matt ordered. "Everybody, sit down and eat." Courtney dropped into a chair as Matt shoveled bacon onto her plate. Silence fell as a pan of fried potatoes slid across the table's rough surface. A thick slice of bread landed on Courtney's plate as she stared at the chipped blue enamel.

There had been light. She remembered the light, so bright she had been compelled to shut her eyes, and even then it had seemed to shine right through her closed lids.

Travis broke the silence as he spread butter on his bread. "Miss James didn't just appear. She had to have come from somewhere."

"Where *did* you come from, Miss James?" Matt asked quietly. He regarded her from beneath long thick lashes, his face expressionless and his dark eyes hiding any hint of emotion.

"I'm not sure," Courtney answered honestly. "One minute I was in one place and then the next thing I remember I was here."

"Don't encourage the boy," Matt warned ominously.

"I'm not. That's the truth."

As silence reigned, Courtney tried to eat. But her appetite had vanished and the food that had smelled so good was suddenly tasteless. She forced herself to swallow a few mouthfuls before she pushed the plate away.

Peter leaned over and whispered, "I'm sorry about the food. That's one of the reasons I wished for you."

"Peter!" Matt's voice cut through the air. "If you're done eating, there's work in the barn."

"Yes, sir." Peter pushed back from the table. He let the back door slam behind him as he went out.

Courtney looked at Matt. He rubbed his brow and when he glanced up and their eyes met, he squared his shoulders. "The boy's got to learn responsibility. He can't be living in a dream world. This land is too unforgiving for that."

Courtney made no reply and Matt looked away, turning his attention to Travis.

"If you're going to town today, you'd better get started." Matt pushed back his chair. "Good-bye, Miss James," he said as he stood. For an instant his eyes locked with hers. "It's been a pleasure." With that, he broke the contact, crossed the room, grabbed his hat and coat from the wall pegs and vanished out the front door.

When Travis came back into the house, Courtney had cleared the table and rinsed the dishes in the washbasin. She hadn't found any soap, but she'd managed to get them fairly clean.

"Are you ready to go?" Travis asked as she wiped her hands on the tattered towel.

"I'd like to say good-bye to Peter, if I could just take a minute." It didn't seem right to leave without speaking to him, especially when the boy had obviously been so thrilled with her presence. His story about the birthday wish had touched her heart. How many times had she wished for parents after her own had died? Perhaps Peter's parents were gone, too.

"Are his parents . . . ?"

Travis looked surprised at her concern. "Grace— that's Peter's mother—lives back East. She sent Peter out here last month. I guess she figured it was time for him to grow up."

"But he's only a boy."

Travis shrugged. "He's old enough, I guess."

"And his father?" Courtney knew she was prying but she couldn't seem to help it.

"Zach's gone. Left the ranch to me and Matt back in eighty-seven."

"And Grace isn't your mother?"

"No. She was Zach's second wife. Kathleen was Matt's and my mother. She passed away in childbirth when I was only four."

"I'm sorry."

"I don't remember her much. Not like Matt does."

"I think Peter misses his mother."

Travis just shrugged. "He'll be sorry he didn't get to say good-bye to you."

Courtney looked at him inquisitively.

"When Matt told him you were leaving, he ran off," Travis explained.

"Well, when you get back, tell him I said good-bye."

"Yeah, sure." He opened the door and let her pass through in front of him. Courtney's attention was focused on the floor, her thoughts tangled with the sadness of Peter's loneliness, something with which she could relate. She drew up short when Travis took her hand. She looked up sharply before she realized that he wasn't making a pass but rather trying to help her up into a wagon.

Yes, a wagon! An honest-to-God buckboard, a horse-drawn wagon. This had to be a joke. Right?

"You've got to be kidding."

"I'm sorry. We don't have much call for a buggy," Travis apologized sincerely. "This has really good springs."

Courtney immediately felt sorry for her outburst. "I'm sure it does," she reassured him as he gave her a hand up and she settled into the wooden seat. These poor guys didn't even have a car or truck. She was going to be overjoyed when they finally made it back to real civilization.

Travis walked around the front of the horse and climbed into the wagon. As he settled into the narrow seat, his thigh pressed against hers and he froze at the contact. Courtney looked away, pretending to be unaware of his reaction. How long had it been since these men had seen a woman? She breathed a sigh of relief when he clucked to the horse and the wagon rocked into motion. Courtney gripped the low edge of the seat railing and braced herself for a long jolting ride.

Matt watched the wagon from his vantage point atop a small rise south of the road. She was finally gone. And good riddance, too. Miss Courtney James didn't fool him one bit. No, sir, not one bit!

He knew what she was: a harlot, a fallen woman, a lady of the evening. Even a fool could have figured it out, what with her walking around with her hair all loose and flowing like that. Said she wasn't used to getting up so early. Matt snorted at the thought. Needed coffee for when she was working late, she claimed. Well, that was probably the truth. Seldom ate breakfast. He guessed not, when she was up half the night entertaining paying men. She hadn't been able to get to sleep last night either. She wouldn't be used to going to bed at a decent hour. She'd tossed half the night, and he could testify to that personally because every time those springs creaked he'd heard them.

She had most likely run away from a brothel somewhere. That would explain the ill-fitting clothes. If she had been forced to steal them, then it figured that the sweater was way too big and the pants too small. Even her jacket wasn't a regular woman's coat. It looked like something she would have gotten from one of those gambling men. Only a soft-living gambler would wear something that impractical out here.

Maybe some man had helped her get away, then changed his mind and dumped her out in the middle of nowhere. Right on top of Anderson's Ridge. Right where Peter had found her. Sure. That was probably what had happened. Good thing they were getting rid of her. There was no telling the amount of trouble she might have stirred up.

Nope, no telling at all. That was the last he wanted to see of Miss Courtney James, he assured himself as the slope of the hill obscured the wagon from sight, leaving only a lingering haze of dust. He pulled the brim of his Stetson down hard and urged Red into a gallop that would take him in the opposite direction, but even the wind whistling past his ears and whipping at his face wouldn't banish the memory of the way she had felt pressed against his back.

# *Chapter Four*

The wagon jolted along the rutted road. Well, it wasn't a road, really, just a packed trail through pastureland. Conversation kind of petered out after the first half hour's discussion about the weather and the land. She supposed cowboys weren't generally known for their conversational skills, and Travis Ward proved to be no exception.

Courtney contented herself with studying the landscape. Verdant spring grass covered the rolling hills, and in the distance the mountains cut into the sky. The mountains. She stared at them, still reluctant to admit she actually saw them. Her thoughts inevitably returned to her predicament. There was no way to explain how she had come to be in Montana or what had happened to her memory. She'd heard about amnesia. Not being able to account for a few hours or days was bad enough; she couldn't imagine how terrifying it would be if she couldn't remember any of her past.

It didn't matter how she looked at it; there was no logical or rational explanation for her being here in Montana. She would just have to content herself with the fact that she was on her way home, albeit the slow way. She folded her hands in her lap and watched the ground creeping by beneath the wagon wheels. It was hard to believe they didn't have an actual car. This wagon ride was probably Matthew Ward's idea of a joke, though why Travis would submit to this kind of torture was beyond Courtney's comprehension.

She shifted on the wooden seat. Already her butt was beginning to grow numb. Any minute now, Matt would probably come roaring by in some souped up four-by-four. She refused to let on that she was annoyed. Nobody made a fool out of Courtney James. A bit longer and she would be gone, away from the Wards and arranging her way home.

The miles rolled by. Courtney gradually relaxed. She even nodded off once or twice. The sun warmed her back and the peacefulness of her surroundings lulled her senses, and she let them be lulled. How long had it been since she'd totally relaxed like this? She seldom unwound. Her volunteer work and her job as a systems analyst kept her busy. Free time only gave her the opportunity to ponder her solitary life, and she preferred not to think about that. It was too depressing.

An extra deep rut in the road jolted her alert as she bounced in the seat. She looked over her shoulder, but there was no sign of relief. For a minute she thought about asking Travis why he was doing this, but what if the wagon really was their only means of transportation? She hadn't seen any vehicles on the ranch, just horses.

"How much farther is it?" she asked instead.

"Just a couple more miles. Over that hill there." Travis pointed to a ridge in the distance.

Courtney propped her boots on the wagon's front plank, shifting slightly to let the circulation return to her backside.

Travis seemed to sense her discomfort. "Did you want to stop for a while and stretch your legs?"

"No. Thanks anyway." She just wanted to get to town and sort this whole mess out so she could get back home.

Travis reached under the seat with his free hand and pulled out a white cloth bag. From inside the sack, he produced a handful of cold biscuits and offered them to her. It seemed impolite to refuse. Besides, it had been hours since breakfast. Getting up so early had given her quite an appetite, or maybe it was all this fresh air. Either way, she accepted a biscuit and took a bite. Gourmet it wasn't. The hard bottom ridge cracked between her teeth, and a large chunk of powder-dry pastry filled her mouth. Courtney had to swallow several times to get it down. She hastily accepted the canteen that appeared in front of her downcast face, and took a big swig of the tepid water.

"Matt?" she asked as she held up what remained of the biscuit.

Travis nodded solemnly.

Courtney smiled. "I guess Peter was right about him not being a great cook."

" 'Fraid so."

She kept the water nearby as she finished the biscuit in small careful nibbles. It proved edible, if you knew what you were up against.

Travis took a drink of the water, then carefully wiped the mouthpiece on his shirt before handing the canteen back to her. He gave her a sheepish grin before his face began to turn red and he pretended to be engrossed in checking the harness straps. Courtney hid a smile at his sudden shyness, and shifted her attention away from him to avoid causing him further embarrassment. She wasn't accustomed to this kind of behavior. The males of her acquaintance were aggressively masculine and competitive or, the opposite, complacent. She had no romantic interest in any of them, though several were good friends. No, Courtney thought, she still hadn't found that man who could make her heart beat erratically in her chest or her face flush or heat liquify her limbs.

Partway up the last hill, Courtney became aware of sounds. Not the roar of city traffic, more like the sounds of a sleepy country town. She could hear children calling to each other and the rhythmic rap of hammering and the general muffled noise of activity.

"You can just drop me off wherever it's convenient," Courtney said as she sat up straighter in the unyielding seat.

"Anywhere is convenient. Was there someplace special you wanted to go?"

"The bank, if it's not out of your way." Hopefully he wouldn't have to maneuver a horse and wagon through a main street's traffic. That would be quite a display, and Courtney had no desire to make a spectacle of herself.

"Bank's right next to the mercantile."

Courtney raised her brows at his terminology. Mercantile? Did people still use that word?

The wagon topped the rise, granting Courtney a clear view of the small town sprawled out over the plateau atop the hill. She went completely still.

Her eyes saw, but her brain refused to accept.

The town was vintage nineteenth century, a replica of Walnut Grove from *The Little House on the Prairie*, right down to the schoolhouse where the children played. The main street—in fact, the only street—was a dirt road flanked by wooden sidewalks and hitching posts on the four blocks that comprised the center of town. There was a bank—she could read the sign, a livery stable and—she conceded to Travis's use of the term—a mercantile. There was even an honest-to-God saloon complete with banged-out piano music and a drunk staggering out the door.

The houses were scattered at both ends of the street. Of the near ones, some painted and some with weathered plank siding, a few had white picket fences, some had verandas and one even sported a courting swing. Laundry flapped in the breeze from several lines.

It was like stepping back in time. Way back. As the wagon rolled slowly past the houses toward the center of town, Courtney stared around. Despite her intense scrutiny she couldn't detect any movie cameras. That ruled out *that* idea.

The wagon creaked to a stop. To Courtney's left was, according to the wooden sign swaying in the breeze over the door, a combination telegraph and newspaper office. Next door to that, the bank and then the mercantile. To her right, a shoemaker's establishment, a tailor's and a barbershop all opened onto the raised boardwalk. Horses were tied to the hitching posts on both sides of the street.

Speechless and numb, Courtney realized that Travis had jumped out and come around the wagon to help her down. She stumbled over the wagon's side. Travis caught and then released her as her feet found the ground. She couldn't seem to tear her eyes away from the sights before her. It was too unreal, too improbable, too completely impossible. The detailed realism was perfect, right down to a pickle barrel that she could see through the open door of the mercantile.

She took a few steps as Travis applied some pressure on her elbow, and she found herself on the wooden sidewalk facing the bank. Through the single window, she could see an old-fashioned teller's cage and, behind the bars, a bearded man wearing a visor. His shirt sleeves were secured tight above his elbows by striped garters. Sorry, not an ATM in sight.

Travis said something that failed to register, just words that couldn't penetrate the swirl of visual sensations that her mind wrestled to accept. It was several moments before she realized he had left and was moving the wagon down to the mercantile.

She pinched herself. A sliver of pain radiated from the offended spot. Yes, this was real. She was awake.

She looked toward the newspaper office, drawn by the clacking sound that came from within. Through a dusty window, she watched a portly man, wearing an oversized leather apron, hand-crank a printing machine. She'd seen similar machines, but only in museums. She took a step in his direction, then another, until she stood before the door. Taking a deep breath, she pushed it open and went inside.

Her boot heels clicked on the wooden flooring.

"Be with you in a minute," the man called without looking up.

Courtney wandered up to the counter that divided the work area from the front part of the room. Trays of metal squares lined work shelves on the back wall, and ink-stained rags covered the counter there. The man grabbed one of the rags and wiped his hands on it. He came forward as Courtney looked down at the piece of folded newsprint on the counter.

The headline jumped out at her. "President Grover Cleveland . . ." Courtney didn't read beyond the name. Her eyes flicked from the headline to the date on the right side of the newspaper's header. Wednesday, April 15, 1896. Wednesday? It should be Monday. But then April 15 wouldn't be on the same day of the week in 1896 as in 1996.

"Yes, ma'am?" The printer looked at her across the counter.

"Is this real?"

"Yes, ma'am, came over the telegraph this morning. The President favors the silver coinage for sure. Lot of people think gold's the only way to go."

"No," Courtney said. "Not the story. I mean the date."

He gave her a look that said she should know what day it was. He planted his ink-blackened hands on the counter with a thump. "April 15th. That's what it says, ain't it?" He spun the newspaper around and peered down at the date. "Yep, that's right."

"1896?"

He raised his brows and leaned over to look at her more closely. He took in her pants with a look of disdain, and muttered something under his breath before turning his back on her and stomping back to the printing press.

Courtney backed out the door. She felt as if she'd just fallen down Alice's rabbit hole and ended up in the middle of Walnut Grove. Only this wasn't television or movies or books or any kind of make-believe. She searched the surroundings for signs of modern civilization. There were no telephone lines, no electrical wires, nothing electrical at all.

A young boy bumped into her on the sidewalk as she spun around. She stepped back with a muttered apology.

Then she had an idea. "Wait," she called as he started to walk around her. She fumbled in her pocket and withdrew a crumpled five-dollar bill. "If you can tell me the day, month and year," she said as she held the bill out to him, "I'll give you five dollars."

The boy gaped at her as if she'd just lost her mind. "Five dollars?"

Courtney nodded.

"April 15, 1896."

"No," Courtney explained. "I don't want you to tell me what they want you to tell me. You only get the money if you tell me the real year."

The boy's brow wrinkled in a frown. "1896."

She waved the bill. "The real year. When were you born?"

He scratched his head and then played with one side of the suspenders that held up his ill-fitting pants. "I was born in 1888." He looked at the money expectantly, then jerked his head up with a scowl. "Hey, that ain't no real money." He back away from her. "Should of knowed nobody would give that kind of money for a dumb question like that. You must be some crazy." He spun on his heel and raced off down the sidewalk, his flat boots pounding on the planks, raising a cloud of fine dust. "Crazy, crazy," he taunted as he ran.

Courtney looked down at the wrinkled bill in her hand. Her stomach was sinking clear out of sight. She rocked back on her heels as dizziness assailed her. It couldn't really be 1896. Could it? Memories flashed: the medicine wheel, the ceremony. The Indian had said she needed to go back. The smoke. The chanting. And then the wind and the feeling of suffocation. A blackout, the bright light, then Montana. 1896?

Numbness began at her toes and fingertips and crept through her limbs like a drifting fog. The last thing she remembered was looking toward the mercantile and seeing Travis standing on the wooden sidewalk. Then everything went black.

Matt adjusted the wick on the lantern and then pulled the ledger a little closer within the circle of light. He scratched a few more numbers and then checked the clock on the mantle again. Travis should be back soon. The sun had set an hour ago. He closed the heavy book, picked it up and carried it to his room. The shirt he had loaned to Courtney the night before was folded neatly at the foot of the bed. He skirted around it and slammed the ledger into the bottom dresser drawer on top of his wool socks and long underwear. He pushed the drawer shut with his foot.

The shirt drew his attention again, and he stared at it with an accusing look. "Damn. It's just a shirt," he muttered as he closed the distance between himself and the bed with a couple of quick steps and snatched up the offending piece of clothing. The cotton fabric was soft against his calloused palm. He could smell her scent, like some fancy French soap or perfume, even before he lifted the cloth to his nose.

His thoughts turned traitorous. He could imagine the softness of her skin, the silken feel of her hair running through his fingers, the sweet smell of her, the taste of her. His body responded.

Matt crumpled the shirt in his fist and then fired

it across the room. Just let a woman in here for a single night and look what happened! She had them all wanting something they couldn't have, something they shouldn't want. But want her he did. It was a good thing that she was gone. No telling what kind of hell might have broken loose if she'd stayed any longer. The kid was pouting as it was, and *he* didn't trust his own response. He had to get this under control. Maybe he should have gone to town. A quick roll with Rosie over at the saloon might have gotten his mind back on track.

The creaking of a wagon distracted him and he welcomed the diversion. Travis was back. Better go help him unload and get the horse settled. He closed the door to his bedroom solidly behind himself just as Travis's footsteps sounded on the porch and he heard the sound of a hat slapping a leg.

Travis pushed the door open and stood there rolling the brim of his hat with both hands.

"Finally," Matt said. "I was starting to wonder if you decided to stay the night."

"Couldn't do that."

"No, I suppose not. There's too much to do around here," Matt agreed as he crossed the room and picked up his boots. He settled himself on the couch and pulled them on. "That was quite the thing, wasn't it? A woman just appearing out of nowhere, like that. Peter hasn't spoken to me all day, but she couldn't stay here. What would people say? Besides, we're better off without a woman messing up our lives."

"Uh, Matt?"

Matt looked from Travis's worried face to the twisted hat brim. "Is something wrong?"

Travis shuffled from one foot to the other, looking down but surely not seeing his hat, for the mauling continued unmercifully.

"When we got to town, things didn't go too good," Travis finally blurted out. "Miss Courtney seemed real distraught."

Matt's eyes narrowed suspiciously. "So?"

Travis shifted nervously again. "So . . . well, I couldn't just . . ."

"Tell me she found a room or got on the stage or something."

"Not exactly."

Matt stood and advanced menacingly. "Then what exactly? Where is she?"

Travis looked up and met Matt's gaze. "She's in the back of the wagon."

"What!" Matt's roar and the accompanying stomp of his foot vibrated the plates in the kitchen. He grabbed his brother by the front of his shirt and pulled him close, nose-to-nose. "Have you lost your mind?"

"Listen, Matt," Travis stammered, "I think something's wrong. She got all white and fainted. She just kept muttering about a rabbit hole and what year it is. She grabbed onto me, Matt, and made me promise to bring her back. I couldn't just leave her there."

Courtney lifted her head and peered over the edge of the motionless wagon. Beyond the corral rails, Anderson's Ridge rose, awash with moonlight. With her gaze fixed on the crest of the hill, she crawled over a couple of sacks, rolled out the back of the wagon and dropped to the ground. Still woozy from sleep and numb with confusion, she staggered toward the hill, toward the medicine wheel. She had to get back home. She had to travel back through time, back to where she belonged. She didn't belong here. She had no family, not that there was anyone in 1996 either. Here she had no job, no money, no apartment, no car, no life. And maybe she was completely and totally insane.

She tripped and fell to one knee as she stumbled at the base of the hill. Bracing herself with her hands, she pushed herself upright and forged ahead, up the incline. At the top, she headed to the circle of smooth stones. She felt numb, mentally detached from her weighted body.

She fell among the stones, feeling them with icy hands, silently pleading to God or the old Indian or her grandmother, whomever she needed, to take her back.

She turned her face upwards to the sky and let out an anguished cry that lifted on the wind. Nothing happened. She dropped her head back down. "Don't let me be crazy," she pleaded. "Just take me back. I have to go back."

There was no answer, only the sigh of the wind and the sound of her own heartbeat. Maybe she needed the sweetgrass and the chant. She beat her hands against the stones in frustration and let out another cry.

Matt stood at the bottom of the hill. The woman's anguish carried on the night air, little snatches of sound that drilled into his chest. It was so like that day six years ago.

Six years ago and it still haunted him. Matt moved numbly up the hill, forcing himself to put one foot in front of the other. He blocked out the memories as he stared at the lone poplar silhouetted against the navy sky. Steeling himself, he looked for Courtney and saw her huddled amidst the rocks, her whimpers a soft mewling as she rocked back and forth, beating her fists senselessly against the stones. He focused his attention on her, forcing the other memories to the back of his mind. In this cursed spot, he doubted that he could ease the woman's anguish, but he suddenly felt compelled to try.

Tears of frustration stung Courtney's eyes. She kept pounding the rocks. Pounding, pounding, ignoring the pain in her hands, until someone grabbed her arms and pulled her to her feet. Strong arms wrapped around her and she buried her face in the rough material of a shirt that smelled of dust and horse and man.

"I can't get back." She looked up into Matthew Ward's dark eyes. "I can't get back." She wanted to keep on hitting, but her arms ached and her hands stung. It was useless. Drained, she slumped against him.

"Promise me you'll never make me come back up this hill after you again," he said stiffly as he scooped her up and carried her down the incline. She couldn't speak and she was helpless to resist his assistance. Shock seemed to have robbed her of all her strength. Everything seemed to pass in a blur. Sometime during the next hour, he cleaned and bandaged her hands, took off her jacket and boots, put her in the bed and pulled the covers up over her. And somehow she fell asleep.

Matt pushed himself and Travis hard the next day despite the rainy weather. He left Courtney in Peter's care. She'd been dead to the world when he looked in first thing in the morning. He figured she probably needed a day's rest. He wanted to finish checking the fence line and round up the last of the strays. As soon as they got all the cattle down from the north pasture, he'd take another day and escort her to town himself. The sooner the better. Tomorrow suited him just fine.

Darkness had fallen when he dragged himself into the house, Travis right behind him. Courtney was nowhere in sight and Peter was peeling potatoes. A neat pile of chopped wood lined the bin and the table was already set.

"Hi," Peter called out. "I got supper started for you."

Suspiciously, Matt eyed the room and then the boy. Peter guiltily avoided his gaze. Something was up and Matt decided now was as good a time as any to find out what.

"So what did you do today?" Matt asked as he hung up his wet slicker and hooked his hat onto its peg.

Peter looked around, carefully avoiding Matt's gaze. "Nothing."

"Is that so?"

Pete gave him a quick sideways look before glancing away.

"Got pretty dirty doing nothing," Matt said as he walked over, pulled a piece of grass from the boy's hair and used it to point to the stained knees of his pants and the rim of mud around the cuffs.

"Sorry, Matt," the boy said, looking at him with wide eyes. "I thought maybe it would help her."

Matt's head jerked up at the reference to Courtney. "Thought *what* would help her?"

Peter ducked his head again. "She wanted to go up the hill." Matt didn't say anything. "And then the rain came and she wouldn't come back down until we were done," he explained.

Matt frowned. "Done what?"

Peter looked guilty. "I wasn't supposed to tell."

"You'd better."

The boy wrestled with his conscience for a moment, then looked back at Matt. "We braided some grass and burned it and she rubbed the smoke around and then I ran around in circles pretending I was an Indian." His head dropped. "And then she cried," he said in a whisper.

A sneeze came from the bedroom.

Matt stomped across the floor and rapped on the door.

"Come in," said a shaky voice.

He opened the door and stared at Courtney. She huddled, shivering, beneath the bedcovers. The lantern light lent a blue sheen to her still-damp hair.

"I'll take you back to town tomorrow."

"I c-c-can't go." Her teeth chattered together.

"You can and you will," Matt stated between clenched teeth before he spun back into the living room and pulled the door closed with a bang.

Two pairs of eyes followed his movement around the room, but no one spoke as Matt took over the preparation of supper. He slammed the iron pan across the stove top and stirred the fried potatoes with a vengeance that left them in mushy chunks. He stabbed the frying steak and slapped it over onto the other side. The meat sizzled. So did his temper. When the meal was cooked, he whacked the pans onto the tabletop and stomped across the room. He wasn't about to deny his guest this last supper. And he was determined it would be her last one under this roof.

The light from the living room spilled into the bedroom and across the bump under the covers.

"Supper," Matt said gruffly.

No response.

He crossed the room and shook the still figure through the layer of blankets. A muffled moan issued from the depths.

"Supper," he repeated.

"Not hungry." Her reply was a hoarse whisper.

He pulled the covers part way back and grabbed the slim wrist that shielded her eyes from the light. Her skin was cold and damp. She shivered and tried to pull the covers back over herself. Matt's hand brushed across her forehead as she pulled her arm away from him. The heat of her face seared against his skin. He laid his palm on her brow. She was burning up.

Looking around the room, he spotted her rain-soaked clothes draped over the back of the chair. At least she'd had the sense to get into dry clothing. But it was too late. The rain and the spring coolness had combined to make her ill. How was he to justify throwing a sick woman out of his house?

Courtney shifted and huddled into a tight ball.

Matt's shoulders slouched and he let out a breath of surrender. All right, she could stay a few more days, but that was all!

# Chapter Five

Alternately shaking with cold, then perspiring with fever, Courtney remained in bed for the next few days. Peter happily took on the responsibility of bringing her food and hot tea and making sure she consumed both.

Late in the second afternoon, Courtney pushed herself upright in the bed. Though still afflicted with a runny nose and achy muscles, she couldn't stay in bed any longer. She needed to move, even if it only meant going as far as the living room. Action might distract her thoughts for a while from the problem of returning to her own time. She'd had too much time to think about her dilemma in the past days, and unfortunately, had come up with no solutions.

Using the wool socks Peter had lent her and wrapping the bed's quilt around her shoulders, she padded out into the parlor.

Peter appeared from the kitchen, braced his hands

on his narrow hips and gave her his best matronly look. "Miss Courtney. What are you doing?"

"I had to get up or go crazy." Courtney accented her words with a sniff. She dabbed at her sore nose with the cotton handkerchief that she held balled in one hand.

Peter hurried over. "Well, sit down here." He gestured toward the couch, and then took her arm and made sure she sat. "Are you cold? Do you want me to make a fire? How about some soup? It's almost ready."

The solid thud of footsteps on the veranda interrupted her reply. As the front door banged open, Matt's voice rang out.

"Peter." His tone was sharp and commanding. Both Peter and Courtney jerked to attention. Matt pinned the boy with an accusing look. "The stalls haven't been cleaned. Or any wood chopped, and Daisy needs milking. What have you been doing all day?"

Courtney struggled to get up, but the quilt tangled around her knees. She jerked it free. "It's my fault. Peter's been helping me."

Matt's jaw tightened. He took a deep breath and then slowly reached back and hung up his hat.

"I'm sorry to be such a bother," she said.

Peter edged toward the door. "I'll go do everything right now." He slipped around Matt. "Now that you're here, you can look after Miss Courtney while I'm gone." He pushed the door open. "There's soup on the stove," he called back. "It should be hot." With that, Peter was gone.

Courtney hitched the quilt up an inch or two, wrapping it more securely around her shoulders, clutching the edge in her fist. She started for the kitchen to take care of the soup.

Matt stepped forward, his voice stopping her. "I'll get it. You just . . ." He gave a jerky wave in the direction of the sofa, shrugged uncomfortably and cleared his throat. "Just sit down."

Courtney shuffled back to the sofa, settling herself in one corner as she fussed with the heavy quilt, untwisting it from around her legs and tucking it beneath herself. Her thoughts drifted to the seniors, and she wondered when people would realize she was gone.

Courtney imagined that they had found her old red Mustang still parked out at the Heritage Center. After everything that had happened so far, she wasn't even certain if the old Indian had been real. Had the authorities found him and questioned him? Or did they assume she had fallen into the North Saskatchewan River? Were they dragging it now, looking for her body, believing she had been caught in one of the treacherous undertows and drowned by the spring-swollen current? Or maybe they would think she had been abducted, her name just another crime statistic, another missing person. Her brows furrowed in thought. Maybe all those missing persons weren't really missing. Maybe, like her, they had been transported back through time. That thought led to one a little more unsettling. She'd never heard of anyone saying they'd gone back through time and then returned. Did that mean she was stuck here forever?

Matt came into the room, carrying a steaming bowl on a folded cloth. His attention was on the bowl as he carefully balanced it so the soup wouldn't slosh over the sides.

He shoved aside the kerosene lantern on the end table beside the couch and carefully set the bowl down.

"I could have come to the kitchen," Courtney said. "I'm not an invalid. I just have a cold."

Matt just shrugged. "It's here now." He stood there as though at a loss as to what to do next, not looking directly at her.

"Matt?"

He looked up, his dark eyes anxious, holding steady on hers. It was only a heartbeat of time, but it seemed to last forever, long enough for Courtney to feel a spark of awareness flicker to life in her chest, for her heart to begin an erratic rhythm that caused a ripple of shivers along her skin. Her heart seemed to compact into a heavy knot. "I need a spoon," she whispered, unable to will herself to look away.

Matt's gaze darted away, down to the soup bowl. He shook his head as if he needed to clear it. "Uh, yeah. A spoon." He turned on his heel.

When he came back, Courtney had taken several deep breaths to compose herself. Hopefully, he would interpret her flushed cheeks as an effect of the cold and not realize how much he affected her.

He stopped well back and stretched over to hand her the spoon. Courtney had to bend forward to reach it. She was careful not to touch him. Instead she wrapped her hand around the spoon handle, feeling the warmth of the metal in her palm, warmth that had come from his hand. A tanned hand, a weathered hand, a working hand, resting now, flattened against the sides of his jean-clad thighs. Well-muscled thighs. She jerked her head aside and fumbled with the soup bowl. She didn't think she needed anything hot right now—her insides were radiating enough heat already—but she definitely needed some sort of distraction.

She moved the bowl into her lap as Matt settled into the chair that sat at a right angle to the couch.

Head down over her soup, Courtney could see his boots and the lower part of his long, outstretched legs.

She shifted. Hot soup lapped over the edge of the bowl. "Ow." Courtney jerked her hand away.

Matt was on his feet in a flash. As she pressed the side of her burned thumb against her mouth, he dropped to one knee beside her and reached for her hand.

"Let me see," he said quietly, his voice smooth and low.

"It's all right," Courtney protested, inwardly cursing herself for her inattention.

He ignored her, reached out for her hand and rolled it gently with his fingers until he could see the slash of red along the base of her thumb. A thick tendril of sensation was winding up Courtney's arm, originating where Matt's calloused palm rested on the smooth skin on the top of her hand.

"I'll get some salve," he said as he laid her hand back in her lap and pushed to his feet.

"No. Really. It's all right."

He gave her a tolerant look. "I'll get the salve."

He returned a few seconds later with a flat metal tin. He dropped down beside her on the couch, unscrewed the lid and dipped his forefinger into the clear gel inside. Taking her hand, he gently spread a thin layer of the salve over the burn. His touch was so gentle, almost a caress. He hesitated for a brief instant, still holding her hand almost reverently.

The back door banged open. Matt dropped her hand like a child caught raiding the cookie jar. He surged to his feet as Peter hurried into the room.

"Good. You're back. Did you finish your chores?"

Peter nodded and smiled at Courtney. She smiled back.

"Okay. You see to Miss James. I've got some stuff to do out in the barn." With that, Matt spun on his heel and was gone.

Peter settled beside Courtney on the sofa, looking from her to the soup until she dutifully began to eat. Each time she looked down at the bowl and the hand that steadied it in her lap, the sight of the burn reminded her of Matt and the gentleness of his touch.

When she finally laid the spoon back into the empty bowl, Peter took them from her.

"You better go lie down now," he suggested. "You need your rest."

Warmed by more than just the soup, Courtney was inclined to agree. For some strange reason, she didn't want to see Matt Ward again right now. She needed time to be alone and mull over the strange reaction his attention had evoked.

As she climbed back into bed and snuggled into the gentle hollow in the mattress, she rubbed the back of her hand against her cheek, mentally comparing the softness of her skin to the coarseness of Matt's. His hand had been rough, but his touch amazingly gentle. An unusual combination that affected her in ways that she had always dreamed of feeling. But why now? She didn't have time for this now. She needed to get back to her own time and once she did, she would never see Matthew Ward again. She settled the quilt under her chin and drifted into sleep, but her sleep was restless, her dreams haunted with foggy obscure landscapes where she wandered lost and alone.

Courtney stared up at the ceiling and sniffed. Matt and Travis were gone, riding out with the first light. Peter had left a while ago; she'd heard the door slam and the dog barking. The house was utterly quiet, completely still in the mid-morning hours. The attic bedroom in her grandmother's home had smelled like this room; the faint odor of kerosene and wood smoke and musky paper permeated the structure.

1896. Her grandmother wasn't even born yet. Courtney squeezed her eyes closed and drew a shaky breath. What was she going to do? She didn't know anything about life in the late nineteenth century. There wasn't any telephone or television or motor vehicles. And there certainly weren't any computers. What had women done for a living in this era? Movies portrayed saloon girls or wives and little else that she could recall. Nurses maybe, though that might not have been until the war. Courtney shook her head. Even the First World War hadn't occurred yet. The Civil War was over, she thought, if she remembered her American history correctly. And the California Gold Rush before that.

Courtney sat up in bed and pushed the covers down. One thing was for certain, she couldn't just lie here and moan about what had happened. Hadn't she secretly dreamed of just this? To have been born in another era when love and marriage and babies were the norm. Maybe she should have been more careful what she'd wished for.

She slid her feet out from under the covers and dropped her legs over the side of the bed. She felt better today, more rested. She sniffed again as she stood. She crossed the room and eased the top dresser drawer open. Folded next to a faded blue shirt, she found the spot where Peter had gotten her a handkerchief from a pile of slightly yellowed cotton squares. She used one, then pulled on her stiff jeans and her sweater. She tucked the handkerchief in her back pocket.

She looked around on her way to the outhouse, but

there was no sign of Peter. He had obviously gone off somewhere. She used the facilities and went back inside the house. Wandering around the rooms only occupied her for a short time. After she'd studied the pictures and some of the cooking utensils, she remained restless. The table was dirty, so she retrieved the cloth by the washbasin and scrubbed it clean. The cupboard got a quick wipe, too. From there she moved to the living room. She carefully lifted the pictures and dusted their frames and then the mantle. Then the end tables, the window ledges and the coat pegs. Pushing up the sleeves of her sweater, she went back into the kitchen to get a basin of water.

Courtney was in the process of rolling up the rag rug in front of the couch when Peter banged in through the back door.

"What are you doing? You're sick."

Before she could speak, he hurried over and got down on his knees beside her.

"I'm well enough to be bored," Courtney replied, struggling with the heavy rug. "I need to do something. I can't just sit around. I'll go crazy." Crazy! That was a joke. Maybe she already was crazy. How else could she explain this belief that she had been swept back through time?

Oblivious to her thoughts, Peter gave her a wide grin as he bent forward to help her roll the rug.

"I knew this would work," he said with a nod as he grabbed the coiled rug under one arm and struggled to his feet. "Where do you want it? On the line outside?"

"Okay." That sounded like a sensible idea. Maybe she would beat some of the mud off it later. That's what the women did in the movies, didn't they? "Do you have a broom?"

With his free hand, Peter pointed into the far corner of the kitchen. As he dragged the rug outside, Courtney retrieved an old battered-looking straw broom. She ran it experimentally across the floor, and was rewarded with a cloud of fine dust. This wasn't going to work; she'd only make more of a mess. She needed something to keep the dust down. She looked toward the bowl of damp sand by the washbasin. It might work like the stuff modern janitors used on cement floors. She scooped out a handful and scattered it in front of the broom, then took another sweep. The sand rolled along the smooth plank flooring, collecting the dirt and dust with it. Courtney grinned at her own inventiveness.

She was finished with half the floor when Peter came back in. Looking at the sand, the broom and the lack of dust, he smiled.

"I can beat the rug for you," he offered.

"Thanks." Courtney swept the pile of dirt out the back door.

"Matt won't recognize this place," Peter said. His grin slowly faded as he glanced at the rifles over the mantle. "Can I do something else before I beat the rug?"

Courtney shrugged. "Sure."

Peter crossed the room and took down all the guns. He juggled them in the crook of his arm until they were properly balanced.

Courtney gave him a questioning look.

Peter glanced away then back. "Matt asked me to take these out to the barn," he explained as he ducked his head and hurried past her.

He probably wanted to clean them or something, Courtney reasoned as she scooped up another handful of sand and returned to the other half of her task.

As she swept, she noticed that Peter made several more trips through the house, into the brothers' bedroom and back outside. Then he began to rummage in the kitchen cabinet, tucking items into his waistband and holding them there as he kept them concealed from her and slipped out again.

Curious, Courtney stopped what she was doing and carried the broom to the back door. Just as she reached it, she heard the clatter of metal, followed by Travis's voice.

"What are you doing?"

Through the window she could see Peter scrambling to pick up the knives that had dropped onto the veranda floor. He glanced quickly back toward the house. Courtney stood still, hoping the darkness of the room's interior concealed her presence.

"You made me drop the knives," Peter accused.

"What are you doing with them anyway?"

Courtney tilted her head and leaned closer to the open door as Peter lowered his voice. Again he checked the house.

"Matt said I was supposed to take all the guns and knives out of the house and hide them in the barn."

Travis frowned. "What the hell for?"

"Because of Miss Courtney."

Travis scratched his head beneath one side of his hat. He didn't get it. Neither did Courtney.

Peter motioned Travis closer and whispered something to the older man.

"Touched?" Travis straightened up with a jerk.

"Shhhh. She'll hear you. And I don't think she's touched. Just Matt does." Peter glared at Travis, then cast another furtive glance toward the house.

Courtney's brows shot up and her hands went to her hips as her eyes narrowed. Matt Ward thought she was touched, did he? And then she smiled. She had been up on that hill beating those rocks like a madwoman after Travis brought her back from town. She couldn't remember if she'd said anything to Matt when he had come to carry her back down. She supposed she wouldn't necessarily have had to say anything for him to think she was crazy. Heck, *she* thought she was crazy. How else did you explain believing that you had traveled back in time one hundred years?

Peter's voice interrupted her thoughts. "Matt said to take anything that she might hurt herself with and get it out of the house." Peter gave Travis a suspicious look. "And what are you doing back here? I thought you were checking cattle."

Now it was Travis's turn to look defensive. "Well, I just thought I better come back and make sure she was okay."

"She's okay," Peter stated as he squared his shoulders and stood straighter. "I can look out for her."

Travis mussed Peter's hair, then stalked back to his horse. "Okay. But I'll be back at dusk to make sure you did," he said before mounting and trotting the buckskin out of the yard.

As Peter hurried off toward the barn to hide the knives, Courtney returned to her tasks with a smile teasing her lips. The concern all three brothers had shown warmed her heart. It was obvious the Wards could use her help. Besides, what else could she do in this era? She didn't know anyone in town. Perhaps she could persuade Matt that she could earn her keep until she figured out a way to get back to the time she belonged in. Being here close to the stone circle seemed necessary. It had to be the doorway through time. Her first attempts hadn't worked. That didn't mean she was going to quit trying.

Matt arrived home after dark. Travis's horse was already bedded down in the barn and looked like he'd been there for a while. Here he was working his butt off, and his brother was back here sparkin' Miss Courtney James. He'd better tell Travis what he suspected about her line of work before his brother made a fool out of himself.

Matt clenched his jaw as he shoved the front door open. His hand froze halfway to the hat pegs.

A fire warmed the hearth, lighting the room with a soft yellow glow. The flickering flames reflected off polished wood and the room smelled fresh and clean. He looked down at the clean-swept floor. Damn woman. Now he'd be expected to take his boots off before he could even come into his own house. He applied one boot to the heel of the other and pried the leather off his foot. He let the boot drop with a thud that drew the attention of the three people gathered around the stove.

Peter huddled on one side of Courtney, leaning over, showing her how to add wood to the fire, while Travis bent perilously near her ear, explaining how to test the oven's heat. All three heads were now turned in his direction.

Peter beamed happily and ran to greet him while Travis, looking sheepish, stepped a pace away from Courtney. The woman herself looked expectant.

"Look at how nice the house looks, Matt," Peter said as he helped his brother hang up his coat. "And supper's almost ready. Miss James had a bit of trouble with the stove, but we got things going good now."

Matt crossed the room. On the stove, a pot bubbled with boiled potatoes, while slivers of carrots cooked in another. Two thick, floured and seasoned steaks sizzled in a fry pan. Their aroma filled the room, combining with the escaping smell of fresh-brewed coffee from the pot steaming on the back of the range. His stomach tightened with a sudden hunger pang that he was reluctant to acknowledge. He didn't want her thinking they needed her. They'd gotten along just fine without a woman for years. Women were nothing but trouble and they all knew it. Well, at least *he* knew it. Travis didn't appear convinced if his ogling was any indication. He eyed Courtney as if she was dessert.

Without comment, Matt crossed the room and ladled water into the basin at the end of the counter. He washed his hands and then wet a cloth and scrubbed the dust from his face and the back of his neck before opening the back screen door and tossing the murky water into the yard. Startled chickens clucked in alarm and scattered from where the water splashed.

"I showed Courtney how to pump water and where the root cellar was. She even knows how to use the cream separator now," Peter said enthusiastically.

"But not how to put all those little metal cups back together," Courtney added, smiling at the boy. "I still haven't mastered that yet."

"You will," Peter said as he beamed at her. "I know you will." He dragged Matt over to the table and pushed him into the chair before running to gather plates and lay them on the spotless surface. Hesitating in front of the cutlery drawer, he gave Matt an accusing look. "I'll be right back," he said as he bolted out the back door.

When he returned a minute later, he dumped a bunch of knives onto the table. "She's not touched," he whispered in Matt's ear, and Courtney forced herself to remain facing the stove to hide the smile that pulled at her lips. She pretended she hadn't heard as she drained the vegetable water into a pail by the back door. She added a dollop of butter to the carrots, and then set the pot on the table.

Peter took his seat as she cut and dished the steaks onto a platter. She added a little flour and potato water to the fry pan and stirred up a quick gravy. Travis helped her carry everything to the table, then held her chair as she sat.

Matt just glowered before bending over his plate. "No biscuits?"

Courtney jumped up. "Oh, yes. I forgot." She opened the stove. A puff of steam and smoke billowed out into the room. Grabbing a cloth, she pulled the tray from the oven. The biscuits were golden on top but blackened on the bottom. Just like the ones Matt had cooked. Courtney stared at the offending crust.

"Just the way I like them," Travis said hastily as he took the pan from her and dumped the hot biscuits into a tin with two cold ones that looked almost identical.

"Matt says they stick to your ribs better this way," Peter assured her as he selected one and placed it on his plate.

"Maybe you aren't used to cooking," Matt said with a look that implied he knew something that he wasn't saying.

"Not on a stove like this," Courtney admitted with a sigh. "I wanted everything to be perfect. Damn it," she added half under her breath.

Three males looked up and stared at her open-mouthed.

"What?" Courtney looked behind her to see if she was on fire. Then she realized that it was what she had said that had silenced them. In this day, a lady probably didn't curse. Good thing she hadn't said anything stronger. Nobody had better be around if she stubbed her toe or hammered her finger. They'd really have something to stare at then, she thought. "Sorry," she apologized as she let Travis hold her chair and she sank into it.

Matt cut into his steak. He had the piece of meat halfway to his mouth when Peter cleared his throat and gave him a reproachful look. "Shouldn't we say grace first?" the boy suggested.

Matt put the meat back on his plate and laid his fork down. Women! Couldn't even eat in peace. He bowed his head while Peter recited a brief verse thanking God for the food. "And thanks for Miss James," the boy added with a sheepish smile at Courtney before he quickly hid his face by ducking his head and hiding behind the lock of hair that fell over his brow.

Muttered amens were quickly followed by the rattle of cutlery. Matt speared a potato and popped it in his mouth. Nothing special. He could boil potatoes. It was just that fried ones were usually faster. A forkful of carrots. Nice sweet taste and a hint of butter. That was just the way carrots were. He'd have to remember to cook them a little more often. He stabbed the piece of steak that he had been in the process of eating before Peter's interruption. He bit down on it, then sat back with a jerk. Never had he eaten meat this tender. Why, you hardly needed a knife. He cut off another piece with just his fork. The taste of onions and pepper and steak filled his mouth with a wondrous flavor. The beef was succulent and delicious. He savored the taste as he chewed. If she hadn't been watching him, he would have closed his eyes with pleasure.

"Mmmm, this is great, Courtney," Peter said with his mouth full. "Isn't she a good cook, Matt?"

"It's all right," Matt said as he sliced the bottom

off a biscuit and used the rest to dab up gravy.

"It's more than all right," Travis exclaimed. "This is the best steak I've ever eaten."

"Thank you," Courtney said with a smile.

Little more was said as everyone concentrated on their meal. Despite his lack of praise, Matt wiped his plate clean. He even took the last biscuit and used it to get the remainder of the gravy from his plate.

Sated, Matt leaned back in his chair. The front legs lifted off the floor as he stretched his long limbs. Courtney looked in his direction. He waited for her to tell him not to tilt the chair. She didn't say anything.

"Aren't you going to tell me to keep the chair legs on the floor?"

She shrugged. "It's your chair. You can break it if you like."

There it was. This was exactly what he'd been trying to tell the others. Women were always telling you what to do. Maybe she hadn't told him to put the chair down, but that was what she'd meant.

"I'm not going to break it." He let the chair come back to the ground with a thump. Rising, he stomped into the living room and planted himself in front of the fire.

Courtney didn't know if it was the cooking or the cleaning or what, but Matt forgot about taking her to town. He even helped clean out the third bedroom at the rear of the house, and volunteered to move into it instead of having her move her things from his larger bedroom.

Peter moved back into the front bedroom with Travis.

And gradually, the family fell into a routine, albeit an uneasy one. Courtney got used to rising to the crow of a rooster as the first pink of dawn streaked the sky. Matt somehow always managed to be up before her and to have breakfast ready by the time she emerged from her room. She suspected it was his subtle way of letting her know that he really didn't need her here.

This morning was no different, though she'd managed to be up a bit earlier. He was just starting breakfast, laying the last strips of bacon in the frying pan. He acknowledged her with a brief nod before he went and poured hot water into the basin as he prepared to shave. A piece of twine dangled from the top button hole of his shirt. It was the second time Courtney had noticed it.

"Let me fix that shirt for you. I found a button and some thread in the cabinet. It'll only take a minute."

He eyed her for a minute, then conceded and slowly unbuttoned the shirt. He seemed to hesitate as the last button popped open, but then he quickly peeled the shirt off and held it out to her. Courtney's breath caught in her throat at the sight of his chest. The muscles were solid but smooth. A fine matt of dark hair tinted his tanned skin an even darker color. Her eyes followed the narrowing swath of fine hair down his abdomen. His stomach muscles twitched as though she had touched him with more than just a look.

Stiffly, Matt handed her his shirt, and then abruptly turned his back. Courtney savored the sight of that view as well. She'd always been partial to men with broad shoulders, and Matt was a prime specimen, all firm muscles and solid flesh. Her fingers itched with the urge to run the tips over the ridges of smooth power. She swallowed, twice.

Matt leaned over the washbasin, roughly stirring the foam in his shaving cup into a lather. The muscles along his shoulders rippled in the light of the rising sun that illuminated the kitchen. Courtney's fingers trembled in the fabric of his shirt. She tried to still them as she redirected her attention with much effort and fumbled with the twine that was twisted through the button hole. By avoiding looking at him, she could retain some semblance of control. She awkwardly threaded the needle, concentrating on getting the thread through the small opening. A rasp of sound drew her attention.

Matt held the skin along his chin taut with one hand as the razor scraped through a thin layer of foam along his jaw. Courtney couldn't keep herself from eyeing that straight firm line of bone and flesh. It seemed to symbolize Matt, solid and firm, rough maybe, but not beyond redemption.

"Ouch." She jerked as the needle speared her forefinger. She stuck the wounded digit into her mouth and her gaze locked with Matt's. A thin line of blood trickled along his jaw, jarringly bright against the white lather. Dropping the shirt, she surged to her feet.

"You've cut yourself." Automatically she reached to touch the injured spot, then halted her hand in midair. Matt watched her with an arresting look, a hungry look.

Courtney backed away a step and reached for the towel on the counter. She felt flustered, unsettled by his nearness, disarmed by the intensity of his look. She handed him the towel without meeting his eyes, and he took it from her without making physical contact. He didn't need to touch her; just the idea that his fingers were mere inches from hers was enough to send a flush of heat over her skin. Her heart pounded in her chest and her breathing grew heavy. What would it be like if he ever actually touched her?

She looked away, afraid he might read her thoughts in her eyes. She couldn't let herself be attracted to him. Not here, not now. This situation was only temporary. She was only here until she could figure out how to return to her own time.

She spun on her heel and went into the living room to affix the button, hoping there would be less temptation if he was out of sight. But every scrape of the razor blade reinforced the mental image of him in her mind. He finished, finally, as Peter and Travis came in from their chores. Somehow, she managed to return Matt's mended shirt and eat breakfast without visibly trembling. But if her hands were steady, her insides were not. She carefully avoided looking at him, and collapsed against the door in relief when he and Travis finally rode out for the day.

# Chapter Six

Matt heard them before he actually saw them. Peter's boyish laugh mixed with the softer more feminine mirth of Courtney's. He pulled Red to a halt in the shade of the poplars along the creek bed and slid from the saddle. Securing the reins around a limb as Red dropped his head and began to crop the lush grass, Matt inched forward. As he caught sight of them, he stopped short, braced his gloved hand on the rough bark of a tree and peered through the branches.

A fallen poplar leaned out over the creek making a perfect seat for fishing. As children, he and Travis had also used it as a platform for swimming and diving. In this spot the water was cool and deep and sheltered. Courtney and Peter sat side by side, heads bowed over their fishing rods while Peter reached over and concentrated on untangling Courtney's line. Matt couldn't help but notice the stark contrast between the two bowed heads, how Courtney's long braided black hair compared to Peter's loose blond-white curls.

Matt's gaze moved downward. Somewhere along the way, Courtney had commandeered his white shirt as her own. He wasn't sure if she still wore it to bed, too. He refused to let his thoughts stray in that direction. Today, she had rolled the long sleeves up past her elbows. Her movements drew his attention to her slender arms and delicate hands. He'd noticed her hands, smooth and soft. While they were easily prone to callouses from the exertions of ranch life, she had never complained, though he'd seen her flinch with pain when they blistered.

Suddenly she bent, intent on helping Peter with the line. The loose neck of the shirt drooped open providing Matt with a startling glimpse of pale white skin rounding gently at the tops of her breasts. A flash of white lace obscured his vision, keeping him from seeing more. He tightened his hands into fists and swallowed against the sudden dryness in his throat, but he seemed unable to tear his gaze from the open neck of the shirt. She shifted and the material bunched, flattening against her chest, leaving Matt with a strange feeling of deprivation.

"I think I've got it." Peter's voice carried crisp and clear in the still air. He leaned back and Courtney ran the thin line through her fingers. Something thick and heavy seemed to settle in Matt's chest as she laughed and wrapped her arm around Peter's thin shoulders, hugging him in a quick movement that normally would have left the boy blushing. But not now, not when he thought they were alone. Courtney had filled an empty spot in the boy's life, perhaps in all of their lives. No. Matt refused to believe that, even as he tried to deny the attraction that had drawn him to this spot, tried to deny his need to just see her, to hear her voice, to watch the litheness of her movements, the nuances of emotion reflected in her expressive face.

"Now do it like this," Peter instructed as he flexed his own stick rod, drawing it back over his shoulder and using a flick of the wrist to send the line soaring out into the middle of the creek.

Courtney nodded, her face set with concentration. Peter moved sideways a bit, to give her room. She drew back, but too far. The line, dangling from the end of the stick, snagged in the dead branches of the tree, almost unseating her when she tried to flick it forward. Peter's laugh rang out as she struggled to keep her balance, the arm without the rod waving frantically in the air. She righted herself and gave the boy a chagrined smile.

"I think this must be a man thing."

Peter shook his head. "It's easy." He reached to unsnag her line. "Try it again."

Courtney leaned back against a stiff branch and shook her head. "You fish," she said. "I'll just watch."

Peter shrugged. "Okay," he said.

Matt watched the way Courtney tilted her head and watched Peter, the faint trace of a contented smile curving her lips. The sun broke from behind a cloud. Light filtered through the maze of branches overhead, glimmering on the surface of the water, shining on a spot directly below Courtney's feet, casting a latticework pattern of shade and light over her and Peter.

She pushed a strand of hair off her forehead, tipping her face to the sun and the warmth. Her bare foot brushed the surface of the water as she swung her leg back and forth. Then, abruptly, she bent over and rolled the cuffs of the pair of Travis's old pants up to her knees. Her legs were smooth, the skin pale, her calves shaped with graceful curves.

Matt's attention shifted just enough to see Peter give her a startled look. She winked at him and pressed a finger to her lips, silently relaying a message not to tell as she slid lower on the tree trunk until her feet were completely underwater.

She let out a sigh, leaning back, her arms braced on the wood. Peter giggled. She gave him an appraising look from beneath her long lashes and then flicked her foot, sending a spray of cool water in his direction.

"Hey." Peter jerked sideways, but too late. The water splashed down the side of his arm. With a mischievous grin, he carefully laid down his fishing rod.

"Peter," Courtney warned, but with little sternness. She scuttled sideways, but his first splash wet her legs past the knees. Her laughter rang across the water as she retaliated, soaking the front of Peter's shirt. Peter kicked back. As she ducked away, Courtney lost her balance on the tree. She grabbed at Peter as she fell. They both toppled into the creek with a loud splash. Peter came up first, sputtering, his blond hair in wet ringlets. Courtney broke the surface a second later with a shriek and a shaky laugh.

"Now look what you did," she scolded playfully as she grinned at him.

"Me?"

She reached out and pulled a piece of twig from his hair. "Oh, well, we needed a bath anyway," she said as she lifted her hand and let water drip into Peter's face. He ducked away.

Matt stood frozen in place, his eyes fastened just above the surface of the creek where the water stopped halfway up Courtney's rib cage. The wet cotton shirt plastered itself to her body in a sheer film of white fabric. Beneath it, her white undergarments did little to conceal her shape. The slight hint of darkness at the tips of her breasts caught his attention and held it riveted in place.

He longed to step from the shadows and into the water. But he didn't want to play in the creek with her. Oh, no. His thoughts were a hundred miles away from that. He wanted to lick each drop of moisture from her skin, from the tips of her toes to the curve of her collarbone and everywhere in between. He wanted to pin her slender arms over her head and tease those barely hidden brown aureoles into tight little buds, to flick them with his tongue until they were rigid, to draw them into his mouth and suckle like a child. He wanted to feel her wet body, skin cooled by the water and then heated by his touch, wanted to caress her into passion, to hear her whisper his name, to look deep into silver eyes aglow with desire.

He ground his arm against the rough bark of the tree, feeling tiny splinters spearing his tanned forearm. The irritation was enough to force his thoughts back into line. He'd never wanted a woman as he wanted Miss James. It was something he couldn't explain and was determined to ignore. He shifted, intending to move away, to saddle up and ride off.

He heard the dog's bark just as the animal barreled into him and wrapped around his legs. His foot slipped in the thick carpet of leaves along the bank. He grabbed for purchase but found none. He stumbled out into the creek with a yelp and a splash. When he looked up, two sets of eyes were pinned on him, one a clear blue, the other polished silver.

He steadied himself and swatted Butch away. "Slipped," he muttered. "I thought I heard voices down here. What are you doing?" He tried for his best stern look, while letting his gaze travel over Peter's wet clothes.

"Uh, we fell in," Peter said with a nod and a quick glance at Courtney.

Matt couldn't continue to stare at only the boy. As much as he knew he shouldn't, he couldn't keep from looking at Courtney. One corner of her mouth was twisted into a hint of a smile.

"We were fishing," Peter added lamely.

"I see." Matt struggled to keep his eyes from straying lower than Courtney's chin. They dipped down for just a second. He jerked them back up, his heart slowing as Courtney's smile faded. She looked down at herself, at the clothes that clung to every curve, then back up at him, something other than laughter in her eyes, something intense and heart-stopping. She remained silent, but her breath came in quick little intakes that told Matt that she was aware of the magnetism between them.

Courtney moved first, plowing through the water to the shore, where she scooped up her discarded shoes.

"I'd better get back and start supper," she muttered by way of an excuse for her hasty departure.

With an annoyed look at Matt, Peter hurried after her.

Matt reached out, caught a branch at the edge of the stream and used it to pull himself out of the water. After only a few sloshing steps, he dropped to the ground, pulled off his boots and poured the water out of them, thinking as it splashed on the ground that it would probably have done more good if he had poured it into his lap. He took several deep breaths to try to get his emotions back in hand and the image of Courtney James out of his head. It didn't work.

He craned his neck in the direction of the house. Peter and Courtney had already disappeared from view. Turning his attention back to the creek, he eyed the water, then peeled his shirt off over his head, undid his belt, shrugged out of his pants and socks and clad only in knee-length underwear, jumped into the water. The shock of the cold water was enough to drive the desire from his loins.

Courtney plucked at the damp cotton, pulling the clinging fabric away from her body. Her skin was flushed and hot despite the cooling effect of the water. She plastered a smile on her lips when Peter ran up beside her. She didn't want anyone to guess how much Matt's intense gaze had unsettled her.

"Shoot." Peter slapped his hand against his thigh. "I forgot the fishing rods."

Courtney didn't slow her steps. "Well, run back and get them."

Peter kept walking with her. "But I have to get Daisy milked before Matt comes back up to the house. You know how he gets if I slack off on my chores."

Courtney looked down at Peter's wet head. He looked back with wide-eyed innocence. She narrowed her eyes, trying to determine if his explanation was genuine or not. For the past few days she'd suspected that Peter was purposely trying to force her into Matt's company, welcome or otherwise.

How could she go back there now with Matt still there? But if she made excuses, Peter was bound to pick up on her nervousness. She wasn't going to let on that Matt's presence affected her.

Peter blinked and smiled sweetly as she slowed her steps.

"Okay. I'll go back and get them."

He flashed her a smile and set off toward the barn on a run.

Courtney let out an exasperated sigh. Stiffening her shoulders, she turned and walked back toward the creek. She'd grab those rods and get out of there. Better yet, maybe she'd just yell down for Matt to bring them when he came. Yes, that was a better idea. That way she wouldn't have to get too close. She looked down at her shirt. The slight breeze still hadn't dried it, though she was clad more decently now that she'd pulled the cloth away from her skin.

Courtney stepped into sight of the creek just as Matt surfaced from under the water, his dark hair slicked back from his forehead, water droplets glistening on the crisp spattering of dark curls on his chest. As if sensing her presence, he glanced up. His eyes locked with hers, the look holding her motionless for an overlong second. Though she'd never witnessed it, it was obvious he often worked without a shirt. His entire upper body was tanned, not just the exposed parts of his arms.

He slid lower in the water, pushing himself back, away from her. His stare never left her, though it traveled down from her face fleetingly.

Get a grip on yourself, Courtney commanded silently as heat blossomed in her abdomen and her fingertips itched with the desire to run them through those crisp strands of dark hair.

"Peter forgot the rods," she stated in a voice that sounded surprisingly calm. "Could you bring them when you come?"

She only waited long enough for Matt to give a quick jerky nod. Turning, she walked away. She waited until she was out of his sight before she pressed her cold palms to her flushed cheeks and let out her breath. Things were starting to get complicated. This feeling she had for Matthew Ward could end in nothing but trouble.

Even the next day, Courtney could still envision the sight of Matt in the water. From her vantage point atop Anderson's Ridge, the creek wound like a blue ribbon through the poplars below. Coming up here had become almost an obsession, and it felt good to have something else to think about for a while instead of the constant concern over how she was to get back through time.

In the distance, the surge of mountains captivated her with jagged peaks and dark purple shadows of rock that faded into the green of the foothills.

The late April sunshine had warmed the smooth white stones in the medicine wheel. She rested her hands on them, absorbing the faint heat, and watched as Peter saw her from down in the meadow, waved and came up the hill.

The boy settled down cross-legged beside her. Neither spoke. It didn't seem necessary somehow. Together they stared off into the northern horizon. Peter had been with her on this hill before, helping her try to reenact the ceremony. He laid a hand on her shoulder, in a silent gesture of comfort that made the back of her throat burn with emotion. She patted his hand.

"Are you very sad, Miss Courtney?"

She blinked her eyes to divert the threat of tears. "Sometimes. I think mostly I'm just afraid because I don't understand what happened. I feel out of place. But I don't know how to fix it."

Peter's thin shoulders rose and fell in a consoling sigh. "What was it like, where you came from? Were you in heaven?"

She smiled down at him. "No. It wasn't heaven."

He waited patiently for her to continue.

"I lived in Canada, about six hundred miles north and east of here. It's very flat there on the prairies. There's a lot of grain farming, more than ranching. We can't see the mountains."

Peter looked toward the Rockies. "We couldn't see mountains in Boston either." His sadness came through in his voice.

Courtney laid her arm around his shoulders. "I guess we both just have to make the best of the things that we can't do anything about."

Peter nodded.

From the side of the barn, Matt could see Courtney and Peter up on the ridge, heads together. For some reason the sight made him think about having a family, something he seldom thought about. There was an odd kind of link between Courtney and Peter, almost the same as the link between a mother and her child, an acceptance and understanding that existed without conscious effort on either of their parts.

The picture of them together on the hilltop almost pushed aside the other image that always filled his mind when he looked at that spot. Almost. He spun on his heel and went back around the barn.

Courtney had expected her lack of clothing to be a problem. All she had was one outfit, a sweater and jeans, and they required regular washing with all the daily labor they were submitted to. She often wore Matt's white cotton shirt, and had also commandeered an old pair of Travis's denim pants, which sufficed while her own things were washed and dried. Instead of being a problem, though, it seemed the limited selection only simplified her life, as did most of the ranch chores.

Things seemed to be settling into a sort of permanence. Matt gradually moved his things into the other bedroom. He left her the hairbrush, but she missed the comforting clutter that she had come to expect on the dresser top. The room seemed empty with only a single change of clothing in the dresser, clothes that weren't even hers. She had taken to rinsing out her underclothes at night and letting them dry over the back of the chair in her room. If "damn it" was frowned upon, she didn't think Matt would take kindly to seeing her private things draped over the clothesline.

Travis was attentive, finding reasons to hold her chair and sometimes brush close to her. Once he caught her hand and held it for a second before blushing and apologizing for being too forward. Peter idolized her and followed her around like she was the puppy he'd always wanted and had finally gotten. Matt basically ignored her unless he couldn't easily do so, like at meals or when she sent a question or a bit of conversation in his direction. But generally, Courtney felt good. She had never felt so needed, as if she really made a difference. She took pride in her accomplishments, mastering the stove and keeping the house in order. For the first time in a very long time, Courtney Anne James felt that she belonged somewhere.

Today, Courtney was completely alone at the ranch. Matt had taken Peter and set off for town at first light, and Travis had saddled up, after Courtney's assurances that she would be fine by herself. But even alone, she no longer felt that old ache of loneliness. It had been replaced by a sense of contentment.

She'd finished her own self-assigned chores and even taken care of Peter's. Spring was in the air.

Everywhere the signs of new life were evident. The early afternoon sun warmed the air and glistened on the new green of May.

Courtney slipped down to the creek and, while Butch barked at her from the water's edge, bathed in the chilly water and washed her hair. She didn't tarry long—the creek was fed by a mountain spring and the water was icy cool—but it felt so good to wash completely instead of relying on only a damp cloth dipped in a tepid washbasin. Memories of Matt here sent shivers of warmth over her goose-bumped skin. The images created such a strange longing that she forced herself not to dwell on them. She quickly dressed in her dry clothes and then wandered up to the ranch.

Today seemed like a good day to air the house. The fresh breeze stirred the worn curtains when she finally managed to pry the windows open. She left the doors ajar as well. And Butch occasionally wandered through to check on her while she cleaned. Intending to air Peter's mattress, she lifted the rag-packed cloth and started for the door. As something fluttered to the floor, Courtney halted in her tracks. The braided piece of sweetgrass was achingly familiar. The end was even charred where it had been burned. It wasn't the twist of grass she had spun for her own use during that first day of desperation. No, this was the piece of grass that the old Indian had held and used in the smudge. Where had Peter gotten it and why was it hidden under his mattress? Courtney had a sinking suspicion that she knew the answer to the second question. It was obvious Peter didn't want her to leave. He still professed that she was here because he had wished for her for his birthday. And Courtney wasn't convinced that he wasn't, in some small way, correct.

She retrieved the piece of grass, twisting it with tense fingers as she looked around the ranch house. Oddly enough, she realized that she wanted to belong here. She took a deep breath and squeezed her eyes shut. She was imposing here. Besides, she had nowhere else to go if the brothers decided they no longer wanted to extend their hospitality. She should go back if she could, back to her rightful place in time.

She dropped down onto the couch, rolling the grass stalk in her hands as she tried to think. The decision to leave caused her stomach to tighten and her throat to burn. Her arms ached as though they needed something to hold, so she crossed them tightly over her chest. It was the right decision. Delay would not make leaving any easier.

She checked her clothes and made one last scan of the bedroom and kitchen to be sure she was leaving with everything she had come with. After pocketing a handful of kindling and several matches, she gathered a few pieces of wood for the ceremonial fire.

She stood at the front door for a long time, memorizing every small detail of the rooms. Maybe she should leave a note. But how could she explain being zapped through time? It was better to just disappear, the same way she had appeared. She stepped outside and slowly closed the door.

By the time she reached the top of Anderson's Ridge, Courtney was breathing hard. She took several calming breaths while she surveyed the landscape around her. Once she got back to where she belonged, maybe she'd come and visit here, see what had become of the Ward brothers. She felt a tightness in her chest. They felt like the family she had never had. But it was selfish of her to stay, to push her unwanted presence upon them.

The murky white stones waited, their strange pattern more pronounced now. She had come here often over the past weeks, each time clearing away some of the tough grass that encroached upon the circle, until now the pattern had become distinct. She squared her shoulders and her resolve and stepped into the circle. With her hands, she smoothed out a hollow in the center and filled it with the kindling. Laying the sweetgrass carefully beside her, she tried to remember all the things that had happened back at the park.

She struck a match across one of the stones and touched the flame to the wood. The wind snuffed it out before it could catch. She rubbed her damp palms on the front of her jeans, then lit another, this time cupping it with her hands to protect the small flame. The dry kindling sparked and caught fire. Carefully she shielded the fire with her body, gradually adding sticks of wood until it seemed substantial enough to withstand the breeze.

She picked up the braid of grass. There was no time to waste. Sage. She had to do a smudge. She glanced around. This was Montana. Sage grew wild everywhere. Jumping up, she found a plant and twisted a few pieces until she broke off a clump of stiff stalks. Squatting back down, she dropped the sage onto the fire. She gathered the resulting smoke in her hands and washed with it as she had done before. Now the sweetgrass, she thought. She picked up the thick braid and held the tip toward the flame. She hesitated for a second, letting her gaze sweep across the expanse of rolling land, across the mountains and finally the roof of the ranch house. Goodbye, she thought as she let the flames lick the end of the grass. A thin stream of smoke curled out of the fire. She closed her eyes and, chanting her grandmother's prayer silently in her head, tensed, waiting for the darkness to descend.

Nothing happened.

She tried chanting softly under her breath, just guttural rhythmic sounds, no words. Still nothing. She opened her eyes and stared skyward. The wide blue expanse stretched away into the horizon, cloudless.

She snuffed the sweetgrass blade in the dirt, rolling the tip to be sure it no longer burned. Sitting back, she stared into the fire. Maybe there was no way to go back. Why had she been provided with the sweetgrass braid then? Did it not represent the chance for a return journey? Maybe she was still missing something. Maybe she'd been sent to find or learn something and she hadn't fulfilled that requirement yet. Either way, her disappointment at not being able to make the ceremony work was softened considerably by a surge of relief. She didn't want to go back yet. Perhaps that was the problem. There was still so much to discover, so many of her own feelings to explore.

She scooped up a handful of dirt and used it to put out the already dwindling fire. She poured an extra handful on just to be sure. Tucking the sweetgrass into her waistband, she leaned forward, planted her hands firmly on the ground and pushed to her feet. She shuffled the burnt ashes around with her boot.

Tilting her face to the sun, she smiled to herself as the light warmed her skin. She felt that she'd been granted a reprieve. Finally, she turned and made her way down the hill and back to the house.

She laid the sweetgrass braid back onto the wooden cot frame and replaced the mattress. Maybe

tomorrow, when they were alone, she'd talk to Peter
about where he'd gotten it.

Dusk was falling and Travis had settled in the living room to repair a piece of harness when Courtney
finally heard the crunch of wagon wheels in the yard.
She headed for the door.

Peter almost bowled her over as he burst inside.
His arms were full of bundles wrapped in brown paper and tied with string. He thrust them into her
arms.

"Here, these are for you." He grinned at her surprised look as she felt the softness of the packages.
They could only contain cloth or clothing. He spun
around and disappeared out the door. "I gotta help
Matt with the rest."

Courtney stepped back as Matt came into the
room. His hat was pulled low over his face and he
carried a sack of flour over his shoulder. He edged
past her and dumped the sack in the kitchen, leaning
the bag against the cupboard. Travis went outside to
help unload. It took several trips to bring in everything. There was coffee and sugar and salt. Matt had
also picked up seed for the garden plot that would
soon need planting. He left the paper seed packets
on the side cupboard. There was some new harness
leather and a pair of shoes for Peter.

Courtney hugged her own parcels to her chest, almost afraid to open them. But Peter wasn't about to
let her delay.

"Open them," he urged as he danced around her.
Matt leaned against the doorjamb, his face hidden
by the lowered brim of his Stetson. Courtney glanced
at him briefly, and then back to Peter when Matt
showed no sign of looking up to catch her expression
of gratitude.

123

The first package contained a bolt of eyelet cotton and several strips of lace.

"Matt thought you might like to make some curtains," Peter explained. "Or maybe some other things." He blushed a deep red, and Courtney quickly guessed exactly what kind of other things he was referring to. She'd never excelled at sewing, but she was willing to give it a try. New curtains would liven the living room up, and she could picture the effect on the windows in her bedroom. Maybe she could also sew some pillow covers, she thought as Peter took the cloth from her and insisted that she hurry and open the other packages.

The second one contained slippers of soft moccasin suede and a pair of stiff leather shoes. She sat down on the couch to try them on. Both pairs fit perfectly. She'd have to wear the shoes a while to break them in, but they were more practical for summer than her boots.

"Matt traced your boot soles when you weren't looking," Peter said.

Courtney glanced at Matt again, but he still stood with his face hidden. Probably didn't want her to thank him, didn't want to admit that this might be an indication that he wanted her to stay. Maybe this was his idea of payment for all she had been doing around the ranch the last couple of weeks. No matter his reasoning, Courtney was grateful and touched by the extra effort he'd gone to while she was unaware. When had he measured her boots, and what man would even have thought to do something like that?

The third package's wrapping fell open in her lap. She let out a gasp and held up an ecru cotton blouse trimmed at the high collar with cream lace. The front was pleated in tiny folds and the back secured by tiny pearl buttons. It was beautifully old-fashioned. Or maybe it wasn't old-fashioned, Courtney realized. Either way it was beautiful. She held it up to her chest. The sizing seemed perfect. It appeared Matt had been measuring other things too, though he must have done it with only his eyes. Ever since the night he'd carried her back to the ranch, he hadn't so much as brushed against her.

"It's a shirtwaist," Peter supplied. "All the women are wearing them."

"It's beautiful," Courtney told him. "Thank you so much."

"There's more," Peter said as he shifted from one foot to the other. And there was.

The second blouse was made of soft white cotton with lace edging in a V across the bodice. Beneath the blouses were a packet of needles and several spools of thread. A lemony fragrance drifted up from a paper-wrapped cake of perfumed soap.

"We figured ladies liked to smell nice," Peter explained with a blush.

There were also two skirts, one a heavy tan fabric and the other a lighter summer cotton in a blue and gray plaid.

"This one matches your eyes," Peter said. "Part gray and part blue, like a far-off summer storm. It's my favorite."

Courtney reached out and gave him a hug. There was a hot lump in her throat that she had to swallow before she spoke. "It's my favorite, too," she confided. "Thank you."

Her fingers fumbled with the strings on the last parcel.

"You'd better leave that one to open in private," Matt muttered.

Courtney's fingers stilled as she realized the parcel must contain items of a personal nature, things that a woman wore under the blouse and skirts. She glanced across the room toward Matthew just as he looked up. A reddish-purple bruise covered the top of his cheekbone on one side of his face, and there was a dark circle under his eye. She was on her feet before she realized it and halfway across the room. "What happened to your face?"

"Nothing. I just ran into a . . . a . . ."

"A fist," Peter supplied.

"Haven't you got chores to do?" Matt growled, and he pointed to the woodpile outside.

"Nope," Peter replied happily. "The wood bin's full."

And it was.

Courtney reached out and took Matt's arm. Beneath his shirt, his muscles were rock hard, his skin warm. The warmth sizzled up through Courtney's fingers. Like a prairie-grass fire, the heat swept through her limbs and pooled in her abdomen.

He started to pull away, but she held firm and finally he stopped resisting. Her pulse pounding in her throat, Courtney struggled to keep her voice normal. The jolt of electric attraction left her feeling weak in the knees.

"Come over here and let's put something on that. It should be cleaned so you don't get an infection." Pulling him into the kitchen and pushing him down into the chair, she focused her attention on the bruise. There were several cuts and scratches along his cheekbone. Nothing serious, but it looked tender.

She wet a cloth and dabbed carefully at the cuts. Matt winced, but didn't moved as she cleaned the area.

"You should have seen it," Peter said.

"Peter." Matt's tone was ominous and threatening, but Peter wasn't about to be deterred.

"Matt laid a whoppin' on Jarvis McKee." The boy swung his fists in a recreation of the infamous battle. "He hit him with so many rights." He swung his right fist, jabbing like a featherweight champ. "Ole Jarvis was practically beggin' for a left."

Courtney retrieved a bottle of alcohol she had discovered in the back of the kitchen cupboard. Uncorking it, she liberally soaked the cloth. She didn't even warn Matt. Anyone who encouraged twelve-year-olds by brawling in the street didn't deserve much consideration in her opinion. She slapped the cloth on the bruise.

"Hold that there," she ordered as he instinctively reached up to jerk the cloth away. His hand covered hers for an instant. There was that flash of lightning again, that streak of unwanted desire. She pulled her hand from beneath his calloused palm and avoided his eyes.

"That's enough, Peter." This time Matt's sharp tone seemed to get through. "Get washed up. It's time to turn in."

Courtney looked down at Matt as Peter went to wash. "I thank you for the clothes," she said stiffly, "but I can't condone a grown man fighting in the street."

Matt rose from the chair. He stood only inches from her, the heat of his body radiating out to warm her chilled skin. Courtney refused to back away from his dark look.

"You're welcome," he finally said. "And sometimes a man's got to do things he doesn't like." As he brushed past her, he dropped the cloth on the table. "I could use a hand with the stock," he said to Travis as he stalked out the door.

"Matt's not one to pick a fight," Travis said, directing his remark at Courtney before turning to Peter. "What happened, Peter?"

Peter shrugged. "Jarvis said something about Miss Courtney living here and then Matt hit him."

# *Chapter Seven*

Matt closed Red's stall door and turned toward Travis.

"Go ahead, call me a fool," he muttered.

"Why? For defending a lady's honor?"

"I don't think Miss Courtney James is a lady. But I can't figure out why I would feel obliged to protect the honor of a prostitute."

Travis stiffened and stepped forward with his fists clenched. "Maybe you'd better take that back before I blacken your other eye."

The woman didn't even have to be in the room to come between them, Matt thought. "Listen," he said. "She admitted that she wasn't used to getting up early. Said she drank coffee at night to stay awake. And look at the way she dressed. I suspect she stole those clothes when she made her getaway from a whorehouse somewhere."

Travis swung but Matt was quicker. He side-stepped into an open stall and put the wood railings between himself and his brother.

"All you have to do is look at her," Travis growled. "You can see she ain't no whore. Watch the way she acts and moves."

"Maybe you've been doing too much of that," Matt said, reluctant to admit that he'd been doing exactly the same thing. He was beginning to doubt his earlier conclusion himself.

"But what if you're wrong?" Travis challenged.

Matt shrugged. "Either way, it doesn't much matter any more. She's got to stay here now. After your trip to town the other week, gossip has spread. There isn't a respectable family in town who would be willing to put her up now. Her only other alternative is the saloon."

Travis banged his fist into the side of the stall. "No! She doesn't belong there. If I have to, I'll get down on my knees and ask her to marry me first."

"You make that sound like you don't like the idea."

Travis's serious expression shifted into a grin. "Here I am making a noble sacrifice and you see right through it." He grew serious again. "Peter's right. We need a woman out here. Look at the house and the way she took over the cooking. Hell, *I* need a woman. You probably do, too, but you're too ornery to admit it."

"Women are just a lot of trouble."

Travis grinned. "Yeah, but you gotta have a little trouble once in a while." Travis looked around at the settled horses, the clean stalls and harnesses hanging in their places on the wall. "We're done out here. Are you ready to turn in?"

Matt strolled back into the tackroom and picked up a brush. "You go ahead. I think I'll give Red another rubdown." There was something about grooming a horse, about working with his hands, that soothed Matt's mind, and right now he needed to think. He was having a hard time seeing Courtney as a whore, too. He'd picked out those clothes assuming she was a lady, and somehow the two thoughts kept getting tangled together until he wasn't sure which he believed anymore.

He lit the barn lantern as Travis went back to the house, and then turned his attention to Red. But brushing the sorrel's smooth coat couldn't quite banish his thoughts of Courtney James clad in the sheer cotton underclothes he had seen the woman at the mercantile wrap quickly in brown paper while he kept his hot face hidden beneath the brim of his hat.

Courtney stood in her room. She had wanted to go out and apologize to Matt right away. He had done something noble and honorable and she had chastised him for it. But Peter had been so insistent about seeing her in the new outfits that she'd allowed herself to be persuaded to go and try them on. Doing so might give her a little time to think about what she should say to Matthew Ward.

The lantern hissed slightly and the light flickered on the plaster wall as she spread the contents of the packages on the bed. She opened the last parcel. It contained what she surmised to be a corset. Up until now she had only seen them in pictures. Stiff bands ran up the middle of the satin fabric and bent into a curve where the waistline went. The top of the corset was shaped to cup the woman's breasts. Tiny pink ribbons and bows were sewn along the white-lace trimmings. The whole affair looked feminine and torturous all at the same time. She set it aside and fingered the soft sheer fabric of a chemise and a pair of bloomers. In keeping with the time period, the legs were long, down below the knees, and gathered with ribbon ties. The waist and neckline of the two pieces were also gathered, with ribbons woven through eyelet holes sewn in the fabric. There were stockings and garters and a ruffled petticoat. Two sets of everything. It seemed Matt Ward knew a lot about ladies' attire. Or perhaps he had let the shopkeeper do the selecting. Courtney discarded that thought as she ran the smooth cotton fabric of the undergarments over her cheek. She could almost imagine Matt's long slender fingers touching the cotton. A shiver of desire danced along her skin as though he had touched her instead.

She unbuttoned her jeans and slid them down over her hips. Next went the socks and panties. She gathered her hair in one hand and peeled the sweater over her head. Unsnapping the front clasp of her molded bra, she shivered as the cool air washed over her skin.

She folded her clothes on the foot of the bed and picked up the bloomers and the chemise, if that was the proper term. Not that it really mattered. She wasn't about to ask anyone here, not if the word "toilet" made them turn red in the face.

She stepped into the bloomers and pulled them on. She tightened the ribbon ties, then dropped the chemise over her head. The sheer fabric smoothed over her skin with a swish of softness. She tucked her arms through the armholes, and pulled the ribbon at the neckline and tied it into a bow. The fabric fell in soft gathers that ran between the peaks of her breasts and around on either side. She closed her eyes against a flashed image of a man's hands, rough tanned hands, touching her where the cloth now rested. She caught her breath as heat radiated through her and weakened her legs. She leaned against the bedpost, steadying herself until the surge eased. What was it about the idea of a man—no, of Matt—buying undergarments that affected her so sensuously?

She shook her head, determined to clear it of such inappropriate thoughts. She snatched the corset from the bed and wrapped it around her waist. In the back, it laced up like a boot. She turned it so the back was in the front, and wove the stiff laces through the slots. She pulled it only tight enough so she could tie it at the top and still turn it around. Carefully twisting the garment while she held the chemise and bloomers in place took a bit of maneuvering, but she finally got it facing forward. She ran her hands up the stiff sides until the garment fitted under her breasts, pushing them upward so they swelled over the top of the formed half-cups.

She looked at the stockings, but she already had the bloomers on and the legs stretched down over her knees. It seemed she should have put the stockings and garters on first. Oh, well, it was a trial run. She'd have to forego the stockings tonight.

The white shirtwaist also fastened in the back, with tricky little pearl buttons that seemed to take forever for her to do up without being able to see them. She ran her hand up the back, feeling to see if she had missed any. The corset dug into her waist as she twisted, trying to get a look behind herself. Not completely satisfied, but unable to check any better, Courtney conceded that it was the best she could do under the circumstances. She smoothed the blouse over her waist.

She chose the gray and blue skirt. Peter's comment about it matching her eyes brought a smile to her face. Stepping into the skirt and buttoning it was the easiest part of donning this outfit. Thank goodness.

She wasn't certain she could take much more. Despite the coolness of the evening, she was warm from her exertions. She brushed a damp tendril of hair from the side of her face, then smoothed the skirt.

Matt had left a small shaving mirror on the dresser. She picked it up and tried, unsuccessfully, to get an idea of the effect of her new outfit. Slipping her feet into the soft moccasins, she crossed the room and opened the door. Travis and Peter stared at her from in front of the fire.

"You look real nice, Miss Courtney," Peter said with a wondrous look on his face. "Doesn't she, Travis?"

Travis wet his lips and nodded.

"Are you sure?" Courtney stepped into the room and did a half turn. "I wasn't sure if I got everything on right."

"I think it's on right," Travis said in a choked voice.

"You look just like a lady now," Peter added as he came over and touched her skirt. He looked up at her and smiled. "I think Matt will want to keep you now," he whispered.

Matt. Yes, she meant to apologize. "I guess I better go out and apologize to him," Courtney said. "For what I said earlier."

Courtney stood at the barn door. She smoothed her hands down over the heavy skirt. She thought about the era she was in. Matt had been defending her honor. No one had ever done such a thing for her before. It made her feel funny inside, a pang of gratitude that ached to be something more.

The lantern's glow lit the inside of the barn. She could see Matt over in Red's stall, brushing the gelding. His back was to her. She watched the play of muscles across his shoulders as he slid the brush in smooth slow strokes over Red's coat, brushing with one hand, following the brush with a sweep of the other hand.

She swallowed and cleared her throat.

Matt's head came up and he slowly turned. His gaze raked over her, his expression unreadable.

Courtney took a hesitant step. "Matt."

He made no move, just stood with one hand resting on Red's broad back.

"I think I owe you an apology."

He looked away and moved out of the stall. He set the brush back on the tack shelf. "No need."

God, she was feeling strange tonight, all soft and feminine. Perhaps it was the clothes. She also had the strongest desire to feel a pair of strong arms around her, holding her. She shook off that fantasy and swallowed against the hollow sensation in the pit of her stomach.

Slowly, she crossed the barn floor. Her skirts swept around her legs with a gentle swishing sound. She halted beside Matt and waited for him to turn and look at her. After a brief hesitation, he did.

"Then I owe you a thank you," she said. She looked up into dark fathomless eyes that did not hint at what he was thinking. "I'm not accustomed to men thinking they need to defend my virtue." She could love this man, she realized. She studied his square-cut chin, his sensuous mouth, those dark eyes. Something tight and warm unfolded in her chest. Her nerve ends tingled with a sharp desire to touch him, to experience again that flash of current that seemed to surge through her whenever they came into contact.

Matt tilted his head slightly, studying her.

Courtney gripped her hands tightly together to resist the compulsion to reach out. "Thank you."

Matt was acutely aware of every detail about her: the gentle swell of her hips beneath the folds of the cotton skirt, the rise and fall of her breasts beneath the gathers of fabric of the blouse. He had thought these clothes would be not only more appropriate but more concealing. He had hoped that they would disguise her shape the way the tight jeans did not. He had been mistaken. If anything, they accentuated her femininity, her beauty, her perfect curves.

The lace of her collar brushed beneath her chin and drew his eyes to her lips. Full pouty lips that begged to be kissed. And her eyes. Sometimes they were gray, like a flash of gunmetal. Peter's description echoed in his mind. Other times they were the gray-blue of a distant rain cloud. Right now they were liquid silver. Quicksilver. He could imagine himself drowning in it, a pool of quicksilver.

He rubbed at his forehead to disguise his attempt to block out the sight of her. But his recollection of her was too vivid. He could still see the hair that rippled down her back. Black hair, silky hair, hair that made him want to run his fingers through it, to twine it around his hand, to clench it in his fist while he pulled her mouth to his. His eyes flew open in a misguided belief that actually seeing her could be less stimulating than his imagination.

A primitive hunger thickened his blood. Silence stretched between them. Even with his eyes open, he could imagine more than he could see. A full-length skirt and long-sleeved blouse did little to impair his visualization of soft smooth skin.

"There you are," Travis said as he stepped into the barn. His voice cut through the static air between them. Courtney took a startled step back. Matt twisted away to face the saddle bench, making a pretense of straightening the saddle there.

"Miss James was just thanking me for getting my face in the way of Jarvis McKee's fist," Matt said as he turned back. He gave Courtney a quick nod and strode out of the barn.

Travis offered Courtney his arm and a shy smile. "Can I walk you back?"

Courtney was too disoriented to refuse. Absently, she rested her hand on Travis's arm and let him lead her back to the house. They followed Matt through the door.

As Courtney entered, she saw Matt's gaze travel to where her hand rested on Travis's sleeve and then back up to her face, but his set expression gave no clue to his thoughts. He jerked off his boots, let them drop by the door, and then stomped into his bedroom muttering something about a fool under his breath.

Courtney excused herself to go to her own room. Inside, she leaned back against the door, weak with unresolved emotion. She knew that if he had touched her in the barn, she would have fallen into his arms. One kiss and she would have lost all restraint.

She stared toward the wall that divided their rooms, and impulsively went and laid her palms against it as though she could touch him through the rough plaster. She leaned her head on her hands and tried to calm her heartbeat with several deep breaths. She was afraid to go to bed, afraid of the empty hollowness in her abdomen, afraid of the pulse of desire that still made her want him, made her want to lay down with him, feel him close to her. She closed her hands into tight fists. Her nails bit into her palms. Slowly the need abated.

She crossed the room to the window, and stood for a long time staring out across the moon-washed fields before she finally undressed and crawled into the cold bed.

The daily routine changed subtly after that. It seemed Matt avoided her as much as possible. She watched him when she thought he wouldn't notice, and sometimes, if she turned quickly, she would catch him watching her, too. Travis took to asking her out for a stroll every evening. Sometimes she went, sometimes she had things to do, excuses. She could see what was happening. Travis's intentions were very clear. It was also apparent that Matt had no intention of giving his brother any competition.

Matt watched her move, watched the way the skirt swayed out from her full hips as she walked around the kitchen, the way her back flexed as she dipped her hands into the wash water and scrubbed the dishes, the way her long curls brushed just where her backside rounded the folds of the skirt.

He let his gaze travel around the room, taking in the clean floors and the dustless furniture, smelling the faint aroma of soap blended with kerosene and the lingering scent of roasted chicken. It was too easy to get caught up in it all, to allow it to happen. He wanted her here, and yet he was afraid. Afraid that just when he found himself needing her as well as wanting her, she would be gone. Like Kathleen and Grace, like Katie and Jeanette, like all the women in his past. He wasn't willing to face that kind of hurt again. Didn't know if he could.

She swept past him and straightened the doily on the arm of the chair on her way. The faint aroma of the perfumed soap he had bought her wafted in the air. Instinctively, he drew a deep breath and held it, letting the scent warm him. It was as tantalizing as the smell of food. Only it wasn't food he found himself hungry for.

She hummed a tune faintly under her breath as she worked. Her company soothed him, filled the house with a presence that had been absent for so long, filled an empty void deep down inside him. No, he couldn't let himself submit to it. He couldn't be lulled into a false sense of security. It couldn't last. Nothing ever lasted.

He stared into the hearth, watching the flame consuming the logs with incessant progression. Like the flame to wood, thoughts of Courtney consumed him, filled his mind even when he was miles away. He'd think of her as he herded cattle, see her as he checked fence lines, wonder what she was doing while he slouched beneath the brim of his hat and peered out through the spring rain across the rolling hills of his land.

He ached to touch her, but didn't dare. He was dry kindling and she was fire. One touch, one spark, and he feared there would be no refuge from the wildfire that would sweep over him, consume him even as the very image of her consumed his thoughts.

He rose to his feet, suddenly needing to be anywhere else, somewhere away from her.

"Going somewhere?" Travis asked. Matt caught the look in his brother's eye. Travis suspected. Several times Matt had found his brother watching him watch her.

"Out for a while." He crossed the room and pulled on his boots.

She was watching him when he looked up. Her eyes followed him as his followed her, asking, wondering. He had no answers. He wished he did. He opened the door and stepped outside. He wanted to stay and to run all at the same time. Even here, alone in the night, he could not escape. He felt her presence as if she hovered over his shoulder.

He crossed the yard and leaned on the corral railing. He rested one boot on the bottom rail and his chin on the top as he stared out into the darkness.

Behind him, the door opened and closed. He shut his eyes and willed whoever it was to go away and leave him alone. But he listened to footsteps approach and knew it was not to be.

"We'd better settle it," Travis said as he leaned on the corral and looked out into the same patch of darkness that mesmerized Matt.

Matt wiped the back of his hand across his mouth and swallowed against the dryness. "Settle what?"

"Courtney." Travis turned, leaned on the rail and looked right at him.

"Ain't nothing to settle."

"I think there is. I want her. You want her. It can't be both ways."

Matt could feel Travis's stare burning into the side of his face. Brother against brother. That was what women did, turned brothers against each other. It was just lust, just plain uncontrollable male lust.

"I been thinkin' about building myself a place over on Calhoun's Creek," Travis said. "Nothing fancy. Just a place of my own. It's time we gave each other some room."

Matt turned toward his brother. The light from the house cast shadows across his features, but the tension in his clenched jaw was still apparent. "You going to live there by yourself?" he asked quietly, knowing the answer but needing to hear it, hoping it would put his maverick thoughts to rest.

"I'm gonna ask her, Matt."

Matt nodded.

"I just don't want to be steppin' on your toes." Travis paused and let the silence hang between them for a moment. "But I will if I have to," he said quietly. With that he stalked away.

Matt stayed, leaning on the corral, staring off into the darkness. It would be the best thing. Travis would take her away from here and then Matt could forget her and get on with his life, go back to the way things had been before she appeared. The plain, uncomplicated, predictable way things had been.

A day later, Courtney still hadn't found a way to deal with her attraction to Matt. It was easier just to avoid him if at all possible. There were already enough images dancing around in her thoughts to keep her in a constant state of agitation as it was. She had no desire to add more.

Matt had returned early. She'd seen him ride up, though he hadn't come up to the house. Now he and Peter were out in the barn. Courtney peeled potatoes and carrots to add to the simmering stew meat while keeping one ear tuned for the sound of footsteps. She added the last of the chopped wood to the stove. As she wiped her hands on the towel by the washbasin, Peter burst in through the back door.

"Courtney, come see the new calf." He took hold of her hand and began pulling her out the door. "Matt said I have to look after him while he's gone."

"Did Matt leave?"

Peter nodded, more interested in getting her to the barn than in Matt's whereabouts. Courtney relaxed, surprised by just how stiff she had been as she felt her shoulders loosen.

"Matt says the mother cow dejected him," Peter informed her as he led the way to the barn.

"Rejected," Courtney corrected as Peter ran off ahead of her.

Courtney stopped just inside the barn, in the open area that served as a tackroom. The late afternoon sunlight slanted in between cracks in the plank walls. Bits of chaff and dust, lifted by the breeze that wafted through the open door, floated in the beams of light. The shaded interior smelled of dust and dry hay.

"In here," Peter called from the last of the three stalls that lined the right half of the building.

Courtney wandered over. Peter was down on one knee, his arm draped over the neck of a white and brown calf. The animal stared at Courtney with wide brown eyes and let out a plaintive cry. Peter picked a large glass bottle out of the hay. The bottle had been filled with milk and fitted with a rubber nipple.

"He's hungry," Peter informed her as he maneuvered the bottle into the calf's mouth. The little fellow tipped his head up and sucked noisily. "Matt showed me how to feed him. It's my responsibility."

Courtney stroked the swirl of hair on the calf's forehead and settled into the straw. He blinked at her, but kept drinking. It didn't take him long to finish off the whole bottle. He nudged Peter a couple of times, then, resigning himself to the fact that there wasn't any more, folded his legs and dropped into the straw beside Courtney. His side warmed her through her skirt.

"He likes you," Peter said as he set the bottle aside and eased down to the calf's side. He stroked the coarse reddish brown hide and then down the calf's white face as the animal's eyes closed.

Courtney waited a few more minutes before pushing to her feet. "I think he's asleep now." She hated to ask Peter to leave the calf when he seemed so content to sit with the animal, but there were chores that needed doing before Matt came back. It wouldn't take the boy long to chop her a little wood; he could come back then. "I used up the last of the wood. You should probably chop some before Matt gets back."

Peter eased carefully to his feet. The calf flinched, his back legs twitching.

"Will you stay here and watch him till I get back?"

Supper was taken care of and Peter was obviously concerned, though Courtney suspected he didn't really need to be. "Okay," she acquiesced. "For a little while."

Peter tiptoed out the door as she leaned her arms on the top of the stall partition and watched the sleeping calf. The sound of the ax didn't disturb the animal, so Courtney stepped away from the stall and wandered down the length of the barn. The other stalls were all empty. A ladder ran up the side of the tackroom, leading to the overhead loft. Lifting her skirt hem, Courtney climbed up and stepped into the low-ceilinged opening. Fresh straw was piled up against the walls in slanting mounds of fragrant golden hay.

There was a pause in the sound of chopping, followed by Peter's excited voice.

"Matt. Do you want me to show you how I did?"

Courtney straightened with a jerk, banging her head on the slanting roof. For some inexplicable reason, she didn't want Matthew Ward to catch her out here in the barn.

"You finish that up first," she could hear Matt tell Peter as his shadow fell across the barn floor. She leaned back, not quite out of sight, but hidden in the shadows.

Matt led Red inside. Stopping in the open area, he undid the leather straps behind the saddle and removed his sheepskin jacket. He pulled his rifle from the scabbard and leaned it carefully against the wall before lifting the saddle and blanket off the horse and draping them over the log beam at the edge of the tackroom. Red wandered into his open stall on his own.

Pulling off his leather gloves and shoving them into his rear pocket, Matt scooped a tin of oats from a nearby bag. He dumped them into the feed bin in Red's stall. Courtney could hear him murmuring to the horse as he started to run a heavy brush over the sorrel's back. His shoulders flexed with the smooth brushing motion, his work-worn hands gentle in every touch. Heat crept up Courtney's legs, snaked tendrils around her rib cage and up to her throat and face. Watching his hands was strangely erotic. She tried not to imagine how they would feel against something other than horsehide. She almost sighed aloud when he finally finished and laid the brush aside. He gave Red one final pat, then left. Courtney slid down into the straw, her knees suddenly weak.

Then she heard Peter's excited chatter and Matt's murmured reply. They were coming back to the barn. She swung her legs over the edge, found the ladder and hurried down, afraid that she would be caught and embarrassed. She dropped the last few feet and ducked out the back door. She pressed herself against the barn wall as Peter's voice grew clearer, echoing slightly within the barn's interior.

She gave her skirt and sleeves a quick brush for any telltale straw, then stepped back into the doorway.

"You're back?" She hoped she sounded surprised. Matt nodded.

"I'm showing Matt how good I did," Peter said.

Courtney smiled at the boy. "I'll leave you to it

then. I'd better go check on supper." She slipped past them and hurried for the house, only letting out her breath when the back door closed behind her. It was foolish to be acting this way, but she couldn't seem to help it.

Matt, Travis and Peter rode out early the next morning to meet the men hired to help with the spring branding. Despite the fact that Matt had strongly *suggested* that she remain in the ranch house until the roundup was over and the hired men had moved on, after the second day of being alone, Courtney couldn't contain her curiosity any longer. She'd spent the morning pacing the kitchen, tidying up though the house really didn't need it, all the while drawn to the view from the back window. Not that she could really see anything. She could, however, imagine.

Dust rose above the curve of the hill, beyond the trees lining the creek where she knew the cattle had been driven in from the surrounding hills into a smaller fenced-in field. She moved from the window to the door, opening it so she could hear through the screen. Calves bawled loudly amid the general milling of noise. The shrill sounds of cowboys' whistles cut the air.

Finally, by late afternoon, she could stand it no longer. No one would see her if she kept herself in the trees along the creek. Before she could change her mind, she hurried out the door.

From her vantage point amidst the trees, Courtney watched, mesmerized by the activity of the spring branding. Systematically, the riders and horses wheeled, cutting selected calves from the herd. Ropes spun in the wide loops, whistling over the roper's heads as the calves were lassoed, sometimes around the back legs, sometimes around the neck. Other riders kept the cows in the tight circle of the herd, allowing only the selected calves to be separated from the mass of milling animals.

The branding was quick and efficient. Several long branding irons were kept heated in the fire. The calf was hauled over, then held down by two men as an older man handed the red-hot iron to Travis, who pressed it into the calf's right flank. Smoke rose from the singed hair and the animal bawled in alarm. Courtney cringed each time the brand was applied. No one could convince her that that didn't hurt. She wondered what these men would think if she told them that in her time some youths went to special salons to get a similar brand, a trend that had replaced tattoos.

Or maybe their reaction wouldn't be so different from her own. She couldn't understand how people could do that to themselves either. The calves had notches cut into their ears, and as the animals surged to their feet, they shook their heads, spraying blood into the dust and onto the men. Then they were herded away from the main group. Once a cow broke loose and the men, after an initial failed attempt to herd her back, let her go to join the calves.

A rider appeared out of the dust on the far side of the herd. Even from this distance, Courtney had no difficulty recognizing Matt. He sat a horse in a way that made him easily identified, though she couldn't see his face. His Stetson was pulled low over his forehead, and a bandanna covered the lower portion of his face to filter the dust roused by the milling herd. He sat straight and tall in the saddle, directing the huge sorrel with only his legs. In one hand he wielded a thick lariat, while he pointed out calves with the other. The men were quick to do his bidding, cutting into the herd, breaking out the selected calf, quickly roping it and dragging it to the fire. But Matt was already wheeling, pointing again. As each youngster was branded and then freed, his mother was cut from the herd and the two were freed onto the open plain.

From Matt's and Travis's supper conversations, Courtney had gathered that these extra men were part of a wandering group that hired out each spring for the branding, and sometimes in the fall if a large number of cattle needed to be cut out for market. They seemed an unruly bunch, unshaven, their clothes stained as well as dusty, most with long unkempt hair. Matt had tried to impress upon her the fact that they were good at what they were employed for, but not necessarily above reproach in other areas. Courtney had gotten the message. That she'd chosen now to ignore his warning probably wasn't the smartest thing she'd ever done, she had to admit, but she'd been too curious to remain locked in the house. And now she found her attention held by the variety of activity, by the diversity of movements, by the cacophony of noise.

A mess wagon was located well back from the herd, farther along up the creek, beyond the holding pens. As Courtney watched, Matt trotted Red over to the wagon and dismounted. He pushed aside the wooden lid on the water barrel strapped to the side of the wagon and dipped a cup inside. He tipped his head back as he drank, and then set the cup back on the board railing of the wagon, leaning against the protective canvas that provided shade and shelter for the inside. Matt wiped the back of his gloved hand across his forehead, leaving a smear in the dust that coated his skin, as he spoke to a short, bowlegged man at the wagon's side. The elderly man passed him a handful of jerky as he talked, and then gestured wildly in Courtney's direction.

"Crap." She jerked back a step, stumbling on the uneven ground, clutching out at a tree limb to steady herself. When she looked back, Matt was swinging into the saddle. He spun Red in her direction, nudging the gelding to a quick trot with a touch of his boot heels.

Courtney assessed her options. She could flee, but she had little doubt that Matt would catch her easily. She could step out into plain sight, but that would just be asking for trouble if Matt's assessment of these hired men was accurate. Or she could step back further into the trees, obscuring herself from the others but still available for the chastising Matt was bound to deliver. She chose the last option. Really, she had little choice. Matt arrived before she could do much else. He dismounted, placing Red between the roundup site and her location, effectively shielding them from the others with the horse's body.

"I told you to stay in the house," he growled.

"I know, I'm sorry," Courtney apologized as she stared down at the toes of his boots.

"Sorry is the least of what you might be if any of these wranglers get any ideas."

A thought flashed through Courtney's mind. Though this wasn't her era of civilization, neither was it a time when men ruled with guns and violence. There had to be some semblance of civility this late in the nineteenth century.

"These are tough men, Courtney. They're used to taking what they want, especially with unmarried women of questionable morals."

Her head snapped up as the implication of his words struck home.

"Questionable morals!" What had she ever done to give Matt the idea that her morals were questionable? All right, she was staying out in the middle of nowhere with three strange men, but she had little choice in the matter. She planted her fists on her hips and glared at him despite the ominous look in his dark eyes. She was just trying to make the best of a bad situation. He had no right to imply that she was immoral.

"I warned you to stay in the house or I can't be held responsible for anything that might happen," he said. "Travis and I would make a poor stand against this many men."

Well, at least he wasn't about to throw her to the wolves, not just yet anyway.

"I suggest you keep out of sight and go back to the house. Now." He raised his voice sternly on the last word.

Someone called in their direction.

"I'll send Peter over to go with you," he added. In that instant, she saw the true extent of his concern. It was revealed by the creases around his eyes and the hard set of his mouth.

Her anger vanished and she stepped backward with a nod. Matt remounted then, and trotted Red back to the branding pit. There he drew up alongside Peter, bending over to say something before leaning back as Peter mounted his pinto and headed in her direction.

Peter maneuvered his horse through the trees lining the creek, reining the animal in at Courtney's side. His face was coated with dust. Sweat had made streaks down through the dirt and flecks of blood. Peter wiped his forehead with the back of his arm.

"Matt says I'm supposed to see you back to the house." He looked back at the branding with longing.

149

"I'm sorry, Peter. I didn't think he'd make you leave. I guess my curiosity got the best of me. I've never seen a roundup before."

"Me neither," Peter said, his face animated. "Isn't it exciting?"

Courtney looked up as she walked alongside the horse. "How about you tell me all about it while I fix you something to eat," she suggested as they reached the house. Perhaps she could appease Peter's feeling that he was missing out on some of the branding.

Peter nodded enthusiastically. "This work really makes a person hungry."

He tied Patch to the back porch post and followed her inside. While Courtney laid pieces of cold chicken in a frying pan to reheat, he dropped into a chair.

"So tell me all about the branding. It looked exciting," Courtney said.

"Where do you want me to start?"

She glanced over her shoulder. "How about at the beginning. What's the first thing you did?"

Peter pushed up his shirt sleeves and slid to the edge of his seat like a storyteller about to start on his favorite tale.

"The first day I helped round up the cattle, ate and went to sleep. But today I heard the cook when he got up. It was way before first light. He let me help him build the fire and get the coffee on."

"He has a stove in that wagon?"

Peter shook his head. "No. The pot hangs from an iron bar over the fire. It's called a pot rack."

"I see."

"He put steaks in some pots near the fire and made biscuits from this big pan on the end gate of the wagon."

"How were they?"

Peter shrugged. "They were okay. Not as good as yours, but Matt says you can't never complain about the food. Hell will pop, though, if it isn't ready on time."

Courtney arched her brows at his choice of terms, no doubt a direct result of the time spent with the herders.

"He's got a sort of cupboard in the back of the wagon with plates and cups and coffee and stuff. Anyway . . ." Peter waved away the importance of the wagon's contents, obviously intent on a more interesting part of the recounting. "Then the nighthawk comes in with the horses. He's the guy who's been out on the flat with them all night. And everyone else starts to get up.

"We sleep right on the ground. Some of the men even use their pants rolled up as a pillow." He nodded to assure her that this was a fact. "In the morning, they roll up their beds and put them by the cook wagon. After everybody eats they go and pick their horses. Oh, I almost forgot. You have to put your dishes in the cook's roundup pan or he gets mighty perturbed."

Courtney sliced bread and set it and the butter on the table. She tested the chicken, got Peter a plate and slid several pieces onto it.

While he buttered his bread and began to eat, she pulled up a chair across from him.

He continued between bites. "They make a corral out of held ropes for the horses, and then each man points out the horse he wants to ride and a roper will go get him. I asked Matt why each guy didn't lasso his own horse, and he said that too many ropes flying would spook the horses."

"Each man doesn't have his own specific horse?"

"Nope."

"How about you? Did you ride Patch or another horse?"

"I rode Patch. Matt let me keep him tied to the cook wagon. And he made me mount up before the rest in case one of the horses decided to start bucking all over the place."

"They do that? Aren't they broken?"

"Matt says some horses just like to buck. He says to watch the way they hump their backs, that's the ones that'll give you trouble. He said he'd have to cover my ears if one bucked through the campfire and knocked over the cook's stuff."

"I bet." Courtney felt relieved. It seemed Matt was making a major effort to explain things to and to keep an eye on Peter. She guessed she really shouldn't have expected less, not from someone as intense as Matthew Ward.

Peter finished one piece of chicken and picked up another with his fingers. After a quickly swallowed mouthful he resumed his story.

"The wrangler takes the rest of the horses away and everybody rides off together to go collect the cattle. It's called riding circle. Then they all herd their cows into the bunch ground by noon. That's what they call the spot where they gather all the cattle." He seemed quite pleased to have remembered all these new names and to be able to relate all this important information to Courtney. She just nodded sagely.

"It's really something to see, all those animals milling around. It's noisy and dusty. And Matt says that sometimes the bulls will fight. We didn't see that, though."

Thank goodness, Courtney thought. She had few delusions about the danger of two charging, territorial bulls locking horns in a battle for supremacy.

"It takes a while, but the cattle finally settle down and there's time for dinner." A broad grin spread across Peter's face. "On the way to the cook wagon, the cowboys have racing contests to see which horse is the fastest. Then they all grab a root and hog down." He smiled at Courtney's upraised eyebrows. "That means they eat."

"Doesn't sound very appetizing."

Peter just grinned. "After dinner they get different horses, cutting horses. Matt says this is where the real work starts. Matt let me watch the branding for a while. Then I got to help the men who keep the cattle in a herd."

Courtney assumed Matt must have become occupied with something and had sent Peter to a safe spot where he wouldn't have to keep as close an eye on him.

"I saw some of the branding," she said. She made a face.

"It's kind of disgusting, some of it," Peter agreed, though it didn't seem to have affected his appetite as he buttered another piece of bread.

"The hands who do the roping are called ketch hands, and two flankers stand by the fire. They catch the calf and hold it for the iron man. It gets branded—our brand is a lazy J over a circled W—and its ear is bobbed and . . . some other stuff." He flushed slightly, and Courtney refrained from comment.

He laid down his fork. "That's about it. On a bigger spread they would drive those cows out and move the camp and start all over in another spot the next day. Here, they leave the camp 'cause it's kinda central, and just ride out in different directions each day. And Matt says he can bring in the few animals that they miss and brand them himself later."

Peter hid a yawn behind his hand. It seemed the late nights and lack of sleep were catching up with him.

"Maybe you should get some rest before you head back out," Courtney suggested as she rose and started to clear away Peter's plate.

Peter seemed torn between sleep and what he might be missing.

"Maybe I'll just sit down and rest for a bit," he said. He went to sit on the couch. Courtney poured a little hot water from the kettle into the washbasin and quickly scrubbed up the few dishes. When she turned around, Peter was slumped over, sound asleep.

The branding lasted two more days, and Courtney stayed in the house. Matt's words had made her realize the foolishness of her actions. The black eye he'd gotten in town was just barely healed. She didn't want to give him a reason to get another one.

Over the weeks, she grew more at ease with manipulating the stove, learning to vary the amounts of wood or the time she let the coals cool before she used the oven. She churned butter and separated cream as though she'd always done it, and found a sense of accomplishment in even those simple tasks. Each night at dusk, when Matt and Travis returned from the range, she had their supper ready. Life was hard. By the end of the day her shoulders ached from carrying heavy buckets of water or from hand-scrubbing wooden floors or from carrying wood. She swore she'd never get used to killing chickens for supper, so Peter did that, but she managed to clean and pluck them. However, there still remained the challenge of trying to milk Daisy, a task that Matt had hinted she might take over to free Peter to help him and Travis.

Well, today was the day, Courtney had decided. She swallowed her nervousness and reminded herself that Daisy was just a cow and a docile one at that. Peter directed her as she carefully positioned the short three-legged stool near the cow's back end. Daisy turned her head as much as the rope that bound her to the stall would allow, and studied her with soulful brown eyes as Courtney settled herself on the stool. Peter looked over her shoulder as she nudged the pail into place with her foot and reached tentatively for the teats. She half expected Daisy to kick or move, but the animal remained placid, calmly chewing on the grass from the wall bin. Courtney squeezed and pulled downward the way Peter had demonstrated, but nothing happened. She jerked back as Daisy shifted uneasily.

Whack. The cow's tail swung around and smacked Courtney along the side of the head. She flung up her arm to prevent a further assault, and gave Peter a stern look as he laughed out loud.

"She still doesn't trust you," Peter explained between chuckles. He reached into his pocket and withdrew a handful of sugar. "Here, give her this."

"Sugar? I thought that was for horses."

Peter shrugged. "Works for cows, too."

Courtney let Peter pour the sugar into her open hand, and eyed the thick tongue that the cow licked over a pink nose. She screwed up her face and showed Daisy the sugar. The cow obviously knew what it was. She reached her neck back in an attempt to get it. Courtney just couldn't accept the idea of letting the animal lick it from her hand. She stretched under the cow's neck and dumped the sugar into the trough. Daisy licked it up, working her way around the bottom of the wooden bin to make sure she hadn't missed any.

"Try now," Peter suggested.

Courtney inched the stool forward, spread her feet on either side of the pail and milked. Nothing. One more try. Still no success. She laid her forehead against Daisy's side.

"I could use a little cooperation here, Daisy. Please give me some milk."

Daisy brought her back foot forward in a quick movement, sending the milk pail flying over Courtney's foot and banging into the side of the stall. Startled, Courtney tottered on the stool, trying to keep her balance. Peter laughed.

"Can't even milk a cow," Courtney muttered to herself as she jerked the stool back into position and gave a frustrated tug. Milk squirted out and across her foot. Peter laughed harder.

"Oh, you think that's funny, do you?" Courtney redirected the stream of milk. Her aim was accurate. Peter let out a shriek as milk sprayed over his pant leg. He jumped back out of range.

"What the hell's going on in here?" Matt's voice echoed off the walls as he stepped into the spot Peter had just vacated.

Courtney jumped to her feet, stumbling over the stool in her haste. Matt's arm snaked out. He steadied her quickly, jerking his hand back to his side as soon as she caught her balance.

Peter watched the way Matt and Courtney looked at each other. His heart settled back into a steady rhythm as Matt seemed more intent on Courtney than on chastising him. He wondered at the way Matt was always looking at Courtney, usually when he didn't think she would see him. It wasn't the same lovesick look Mr. Wesson gave his mother back in Boston. And Matt certainly never touched Courtney the way Mr. Wesson was always touching Mother. Mr. Wesson would use any excuse to offer her his arm, or put his hand on her back to escort her from a room. He'd let their fingers brush when he passed her food at the table, and had held her hand when she got up off the sofa. And had smiled. They'd always been smiling at each other.

Matt never smiled at Courtney. Nor she at him. And touch—Peter looked down at Matt's hands, knotted into fists at his side. Matt acted as if he would get burned if he touched Courtney. More often than not, he went around her with his hands jammed into his pockets or clenched into fists as they were now. If Matt would smile at Courtney once in a while, maybe she wouldn't be so sad, maybe she would want to stay here forever.

Maybe they just needed to spend more time together. That was what his mother had suggested he do with Mr. Wesson when he told her that he didn't really like him. Spend some time together. Peter would have to see if he could arrange that, without either of them suspecting, of course.

Courtney excused herself and went back to the house, while Matt turned and began to unsaddle Red.

"Better get that cow milked," Matt said without glancing at Peter. Tension underscored his tone. Peter retrieved the bucket, righted the stool and did as he was told. He had some planning to do.

# *Chapter Eight*

Courtney's long skirt brushed the top of the grass as she wandered along the rise beside the creek. All around her, new life burst forth, from the bright green leaves to the new shoots of grass amidst the brown tangle of last year's vegetation. Nature's renewal mirrored her own feelings of rebirth. It almost seemed she had been given a second chance, another shot at life, definitely a new view of things.

She followed the curve of the land, down a slight incline. There she stopped, just inside a stand of cottonwood trees. A sheltered circular retreat had been formed by the trees, and in its midst stood a private family cemetery. The rock headstones were a light tan color, ground or polished smooth on the faces where names had been chiseled. A white picket fence enclosed the area that was already made private by the surrounding trees.

Courtney stepped closer, to the edge of the fence.

She read the inscriptions on the markers: Zachariah Ward 1831–1884, Kathleen Hayden Ward 1844–1872, Katie Marie Ward 1872–1890. Eighteen years old. A sister. The realization reminded her of the harshness of this era. Yet things were so much simpler here than in her own time. While death was still grievous, the causes were easier to comprehend.

She stared at the gravestone and wondered what had killed Katie Ward at the age of eighteen.

She started as a horse nickered just beyond the cottonwoods. Through the trees she saw Travis as he dismounted and tied his buckskin's reins around a branch. She felt slightly guilty being found here, as if she had invaded some special private part of their lives.

"I just sort of stumbled across it," she explained as Travis walked up beside her. "I didn't mean to intrude."

"You're not intruding," Travis assured her in a lowered voice. "You can come here anytime you like."

Courtney turned back to the markers. "I didn't know you had a sister."

Out of the corner of her eye, she saw Travis nod his head.

"She was so young," she murmured, almost to herself.

"Eighteen," Travis said, his voice tight with sadness.

Courtney turned toward him, refraining from asking what had happened for fear it would dredge up more pain. She laid her hand on his sleeve.

"I'm so sorry."

Travis's gloved hand came up to cover hers. She looked up. His expression of grief had changed to one of hope and adoration. She suspected he had misread her compassion, but wasn't certain what to say to tactfully let him know she wasn't interested in him that way. She withdrew her hand and moved one step away.

"It must have been very hard losing her," Courtney said, leading the conversation back to where they had started.

He gave his head a little shake as though to get his thoughts back on track with her words.

"Katie was full of life, spirited like a yearling filly before a storm. You never knew which way she was going to run or what she was going to do. And a temper, too. The Irish coming out in her, Zach always said. Maybe if he'd taught her to control her temper, she'd still be alive."

He paused, his brow furrowing as he pondered the memories. "Matt is only now starting to get over the anger."

Courtney frowned. Anger? Matt hadn't seemed angry to her. What she sensed had been more like restraint and maybe pain, deeply buried pain. Perhaps Travis confused that with anger.

"It wasn't his fault," Travis continued. "But he's determined to blame himself. Both for Katie and for Jeanette."

"Who's Jeanette?"

"Jeanette was the daughter of one of the ranch hands Matt hired to help with the roundup and branding. Her father was one of those Mexican cowboys, and he never said no to his daughter. She always got what she wanted, either before or after a screaming fit. She was a year or so older than Katie and they became fast friends, even when Jeanette set her sights on Matt. Like I said, Jeanette always expected to get what she wanted. She wanted Matt and she tried everything to get him. Funny thing was,

Matt might have been interested at the beginning, but the more determined and pushy Jeanette got, the harder Matt fought it. Matt's gotta do things his own way, in his own time, and that wasn't sitting well with Jeanette.

"They had some kind of an argument. I'm not sure about what exactly, but I suspect Matt spurned her advances. It doesn't matter what set her off. What mattered was what happened after." He took off his hat, ran a hand back through his ginger hair and then returned the Stetson to his head.

"Matt had a big black stallion that he had broken. That horse was still plenty green and Matt was the only one who could control him. The horse was tied up outside the barn and when Jeanette stormed out, she saw him there, all saddled and ready for Matt to ride. Out of spite, she stuck burrs under the horse's blanket, thinking Matt would be in for the ride of his life. She probably hoped he would get thrown, she was that mad."

He looked at Courtney, his blue eyes dark with emotion. "It was just one of those things. You know, those things that afterward, you look back and think that if this would have happened or that, just one small change in the course of events, everything would have worked out different."

Courtney waited while he took a deep breath and expelled it in a heavy sigh.

He shook his head. "Everything could have been so different," he said as he gazed off beyond the clearing, seeing something in the horizon, reliving the past in his mind until Courtney couldn't stand the suspense.

"What happened?"

Travis straightened, seemed to come back from some place in his thoughts. He indicated the grass at her feet, silently gesturing for her to sit. She dropped down, tucking her skirt around her crossed legs. Travis settled down beside her, turning so he could see the family plot.

"Katie'd been pestering Matt for weeks to ride the stallion. When she came into the barn and started at him again after he'd just had the fight with Jeanette, he lost his temper. Told her something like she wouldn't be able to handle the horse, that she wasn't a good enough rider yet. Well, Katie wasn't the type to take that lying down. She decided she'd show him.

"She used the corral rail to help get up on that animal. He was hard enough to handle at the best of times—even Matt had to keep him on a tight rein. But when Katie's weight settled into the saddle and the burrs dug into his back, all hell broke loose.

"She was determined to ride him, but he threw her off like she was a rag doll. She landed against the corral post. I guess the blow must have stunned her. The horse went wild, bucking blind. Her foot got hung up in the stirrup. He came down on her before she could get out of the way." Courtney gasped, but Travis continued on as if he hadn't heard her.

"By then everyone had heard the ruckus and came running, but it was too late for Katie. I remember Jeanette cradling Katie's head in her lap and the blood covering her skirt. I think we were all just stunned. Jeanette started to cry. Matt was shaking and the horse was shaking. I just stood there unable to believe what was happening. Matt picked Katie up and carried her into the house. Nobody thought too much about it when Jeanette walked off.

"After we knew Katie was gone, Matt got his gun and went out to find the horse. The stallion was standing there right by the corral, his eyes wide, his flanks still heaving. I would have shot him right there, he looked so evil. But not Matt. He took the beast into the corral and unsaddled him first. That was when he found the burrs and realized or guessed what had happened. He left the horse and went to find Jeanette instead. He walked away from me with that gun hanging from his hand and that cold, blank look in his eyes. And I didn't know what he might do.

"We found Jeanette on top of Anderson's Ridge. To this day, I'll never forget that sight. Matt still won't go up there unless he absolutely has to. I don't think he's been on that hill more than a couple times since that day." He paused again, once more mired in the memories.

"He didn't shoot her." Courtney shook her head, refusing to believe Matt capable of such a thing.

Travis took off his hat and twisted the brim in his lap. "No, he didn't shoot her." He looked up at Courtney, his eyes sorrowful. "She was already dead."

Courtney stared at him in shock.

"She had smeared the blood all over her face and hair." He lowered his voice so Courtney had to strain to hear his words. "Then she'd hanged herself from the lone poplar tree there."

"Oh, God." The words escaped from Courtney though she clamped a hand over her mouth to try to contain her stunned disbelief.

Travis's face was tight as he struggled with his own emotions. "Matt made this sound." He swallowed and looked away, staring across the meadow with unseeing eyes. "Part growl, part cry, part shout. Like an animal in pain almost. It was the worst thing I've ever heard. He said he had killed them both. He walked away and disappeared for three days."

"It wasn't his fault," Courtney protested. "How

could he have known what would happen? How could he have changed things?"

Travis shrugged. "Jeanette's father took Jeanette away with him. We buried Katie. Matt sold the stallion and he never spoke about what happened ever again. But he went to work with a vengeance, driving himself past a normal man's endurance. I think maybe that was the only way he could keep the anger at bay, by exhausting himself, working himself till he dropped."

Courtney pondered the events that had shaped Matthew Ward, the things that had forged his reluctance to allow women close. First his mother had died when he was young, in the child's mind deserting him. He probably blamed himself for that somehow. Then came Jeanette's betrayal and vengeance. In one senseless act he had lost his sister and her friend. His feelings for Jeanette were still unclear, though Courtney suspected there had been some kind of attachment. Clearly he blamed himself for this horrendous turn of events. And so it seemed he meant to hold himself in check, to keep from getting too close again in an effort to protect what was left of his feelings. Courtney wondered which was worse, to have known your family and then lost them, or like herself, to have never had family: no parents, no siblings, no close relationships. It didn't take much consideration. She decided Matt's experiences were far worse.

Travis's story explained a lot of things and gave her a new insight into Matthew Ward's behavior.

"It'll be getting dark soon," Travis said as he pushed to his feet and extended a hand to help her up.

As she accepted and got to her feet, Courtney noted the long shadows cast by the cottonwoods.

They returned to the house, Travis walking his horse alongside her. They were both quiet, each lost in thought, Travis probably in retrospection and Courtney in consideration of how the past had shaped the Ward brothers.

Courtney discovered the bathtub in the root cellar. It was leaning against the dirt wall behind the stairs. For a moment she forgot her mission to collect potatoes for supper as she fingered the dusty aluminum. It wasn't much by twentieth-century standards, merely a tin oval barely wide enough and long enough for a person to sit in. But a bathtub. A real, honest-to-goodness bathtub. The notion that she could be enthralled by something she had once accepted as commonplace made her smile.

Water would have to be hauled from the well and heated on the stove. The bath would probably be tepid at best, but even that would be better than a dip in the icy stream or the nightly sponge bath she had managed with so far. And the tub would make it so much easier to wash her long hair than it had been in the washbasin. She started to set down the pot in her hands and then looked down at it, remembering the purpose of her trip. She cast the tub a last glance, knowing she would be back as soon as she had supper started.

Lately, Peter had started to accompany either Matt or Travis on their daily excursions, but the older brothers usually sent the boy back early as he still wasn't used to a full day of horseback riding and grew easily bored with hours of checking fences or searching for lost cattle. She decided that when Peter returned, she'd enlist his help in bringing up the tub.

She crossed the small root cellar and filled her pot with potatoes. The sooner she got supper on, the sooner she could start contemplating the luxury of her bath. She'd use the sweet-smelling soap Matt had brought her from town, not just for her skin but for her hair as well. It was going to feel so good to settle into a tub of hot water, or even just warm water. As she climbed back up the stairs she gave the tub a last glance before she let the closing door plunge the cellar back into darkness.

As she expected, she heard the sound of Peter returning just as she had set the potatoes to boil. She checked the roast in the oven. It was almost done and still had enough water to keep it from scorching on the bottom. She took it out and set it on the cooler corner of the stove.

She stepped outside and discovered that Peter wasn't alone. Matt had come back early, too. She looked away from him. She considered forgoing her request, but she'd been anticipating the bath just long enough to really want one now. She directed her words to Peter, who was already dismounted.

"Peter, would you give me a hand carrying up the tub that's in the root cellar."

Saddle leather creaked as Matt turned, but Courtney purposely avoided looking his way.

Peter looked up, his gaze flicking from her to Matt and then back. She thought she saw a gleam of speculation in his blue eyes.

"I have to rub Patch down," he insisted quickly, grabbing the horse's reins and starting to lead him back to the barn at a trot. "Matt will help you. Won't you, Matt."

Before she could even sputter out a protest, Peter was across the yard. Courtney heard a mutter as Matt dismounted. She was going to have to have a serious talk with that boy.

"I'm going to have to have a talk with that boy,"

Matt said, echoing her thoughts. He secured Red to the veranda railing and headed for the root cellar without so much as a glance in Courtney's direction. With no other choice available to her, Courtney followed as he descended the steps.

The metal edges of the tub clanked against the stairs as he picked up the end and maneuvered the tub to the bottom step. Though not heavy, the thing was awkwardly shaped. Standing on the bottom stair, Courtney reached down automatically and grabbed the handle on the end closest to her.

The cellar door dropped down with a crash, plunging them into darkness. Matt muttered a curse under his breath and dropped his end of the tub. Disoriented by the sudden darkness, Courtney groped around for something solid to hang on to. Her hand closed on fabric and warm skin. She felt Matt stiffen and go still. Then his hand was on top of hers, moving it away from him, placing it on one of the pillars flanking the stairs.

"Let me get by and I'll get the door," Matt said.

"I'll get it," she said as she edged up a few steps and pushed against the fallen door. It refused to budge. "I think it's stuck."

She heard the tub scrape in the dirt as he shoved it aside. She felt the warmth of his body as he reached past her to push on the door. From outside came a grunt. Matt leaned against her as he pushed harder. Trapped in the cramped confines of the cellar, she should have been afraid, but all she could think about was being alone in the dark with him, of all the things they could do without having to see or be embarrassed, all the things she'd like to do but was prevented from doing by propriety. Instead of reaching for him, she gripped the post at her side.

She heard his step on the riser as he moved higher,

his body now pressed into her own. As he pushed on the door, she could feel his muscles flex. Then he banged on it, the pounding echoing in the darkness around them.

"Someone's pushed the latch closed," Matt said. "It wouldn't catch on its own." He called out. "Peter?"

For a moment there was only silence.

He called again, louder. "Peter!"

After a long second, there came a reluctant, "Uh-huh?"

"Open this door," Matt demanded.

"Uh. It's stuck."

"Open . . . this . . . door . . . now!" Even Courtney had no trouble reading the implications in that command.

"I just want you and Miss Courtney to spend some time together so you will like each other," Peter explained through the wooden door.

There was dead silence for a second. Then Matt answered. "We like each other fine," he asserted. "Now open the door."

"Miss Courtney, do you like Matt yet?" Peter persisted.

"It's hard to like anyone when I'm locked in a dark cellar and scared half to death."

There was another moment of silence.

"Peter, open this door." Matt had toned down the anger in his voice.

"I'm sorry. I didn't mean to scare you, Miss Courtney."

The latch clattering away to the side of the door was followed by the sound of running footsteps.

Matt pushed the door open, shielding his eyes from the outside brightness.

"When I catch him, I'm going to whup him," he

announced as he grabbed up Courtney's end of the tub and began to haul it up the stairs.

"No, Matt, don't. He was only trying to force us together so we would get to know each other."

He gave her an incredulous look, his eyes stormy.

"I know his methods were a bit underhanded, but his intentions weren't so bad," she added. "Promise me you won't punish him."

He gave her another silent look.

"Promise me," she insisted.

"Okay," he agreed reluctantly.

"Good," Courtney said looking at the tub, "I just want to take a long hot bath and forget the whole incident."

Out of the cellar, Matt shifted his eyes away from her and downward. Just as quickly, he looked away from the tub as though the sight of either her or the tub caused him pain. Courtney felt the heat rising in her cheeks as she wondered if he was picturing her bathing. He stared off across the yard, averting his eyes when Courtney moved in front of him and stooped to grab the tub handle. He stumbled slightly when they reached the step rather than turn his attention back toward her and their burden.

Courtney backed through the kitchen door and proceeded to carry the tub to her bedroom. She glanced at Matt. His neck was red, and it seemed he wasn't sure where to look now. Obviously, he wasn't comfortable looking around her room even though he himself had occupied it only a few months ago.

His relief was almost palpable as she finally set her end down on the floor. He dropped his end, spun on his heel and fled. Strangely, Courtney's earlier embarrassment had faded as she watched him. A languid current of heat was drifting along her veins, warming her from the inside out at the thought of

Matt's need to avert his eyes. She imagined what he had envisioned, and somehow her mind put him into the picture, too, his strong calloused hands lathering soap down her back and her legs, long tapered fingers slipping along her sleek wet skin. Her body began to respond to the images, heat pooling in her abdomen, her legs quivering, her nipples stiffening as her breasts grew sensitive to even the pressure of the fabric of her blouse against them.

She forced the thoughts away. There was supper to prepare.

But as she busied herself with that task, her thoughts refused to remain subdued and she had to fight to keep from looking at Matt.

Relieved when the meal was finally over, she occupied herself with the job of carrying water and heating it. A subdued Peter helped, while Matt and Travis went back out to the barn.

When the tub was filled at last, Courtney closed the bedroom door and sank back against it. She eyed the water and her thoughts quickly turned traitorous. She gave her head a shake. This was ridiculous. It was only a bath. With stubborn determination, she quickly peeled off her clothes and tossed them across the foot of the bed.

She sank into the warm water with an audible sigh, letting the heat seep into her bones and the liquid caress her skin. Courtney reached out of the tub and picked up the soap and washcloth she had set on the floor. As she lathered the soap, the soft aroma of lavender wafted up to her. As she began to work the soap over her skin, she closed her eyes, visualizing the ivory bar in other hands, in rough, workcalloused fingers. Shivers of sensation danced across her flesh and pooled in her abdomen. The sudden urgent rush of desire startled her. She drew in a harsh breath and dropped the soap. She gripped the cold edge of the tub until the sensations subsided.

It was several minutes later before she felt enough in control to finally slip down entirely into the water, bending her knees so she could submerge her back and wash her hair. Already the water was cooling. She stood up and reached for the towel, determined to keep thoughts of Matthew Ward from her mind.

As she dried, she eyed the stiff corset and the long heavy skirt and dismissed the idea of putting them back on. It was almost time to call it a day anyway. She finished drying and wrapped the towel around her hair, giving the cloth a twist to hold it in place as she flipped it back. She reached for Matt's white cotton shirt. Fresh from the line, it smelled of spring breezes and sunshine. Little trickles of desire simmered through her veins. Ignoring them, she slipped into the shirt, rolling the sleeves to her elbows, leaving the collar open at her neck. The cotton felt smooth against her skin.

She inhaled deeply of the sweet perfume smell that surrounded her. Feeling very feminine all of a sudden, she wondered if Matt would notice. Would he like the scent? He had chosen it, she reminded herself. She pulled on her jeans and realized she felt uncomfortable now with the constriction of her limbs. The denim was worn but still thick and heavy, unlike the linen of the bloomers that she had been wearing. But she needed to empty the tub before she turned in, and jeans seemed appropriate for the chore.

She stepped out into the living room expecting all three brothers to be there, but instead she saw only Matt. She glanced around.

"Peter asked Travis to help him in the barn," Matt explained as he saw her survey the room.

"And you didn't go?" Courtney recognized the sarcasm in her voice, but it was too late to take back the words. Matt had been avoiding her so much lately that she was surprised that he had chosen to remain behind, alone in the house with her.

Matt was surprised, too. After the lengths to which he had gone to keep away from her, he couldn't believe he hadn't escaped to the barn with his brothers. But he had been so distracted by thoughts of Courtney in that bathtub that, when Peter had persuaded Travis to show him how to lace harness, Matt had listened only halfheartedly. Even as they left, his mind had barely registered their parting. He'd been too distracted by an array of tantalizing images to pay his brothers much mind. Now he didn't have to rely on mental impressions.

She stood before him, her skin flushed from her bath, her oval face framed by the towel twisted around her hair. With her hair pulled away from her face, her features were more striking than ever, a perfect oval face with high cheekbones, her mouth full, her lips soft and inviting, her eyes a cloudy gray, darkening even as he stared at her. The sun had tanned the tops of her cheeks, her nose and her forehead.

He let his gaze stray to the open collar of the shirt. Her neck was long and graceful, and he had the irresistible desire to kiss the spot in the curve of her jaw just below her ear, to work his way down that smooth column of skin to the hollow at the base of her throat and then even lower. His eyes drifted downward with his thoughts, sweeping over the rise of her breasts. The fabric of the shirt wasn't anywhere near sheer enough. He wished it were wet, that she hadn't dried after her bath, that the cotton fabric was soaked and transparent, but it didn't really matter. He could envision the curve of her breasts with only his imagination. His palms itched. He longed to feel the weight of her in his hands, to close his fingers over the softness, to feel her nipples, taut, jutting into his palm.

Her scent carried to him. His nostrils flared slightly as he drew the odor deep into his lungs. The hint of flowers mingled with another scent, that of the woman beneath those clothes, beneath the layer of perfumed soap. He felt the heaviness in his loins and thanked God he was sitting down. To relieve the pressure, he stretched out his legs, crossing them at the ankles. He forced himself to look away. It wasn't easy. He wanted her with a fierceness that had been driving him to distraction for weeks.

"I could use a hand emptying the tub." Her voice was slightly hoarse.

He nodded and reluctantly pushed himself to his feet. He turned quickly so his back was to her, and went to get a bucket.

Matt inhaled sharply as she fell into step beside him, bending as he did and reaching for the other bucket by the stove. The strange sense of oneness, of togetherness, struck him, driving a nail of possessiveness into the middle of his chest. It was almost as if they belonged together. It felt so right to be working side by side with her, as if he had suddenly found a hidden piece of his own person, a piece that until now he hadn't even realized was missing.

He straightened slowly, overwhelmed by a sense of loss, as she moved away and headed back toward the bedroom. His insides tightened urgently, his mind spurring his legs into motion, forcing him to hurry after her in some inexplicable desire to fill that void.

He worked by her side without speaking, occasionally catching her eye, reading in her look the same mix of uncertainty and desire that he felt inside. But then she muttered a hushed "Good night," slipped into the bedroom and closed the door.

Courtney leaned back against the door and stared down at her trembling hands. She clenched them tightly together to dispel the powerful ache of needing to touch Matt. Her fingertips tingled with the desire to run them over his skin. Just the thought sent a sizzle of awareness up along her arms. Her breath felt heavy in her chest.

She'd tried to avoid him, telling herself that she didn't want him near. But when he was, it was never near enough. She drew in a deep breath and imagined how she would feel enfolded in his embrace, those strong arms wrapped around her. She shook off the image. It wasn't comforting. With it came an awareness of a huge hollow spot, an empty aching void just beneath her rib cage.

Were these the pangs of love? She looked upward and whispered to the empty room and to her grandmother, "I never knew it would hurt this much."

The afternoon was quiet as Courtney snapped the cleaned pieces of the cream separator back into place. She covered the full milk pail with a cheesecloth before pulling the butter churn in front of her chair. Travis and Peter were making the monthly trip into town today, and Matt had disappeared out onto the range early. The house always seemed so quiet without Peter here during the day. Even when he was outside, there was usually some sort of noise: chickens or the dog or Peter's own high-pitched voice.

As she worked the churn paddle up and down, she surveyed her kitchen. Yes, she'd begun to think of it as her kitchen. She'd started to feel as if she really belonged here. She'd even added a few items to the shopping list, after a careful conversation with Peter to see exactly what was available. She didn't want to look like an idiot by asking for something that hadn't even been invented yet. She was tiring of the usual diet of potatoes and vegetables and meat and biscuits. And she was afraid to experiment with precious supplies. She acknowledged that she needed a recipe to make bread or cakes. She had made Peter promise he would look for a cookbook, but she didn't want to get her hopes too high.

She was scraping the last of the butter out of the churn when she thought she heard the sound of hooves and the creak of saddle leather. Matt? Nervously, she wiped her hands on her apron and crossed to the front door.

Matt was kneeling beside a calf. The frantic animal was kicking, struggling to get to its feet while Matt tried to hold it on the ground.

"Courtney." He called to her just as she pushed out the door. "Can you give me a hand here? Damn it, I wish Travis or Peter was here," he muttered.

"I can help," Courtney stated defensively. "Just tell me what you want me to do."

"I need you to hold him down," he said, jerking his head in the calf's direction. "Put your knee across his neck and hold his head and his back legs still. I need to get the wire cutters from the barn."

Blood matted the calf's back legs. A strand of twisted barbed wire encircled the animal's hind quarters, cutting a deep gash in his hide.

Matt eased off the calf as Courtney brushed

against him and leaned into place. The calf's eyes rolled wildly.

"I'm hurting it." She started to lift her knee. Matt bent and pressed her leg back down.

"He's just scared. Letting him struggle will hurt him more than your weight will." He laid a hand briefly on her shoulder as she nodded her agreement. "Good girl. I'll be right back." He sprinted toward the barn and returned seconds later.

Matt looked at her as he knelt by the calf. "Hold him firm. This will probably hurt. I expect him to kick."

Courtney nodded, letting Matt press his hand onto the calf's flank alongside her own. Their fingers touched in the sticky fur, but she didn't pull away. There were other things to concentrate on, though she was acutely aware of the contact. Courtney turned her head away as Matt began to dig through the matted fur to reach the tightened wire. She ran her free hand over the calf's neck.

"Shhhh," she whispered. "It's all right. Just a couple minutes. Shhhh." Then there was a snap. Courtney focused on holding the calf as it struggled under her. She looked back as Matt finished pulling the wire free, and then she started to ease her weight off the animal.

"Hold him another second," Matt said as he pulled a tin of salve from his back pocket, scooped out some of the ointment with his fingers and spread it over the cuts.

"Okay," he said when he had finished. He maintained his grip on the calf's flanks while she stood. As the animal began to struggle to its feet, Matt helped it up.

Shaking, the calf tottered off a few steps before letting out a plaintive cry. Courtney smiled. "He wants his mother, I think." She looked at Matt. "Are you going to take him back?"

Matt shook his head. "Not for a few days. I want to keep an eye on that cut. The cow is following me anyway. She wasn't about to let me take her calf from her. I suspect his cries will bring her in a minute." As they finished rinsing their hands in the horse trough, the calf's cries drew a reply. A white-faced heifer halted beyond the corral and eyed Courtney and Matt warily.

"Let's get the calf into the corral out behind the barn. I think if we leave the gate open she'll go in."

Together they herded the calf, arms spread, making clucking noises until they got him into the corral with Daisy. Matt steered Courtney into the barn and after a brief hesitation, the calf's mother found her way into the corral and the calf immediately began to nurse.

"I guess it's a good sign that he's hungry," Courtney said. She was aware of Matt standing right behind her. A single step back and she could lean against his broad chest. Even now she could feel his breath whisking across the back of her neck where she had gathered her hair in a ribbon. She looked back over her shoulder, turning just slightly, enough to see him. He was looking down, intently studying the dark tail of her hair. And then he reached out a hand, touching the hair carefully with the tips of the two middle fingers. Slowly he spread his hand and pushed it through the wavy strands, letting the tresses sift between his fingers.

Courtney's breath caught in her throat.

"I've wanted to do that for a long time," he confessed in a harsh whisper.

Courtney could feel her heart pounding in her chest as he slowly met her gaze. She swallowed against the lump that filled her throat. Her nipples tightened in instinctive response to his touch.

"And this," he said as he pulled the ribbon free. His fingers slid along her jaw, then through her hair, cupping the back of her head.

Courtney turned and stepped into his embrace. "And this," she whispered as she tilted her head and offered him her lips.

"Especially this." His lips touched hers and her eyes drifted closed. She expected his kiss to be rough, like him. All rawhide and saddle leather. But instead it was gentle, a brush of a spring breeze, the softness of a rose petal. Tentative, exploratory, hesitant.

She melted against him, letting her body mold to his. She felt the hardness of his muscles, his chest and thighs pressed against her own. She wrapped her arms around his neck and returned the kiss. He started to lean away from her, but she moved her hand to the back of his head and held him against her lips. His resistance faded. He surrendered with a moan that came from deep in his throat. He tightened his hold, pulling her closer, urging her lips apart with his tongue. And suddenly he was kissing her with unbridled hunger. His fingers knotted in her hair as his lips crushed hers and his tongue sparred with her own. His breath was hot on her cheek, his kiss urgent and demanding. Liquid heat pulsed through her blood.

His hand slid down her back, over her waist to her buttocks. He pressed her against his arousal. Her body jerked with response as she moved against the hardness.

He broke away from the kiss and buried his face in the hollow beneath her ear, breathing in deep quick gasps. His right hand found her breast and cupped it. He ran the tips of his fingers over the taut peak. He ducked his head, pressing his lips to her breast, warming it through the cloth with his hot breath. Courtney wanted more, wanted to feel the touch of his lips against her skin, to feel his mouth drawing on the turgid tip. Bands of sensation wrapped around her rib cage and she arched her back, pressing against him.

"Oh, God," Courtney murmured as she leaned her head back and reveled in the instinctive response he elicited from her body. Her skin tingled from his touch, every nerve ending taut and aware and over-sensitive. She was damp and ready. She let her hands move down over the ridges of muscles on his back, reveling in the feel of his sheer strength. He straightened, ground her against him. Pleasure surged up through her body, tightened in her abdomen, building into an urgent need.

With a small step, he pushed forward until the wall of the barn was at her back. He found her lips again as he shifted, maneuvering his thigh between her legs, his arousal pressing into the soft line between her hip and thigh. He pushed upward with his thigh muscle, and she cried out, feeling herself contracting and pulsing inside. Again he lifted her, his muscles quivering, rippling, hard where she was most sensitive. Instinctively, she clung to him, gulping in air as her body trembled, shook with desire, surged toward fulfillment. And then she peaked. Right then, right there, with all her clothes on, pushed to release by only a touch dulled by layers of material. A cry of pleasure escaped her. God, what would he do to her if nothing separated them but their fevered skin?

Courtney went limp, and Matt slowly lowered his leg. He braced one arm on the wall beside her head and looked down at her with arched brows and dark smoldering eyes as she struggled to calm her frantic breathing.

"Well, if that isn't the darnedest thing," he murmured.

"Sorry."

"Hell, don't apologize just when you got my ego all built up. With an act like that you must have been one of the top girls wherever you came from."

"Top girls?" Courtney stared at him and the coldness that darkened his eyes. She was certain it hadn't been there only a moment ago.

"Is this what you do to Travis on your evening strolls?"

She just stared at him, a shiver passing across skin that had been heated by passion only moments earlier. He pulled away and she took a quick step, struggling to remain standing without the support of his body.

"No wonder he thinks he wants to marry you." Matt jammed his hat down tighter on his head. "Tell Travis I'll be gone for a few days," he said as he stomped out of the barn.

Courtney stared after him in disbelief. What should have been a joyous moment of shared passion had just shattered into sharp shards of regret and hurt. It filled her chest, painful and thick. She loved Matthew Ward, she realized, and love hurt.

Matt was so angry with himself he could just spit. What the hell had he been thinking? It was bad enough he'd touched her, but the rest? He should be horsewhipped.

Crossing the yard, he grabbed up Red's reins and mounted in a single effortless bound. He jerked on the reins and kicked the big sorrel into a full gallop.

He shifted uncomfortably in the saddle. She might

have found release, something that had startled him back to his senses, but he sure as hell hadn't. He turned Red for town, ignoring the road and cutting across the grassland to avoid any chance of meeting Travis and Peter. He had to get away, and get away now.

All the way to town he tried to push Courtney from his mind, tried to deny the genuine emotion in her response to his touch. It didn't work.

He sought his release first in alcohol, then in a room above the saloon.

Matt tossed Rosie's chemise aside and drove into her. Like a good whore, she was ready. The muscles on his forearms tightened as he raised himself up. His thighs pounded with the force of his thrusts. But it wasn't the image of Rosie's pudgy, painted cheeks or sandy-colored ringlets that filled his head as he rolled away and fell exhausted onto the pillow. Somewhere etched on the back of his eyelids was a woman with black hair and silver eyes.

He dropped his arm over the edge of the bed and fumbled around until he found the half-empty bottle of whiskey. Taking a deep swallow, he wondered at the way he was trying to drink himself into oblivion. He slammed the bottle down on the night table with a bang. If the first half of the whiskey hadn't erased her from his thoughts, the second half wouldn't either.

He swung his legs out of the bed and reached for his pants. He swayed slightly as he stood and pulled them on. Jamming his feet into his boots, he reached into his pocket and tossed a couple of coins onto the bedcovers.

Rosie lit one of the little cheroots she had a preference for. He wrinkled his nose at the smell as she blew a stream of smoke into the air.

"You runnin' away from that girl I heard you had out at your place?"

"I ain't running away from nothing," Matt said as he crossed the room and slammed the door behind him. "Ain't running from nothing," he muttered to himself, though he knew it was a lie. He was running from something that he couldn't escape, his feelings for Courtney James.

# *Chapter Nine*

Courtney stood in the doorway as Travis pulled the wagon into the yard and Peter spilled out. She'd had a lot of time to think about what had happened between her and Matt. Time to think about what he had said about Travis wanting to marry her. Time to recognize what Matt meant about being a top girl. When she thought back now, she saw how he might have come to that conclusion. She wasn't used to getting up early, she drank coffee to keep awake at night and she couldn't explain where she had come from. What occupation did those things apply to in this day and age, if not a prostitute? And her behavior in the barn had surely convinced him, once and for all, of her promiscuity. She couldn't explain it, but he did something to her. With his dark looks and withdrawn attitude, she'd ached to touch him from the moment she'd laid eyes on him. Might as well admit it, at least to herself. Maybe that would make it easier to deal with.

And Travis. She watched him smile at her and tip his hat before he started to unload the supplies. She'd been afraid of hurting his feelings and so she hadn't rebuked his shy compliments or refused his invitations for an evening stroll. Now she realized just what those actions had telegraphed to both brothers. Matt didn't want her, but she sensed he was drawn to her just as she was drawn to him. And Travis wanted her, but only because he appreciated having a woman around. They'd never so much as held hands, let alone kissed. Or anything else. She recalled her response to Matt's passion with a flush of embarrassment. What a harlot he must think she was.

Peter bounded up the steps. "Guess what, Miss Courtney?" he said as he hopped excitedly from one foot to the other.

She couldn't help but grin back. "What?"

"They're having a spring picnic and dance this Saturday at the schoolhouse."

It was obvious that Peter expected them to attend. Courtney remembered Matt's bruised face. She shook her head. "I don't think that's a good idea. Matt might not welcome another black eye."

"Oh, it's okay," Peter said with a wide grin. "Travis fixed it all."

Travis clamped a hand on Peter's shoulder as he reached the doorway. "Why don't you go unhitch ol' Blue?"

Peter gave Courtney a smile and Travis an ill-disguised wink as he hurried off to do Travis's bidding.

"Fixed it?" Courtney asked suspiciously, her eyebrows lifting.

Travis avoided her look and scanned the interior of the house. "Matt not around?"

Courtney ducked her head. "Uh, no. He said to tell you that he'd be gone for a couple of days."

"Where'd he go?"

"I don't know." Courtney crossed the room and began to fuss with the cloth covering the cold sliced beef. "There's some cold meat if you're hungry."

"Maybe later."

She looked up. It wasn't like Travis to refuse food. He twisted the brim of his hat in both hands and stared at his boots.

Courtney leaned back against the counter, suddenly concerned more with Travis than with explaining Matt's absence. Something was up. Peter had said Travis had fixed it. Fixed what?

"What did you do?" she asked quietly. "To fix . . . it."

Travis looked up, his blue eyes pale against tanned cheeks, a shadow over one eye from the lock of ginger hair that persisted in falling across his forehead. He swallowed and then squared his shoulders and walked across the room until he stood directly in front of her. Courtney couldn't move. She realized she had stopped breathing. She inhaled and waited.

Travis shifted nervously, looking everywhere but directly at her. Finally he cleared his throat. "This isn't how I thought this would happen. But I see you need an explanation, and I can't give one without doing something else first." He fumbled in his pocket and withdrew a small packet. A ring-sized packet.

A sinking sensation swept through Courtney's stomach and weighted her limbs. Oh, God, he was going to ask her. What was she going to say?

"I told them that your aunt was staying at the

ranch with you. That should fix any damage done to your reputation."

Courtney waited while he turned the paper packet over and over in his hand. "I explained why you were here."

Her head jerked up and she frowned. He hesitated a bit too long. "What did you tell them?"

He looked up then, studying her with a hopeful expression that sent Courtney's heartbeat plummeting.

"I said you were a mail-order bride."

Courtney choked on her own breath. "What?"

"I don't care where you came from." Travis clutched her hand and rushed ahead. "I don't care what you did before you came here. It doesn't matter to me." He stepped back a pace and pushed the chair out of his way as he dropped to one knee. "I'd feel very honored, Miss Courtney, if you'd be my wife."

Courtney looked down at his upturned face. She felt the sting of tears at the edges of her eyes. Here was a good man, a man who wanted to marry her. All her life she'd wished for this, to have someone of her own, to be loved, to belong. But now something was missing. She closed her eyes. It wasn't Travis Ward she wanted before her on bended knee. It was his brother, Matt, the man who could stir her passions with a glance and satisfy them with only his touch. She clenched her fists, blinked back the tears and told herself that she was wishing for the moon.

Travis slowly rose to his feet and raised his hands to grip her upper arms. She watched detached as he leaned to kiss her. His lips were warm and soft, but completely undemanding, completely devoid of passion. It felt as if he was kissing someone else, as if she was a spectator rather than a participant. Nothing stirred in her, no response, no feelings. Had she hoped she would feel something? Hoped that she could justify marrying someone she didn't love just for the sake of having the family she had always wanted?

She flattened her hands on his chest and pushed him gently away. "Travis, you're my friend. But I can't. . . ."

Peter burst through the door with Butch jumping around his legs. "Blue's all settled," he said as he raced into the kitchen and headed for the covered dishes on the table. At the ensuing silence, he stumbled to a halt and looked from Courtney to Travis.

Travis stepped back under the boy's scrutiny. "I'll check the stock." He gave Courtney one last searching look and then turned on his heel. Courtney let out a deep sigh as the door closed behind him. She covered her disquiet by fussing over Peter, brushing her fingers through his tangled hair and patting his back as he folded some meat onto a piece of bread.

He chattered about the trip to town and the upcoming dance. Courtney let her thoughts stray to Travis, somewhere outside alone in the night. And Matt. And herself. They were all alone. When Travis didn't return as darkness fell, Courtney turned in. Peter called a sleepy good night as he settled into bed. But Courtney didn't sleep. She stared at the shadows and wondered why life could never be simple.

Matt returned the Friday before the dance. If he knew of Travis's efforts to save her reputation, he said nothing. He spoke to her only when necessary. He tried to act as though nothing had changed in the ranch house, but everything was different, the atmosphere strained and stiffly formal.

He'd been wary of her before, and now his discomfort was even more pronounced. He spent as little time inside as possible, finding any and every excuse to return to the barn or the yard at night. He remained there until darkness fell and everyone had gone to bed before he came back in.

Saturday morning, Peter approached Courtney early with a sheepish look on his face. He stared down at the toes of his boots as she finished straightening the kitchen and waited for him to get to whatever it was that was on his mind.

She knew it couldn't be about what they were going to wear. She'd already laundered and mended everyone's good clothes, even Matt's, though she wasn't sure he had even noticed.

"Was there something you wanted, Peter?"

He looked up then. Still biting his bottom lip, he swallowed noticeably before he spoke.

"Miss Courtney." He frowned before continuing in a rush. "Do you know how to cut hair?"

She looked from his face to his tangle of blond curls. He hadn't gone to the barber on the last trip to town.

She shrugged. "I think I could probably manage a respectable trim."

Peter's expression changed to one of elation. "Miss Courtney, you can do everything."

Courtney ruffled his hair. "Maybe you better save the accolades. I haven't done anything yet."

Peter's brow creased into a frown. "What's acco . . . acco . . . ?"

"Accolades. It means praise," Courtney explained as she pulled out one of the kitchen chairs and rummaged through the drawer for a pair of sewing scissors.

Peter settled stiffly into the chair. She started slowly, carefully trimming a little off the top and along his ears. Gradually gaining confidence, she worked around to the back. She didn't cut it too short, just enough that it was off his collar. She retrieved the square mirror from behind the washbasin and handed it to him.

"How's that?" she asked as she stepped back and surveyed her work.

Peter ran a hand down the back of his head and grinned at her. "I think it's great. Thanks."

"Have you got time for another one?" Travis asked from the doorway. He regarded her hopefully.

"All right." Courtney hoped cutting a man's hair didn't constitute some kind of personal commitment that she wasn't aware of. As Travis exchanged places with Peter, Courtney moved into position. She noticed that he had washed his hair and smelled slightly of soap. While she could remain detached while the clippings fell to the floor, she saw the way Travis kept his hands clenched tightly in his lap. He avoided looking at her, even as she moved around him. When she finished and stepped back, he thanked her, rose stiffly and headed out the back door.

Courtney realized she was having the same effect on both the elder Ward brothers. It seemed neither of them wanted to be in her presence, Travis because he wanted her so badly and Matt because he didn't.

She was studying the scissors when Peter spoke.

"How about you, Matt? Do you need a haircut?"

She raised her head slowly as blood surged through her veins in a warm rush. Her eyes met Matt's over Peter's head, and held for indeterminable seconds. His dark look revealed nothing of his thoughts. Courtney felt the blush creeping into her cheeks. Her fingertips tingled at the thought of running them through the dark strands of his hair.

They'd been there before. They knew the silky softness of those raven locks.

"I don't think so." He turned sharply and was gone before she could speak.

Her heart settled in her chest like a lead weight as she realized how much she longed for even such an insubstantial contact. She busied herself getting the broom so Peter would not see the disappointment in her eyes.

When Peter disappeared outside, she leaned heavily against the counter, bowing her head against the hollow ache in her chest. She'd ruined whatever chance she'd had of gaining Matt Ward's respect.

She had cleaned up when Peter came back in a while later.

"Matt needs help in the yard."

She regarded him with suspicion. "Well, you can help him," she suggested.

"He needs somebody else, too. I have to get the part. Can you bring water?" He turned and vanished back out the door before she could protest.

With a deep sigh, she got the bucket, filled it with water and went out.

Matt was sprawled flat on his back under the wagon, fiddling with something near the front axle. Courtney's breath hissed out between clenched teeth at the sight. His lower body was exposed, giving her a very nice view of his thickly-muscled, jean-clad legs. That view was more than enough to instill a few traitorous thoughts in her head, thoughts that quickly translated into reactions in the lower parts of her body. The water in the pail she was carrying sloshed against her leg, wetting her skirt and bringing her attention quickly back to the matter at hand.

She stopped beside his outstretched legs and carefully kept her gaze pinned on the distant hills.

"Here's your water."

Whomp! A distinctly involuntary curse followed the sound. Then Matt, seemingly becoming aware of his position, scrambled out from under the wagon. He took a minute to brush the dirt from his pants before he looked at her.

"What water?"

"Peter said you needed a bucket of water."

"What for?"

"I don't know. Fixing the wagon, I guess."

"I sent him for a bolt." Matt looked at her as though she had somehow instigated the misunderstanding.

She looked away uneasily. "Well, he must have misheard you."

"I don't think so."

Her head came up at his quiet tone.

"Where is he? I think I need to straighten him out on a few things."

Comprehension dawned. "Matt," she warned quietly.

He didn't answer. He marched toward the house. Courtney lifted her skirt hem and followed, afraid suddenly that Matt intended to do bodily harm to Peter.

"Matt," she called after him. "Matt. Don't you hurt him. You promised."

But Matt refused to be so easily calmed.

He was advancing on a back-stepping Peter as she came into the kitchen.

"This has got to stop, Peter," Matt was saying. "I see what you're trying to do and it won't work."

Peter's blue eyes were wide.

"You can't manipulate Miss Courtney and me by pushing us together every chance you get."

Peter still offered no defense.

Courtney silently acknowledged that perhaps if it weren't for the incident in the barn, Peter's manipulations might have worked. Just being near Matt was enough to send her senses into overdrive. There was something that sparked between them every time they were near each other, a chemistry that they were both doing everything in their power to ignore.

"You'll stop this immediately. Do I make myself clear, young man?"

Peter nodded, his blue eyes widening even more at Matt's stern tone.

"Get out of here then," Matt ordered. And Peter fled. The screen door banged shut behind him. Silence filled the room. Slowly, Matt turned. He looked right at her, and for a moment he seemed about to speak. Then his gaze shifted away.

"Got work to do," he said as he stepped around her and followed Peter out the door.

Later, when it was time to head to town and only Peter and Travis appeared, she silently asked herself what else had she expected.

Lanterns hung from the schoolhouse stoop and several nearby trees. The flickering yellow light warmed the gathering of noisy people. Wagons lined the street, and the horses that wouldn't fit into the overcrowded livery were tethered on a length of rope stretched between two tall poplar trees. Numerous tables had been set up and covered with white linen, and the townsfolk had hauled their chairs from home to provide seating in addition to the planks that had been laid across pails and blocks of wood.

Courtney helped the women clear away the last of the potluck dishes and cover the desserts. The residents had quietly accepted her into their midst. The schoolteacher, Mary Emmery, had even offered

Courtney a bed for the night. The men would sleep in the wagons and on the ground, providing the weather remained clear, or in the livery if it rained.

Courtney had been unbearably nervous, but after the first few hours when everyone went out of their way to make her feel welcomed and no one questioned Travis's story, she began to relax. Of course, rumors circulated. Everyone knew about the Wards' mail-order arrangement and her chaperoning aunt, whose absence tonight Travis conveniently attributed to poor health. She heard them discussing the betrothal when they didn't think she was listening, though no one approached her and asked her outright. Courtney was relieved. She wasn't certain she could have gone along with the story if she had to look someone in the eye and lie.

As dusk fell, the people began to gather around a packed piece of ground that Courtney guessed was to be the dance floor. Someone tuned a guitar. Another man played a few strains on a violin.

Courtney followed the other women's example and untied her borrowed apron and folded it onto the tabletop. She tucked her hands into her skirt pockets and watched Peter playing tag with the other children. His blond curls caught the lantern light as he raced by and flashed her a crooked grin.

From across the yard, she could see that Travis watched her from where he stood with a group of men. A number of them were dressed in striped gray trousers and jackets. Others, the ranchers of the area, she presumed, wore clean denims and starched cotton shirts, some with, some without, vests. A few sported cowboy hats, but most had forgone hats and slicked back their hair. Courtney felt as if she was watching an old movie rather than participating in an actual event.

She reached a hand up to smooth her own hair. A few stray wisps curled around her face and tickled against her cheek, but the rest remained constrained in the twist that she had gathered at the nape of her neck. She felt pretty and feminine. Attired in the white blouse and the plaid skirt, she blended in with the other ladies. The smell of Matt's gift soap perfumed the air around her.

She caught snatches of conversation: how the sheep ranchers were doing, if all the calves had been branded, whether anyone had seen any more of that mountain lion that had been around a while back. The women talked of children and babies, of cooking and sewing. The air was filled with the smell of apple pie and the sweet aroma of tobacco from an after-dinner pipe.

It seemed everyone had turned out. She had met so many people that she couldn't remember half of their names. She suspected that this wasn't an everyday occurrence. The people took seriously an opportunity to get together. With the rarity of this kind of event, no one wanted to miss the excitement. Yes, everyone was here. Everyone but Matt.

Even when he was absent, she ached for him. She longed for his touch, dreamed of it, was tormented by it.

She shook her head. She had to accept that Matthew Ward wanted nothing to do with her. And since she couldn't, in clear conscience, marry Travis without loving him, she had to come up with something else. Maybe she could say her aunt was forced to return home and she could convince one of the local residents to give her a job. She could help cook and clean. Or even teach maybe. She had to find a way to leave the ranch. Things couldn't go on as they were now. If there was no way to get back to her own time, she needed to get on with her life in this era, to make the best of the situation, to give up on unrealistic dreams.

After a rough beginning, the makeshift band swung into a lively tune. Across the yard, Travis stepped out of the group of men. Laughing, they called after him, something she couldn't hear. He'd only taken a few steps when Peter appeared before Courtney and distracted her attention.

"Would you dance with me, Miss Courtney?"

She tousled his blond curls. "I'm not sure I know how to dance to this," she admitted in a whisper while she breathed a sigh of relief at being rescued from having to dance with Travis so early in the evening.

Peter puffed out his chest. "I can show you. My mother taught me." For a second a shadow passed over his eyes, but then he forced a smile and the sadness vanished. He held out his hand and, unable to refuse, she laid hers into it. She cast a quick glance in Travis's direction. He had veered off toward the punch table. Courtney gave a sigh of relief, and turned her attention to Peter's attempts to teach her the steps of the reel. Soon the music made her forget everything else. She skipped along, laughing and tripping after Peter's boisterous lead.

When the music stopped, she pressed one hand to her heaving chest and fanned her heated face with the other. Peter thanked her graciously for the honor of the first dance. His look flicked to a young girl at the edge of the crowd. She was wearing a frilly pink dress, and her long blond ringlets were tied with matching ribbons.

The music started again, slower this time. "We could do another," Peter offered.

Courtney nodded her head in the girl's direction. "I think you should ask her."

Peter blushed.

"May I have the honor of this dance, Miss James?" A man Courtney recognized as the local banker stepped in front of her. A quick look told her that Travis was again headed in her direction. Despite the fact that she had turned down his marriage proposal, he seemed to have decided tonight that he just needed to be more determined. Perhaps he had convinced himself that he could get her to change her mind. On the ride into town, he'd doubled his efforts to be polite and helpful and gentlemanly. Courtney suspected that she shouldn't have come but, besides not wanting to disappoint Peter and feeling obligated to uphold Travis's story, she had hoped she might discover a way to get off the ranch.

She allowed herself to be escorted back out onto the dance floor. Mr. Charles made polite conversation over the music, and she followed him easily in a regular waltz.

She had no shortage of dance partners. Everyone mixed. All of the women danced with all of the men in an atmosphere of general cordiality and merriment. The only time she felt awkward was when Travis finally caught up with her. She smiled and tried to pretend everything was all right, that dancing with him was no different from dancing with any other man there, but she felt stiff and guarded.

Relieved when the dance finally ended, Courtney thanked Travis and stepped back into a group of women who had gathered on the steps of the schoolhouse. She folded her skirts and dropped down beside Mary Emmery. The teacher fussed with the braided blond coil that rested at the nape of her neck. But her attention was on the dance floor. Her pale blue gaze strayed time and again to Travis as he spun one of the married women into a reel. Subdued emotion was apparent in the look.

Courtney looked away. Too bad Travis couldn't read the interest in Miss Emmery's eyes. Maybe Courtney could redirect his attention. She stared at the ground, pondering a way of accomplishing that, while the dance ended and the guitar player strummed the first notes to another waltz.

A pair of scuffed boots appeared in her line of vision and a hand came into view. Rising to accept the dance offer, Courtney found herself staring into a pair of dark eyes that were only partially concealed by the low brim of Matthew Ward's hat.

She started to draw her hand back, but he grabbed hold and tightened his grip. She couldn't decline his offer without making a scene. As he led her into the dance, she wasn't convinced she wanted to refuse. His touch sent a shiver of warmth through her fingers and up her arm. When he pressed his flattened palm to her waist and guided her into the waltz, heat erupted, sizzling up her spine and down her legs. She stumbled and missed a step, but he held her firm.

She detected the faint odor of whiskey as his breath feathered past her ear. He wore the clothes she had laundered, the soft white cotton shirt that she still used at night and a pair of rough denim pants. She let her gaze stray to his chin. A shadow of whiskers darkened his jaw. His hair did need cutting, and the waves at the back brushed his collar. His mouth was set in an angry line.

"You don't have to dance with me if you don't want to," she said under her breath. His displeasure was obvious to her, though his hat hid his expression from the others around them.

"I figured it was the only way I could talk to you. What with your sudden popularity."

Courtney forced herself not to respond to his growled comment. There was an insinuation in his words, but she refused to be insulted, refused to take the bait.

"Just what the hell do you think you're doing?" he breathed angrily against her neck.

"Doing?"

"Yes," he bit out, and almost came to a halt. Then realizing that he was in the middle of a crowd of curious people, he fell back into step. "Passing yourself off as a mail-order bride."

Courtney twisted so she could look up at him. "That was not my idea," she informed him.

"Really?" His sarcasm and disbelief were apparent in the tone of his voice.

"Travis made that up to restore my reputation. Unlike you, he thinks with his head instead of his fists," she retorted.

Matt swirled her around in time with the music and danced her closer to the edge of the crowd. "There seems to be a flaw in Travis's plan."

"And what is that?" Courtney affected a politeness she didn't feel, smiling as another couple nodded to them on their way past.

"It seems there is a fair amount of speculation over which of the Ward brothers you are to wed."

"What?" Her feigned politeness vanished.

"My brother failed to mention, in his little tale, which brother had sent for you. No one is so impolite as to ask you directly, but they sure as hell don't mind asking me."

Courtney smiled.

"This isn't funny."

His thighs brushed against hers through the material of her skirt. The imprint of his hand burned into her back. Her fingertips tingled where they touched his soft cotton shirt and felt the solidness of muscle across his shoulder. She took a deep breath to still her mutinous thoughts, and forced her attention back to the conversation.

"And what did you tell them?"

"That it was none of their damn business," he growled.

Courtney felt a faint glimmer of hope inside her chest. He hadn't declared outright that he didn't want her. He hadn't said anything that indicated that he thought she should marry Travis.

"I turned him down," she said.

Matt tilted his head slightly and looked at her through narrowed eyes.

"Travis," she explained. "I turned down his proposal."

"Is that suppose to make me happy?"

"I don't know, Matt. How does it make you feel?"

For a second, he just looked at her. "You're throwing away a chance at happiness," was his eventual reply.

Courtney studied the opening at his collar. What did she say now? Profess her love for him and look like a complete fool when he didn't reciprocate her feelings? She didn't think so. But maybe she could change his opinion of her.

"I'm not . . . what you think."

She looked up into his face. She couldn't read anything in his shaded eyes. He just shrugged.

"If I was, I'd marry Travis."

The music faltered to a halt and Matt's hands dropped from her back. She stepped away. "Thank you for the dance," she said, and then turned and walked away.

The hours passed in a blur. She danced once with every man present, and with Travis several times—as her aching feet confirmed. Matt avoided her, though she caught him watching her more than once.

When the guitar player announced the last waltz, Mary Emmery coyly asked Courtney who she would dance it with. Courtney immediately recognized the significance of the question. The group of women around her suddenly fell silent in an expectant hush. No one had wanted to be so forward as to inquire which brother she intended to marry. But even if she didn't answer, Courtney knew everyone would draw their own conclusions depending on who she chose as a partner for this waltz.

"I haven't decided yet."

There seemed to be a group exhalation, which Courtney chose to ignore.

Across the clearing, Travis broke off his discussion with a group of ranchers and looked in her direction. Matt leaned against a tree directly behind his brother, his hat brim concealing his face and his intentions. Courtney glanced around, looking for Peter. She spotted him, asleep in the back of the wagon. So much for that avenue of escape.

Matt studied Courtney from under the brim of his hat. Her cheeks were flushed from dancing. He could find her easily. She stood taller than any of the women here. He noted her hair, the way she had tucked it into a bun. The clothes he had bought for her draped her figure but did not hide it. He remembered the smell of her, how she had felt in his arms, how she had made him want to crush her to him. It was a battle to refrain. Now they had announced the last dance. When the music started every eye would be trained on her. At last the townspeople would know the answer to the question they all were asking. He shoved himself away from the tree and tapped Travis on the arm.

He jerked his head, silently directing his brother away from the group. He stepped into the shadows and Travis followed.

"Make it quick," Travis said. "The last dance is starting."

"So far, no one knows which brother Courtney is supposed to be marrying. I think we should leave it that way."

"I mean to dance with her," Travis declared in a lowered voice.

"She turned down your proposal," Matt reminded him. "You'll only be embarrassed if she turns down your offer for this dance."

"She'll change her mind about the proposal. I just need time to convince her."

"I kissed her," Matt announced coldly. "And she let me." Maybe that would sway his brother's opinion of Courtney James.

Travis's eyes flashed fire and he clenched his hands into fists. Matt grabbed his wrists and held them. "Not here, Travis. If we need to settle this, let's do it back at the ranch."

Travis glared at him. "I want her, Matt. You don't. She'll make a perfect wife. If you screw this up for me, I'll never forgive you." Travis jerked his hands loose. "I'm going to ask her to dance."

The guitar player strummed a chord. The crowd milled as partners filed out onto the packed ground. Travis and Matt stepped back into the light together. Matt had done what he could. It wouldn't be his fault if Travis made a fool out of himself now. Courtney, he decided, had brought this on herself. He had hoped to spare her any embarrassment now that she had established herself with the locals. But it appeared that was not to be.

Courtney heard the waltz's first chord. It reverberated in her head. She lurched to her feet just as the brothers emerged from the shadows. It appeared the discussion was over. She wondered what had been said. Both Matt and Travis wore equally grim and determined looks. She couldn't afford to wait for them to decide her fate. Beside her, Mary Emmery had risen. The teacher turned toward Courtney, a glass of punch gripped tightly in her hand.

Courtney took a step forward and stumbled. Mary's punch splashed over Courtney's sleeve and the side of her blouse.

Mary's face contorted with disbelief. "Oh, I'm so sorry," she apologized as she brushed at the stain with a handkerchief she pulled from her sleeve.

"Perhaps I'd better put some water on it before it sets," Courtney suggested as she edged her way toward the schoolhouse door.

She needed to get out of here now. She didn't allow herself even a single backward glance to see if Travis or Matt had moved, and she didn't relax until she had put the heavy wooden door between herself and the Ward brothers.

The last strains of music had faded. The last bowls of food had been cleared away. The rural partygoers had been billeted out throughout the neighborhood, or had dropped off to sleep in the wagons or on the grassy lawn of the school. She had bid Matt and Travis equally unemotional good nights as they stood together at the side of the wagon. Now she lay in the cot in Mary's small bedroom in the suite at the rear of the schoolhouse and stared up at the ceiling in the darkness.

"Courtney?" Mary whispered quietly into the silence of the room.

For a moment Courtney contemplated feigning sleep, then discarded the thought. "Mmmhm."

"I'm sorry you didn't get to dance the final waltz. I should have been more careful with my punch."

"It was my fault," Courtney said. "I've always been too tall to be graceful."

"That's not true. You seem very graceful to me."

Courtney waited for what she was sure would prove to be the real gist of this conversation.

"I just wondered . . . I mean. . . ." Mary hesitated, then forged ahead. "Which of the Ward brothers sent for you?"

Courtney contemplated her answer and then smiled into the darkness. She didn't need to deceive Mary in order to answer this question. "Actually, it was Peter," she said as she rolled over and snuggled under the feather quilt. "Good night, Mary."

# Chapter Ten

When they returned to the ranch, Matt continued to avoid her like the plague. If she came in one end of the barn, he went out the other. At the table, he ate in silence, directing the occasional remark to Peter or Travis. He discussed the operations of the ranch and little else. Even if she had managed to tie Matt down, Courtney wouldn't have been able to talk to him alone. Travis was always just a few steps behind her. He found excuses to go where she went, he stopped by the house at all hours of the day, he praised and complimented everything she did, and Courtney knew that it was just a matter of time before he proposed again. She also knew that her answer hadn't changed and that it never would. For years she had thought she would never find a man who was right for her. Now she had and she still couldn't have him. If she couldn't have Matt Ward, Courtney didn't want anyone else. She'd never settled for second best, and she wasn't about to start doing so now.

"I'm going to town tomorrow," Travis mentioned as she cleared away the supper dishes. "Is there anything you need?"

Over the past few days, Courtney had given a lot of thought to her situation. She had an idea, a plan of action that might provide a way out of her current dilemma. "Could you deliver a letter for me?"

Matt looked up, and then quickly turned his attention back to the piece of harness he had brought to the table with him. Courtney could see that his attention was no longer focused on the leather. He waited, probably expecting to catch her sending a letter to some family member. He could then figure out where she had come from, could prove that everything she had told him was a lie.

Travis voiced his curiosity. "To who?"

Courtney pulled a piece of paper from the cupboard drawer and rummaged around until she found a pen and a bottle of ink. "Mary Emmery."

"What do you want to write her a letter for?" Travis asked.

"I'm curious about schooling for Peter in the fall. It's too far for him to go to town each day, but maybe Mary can arrange something so that he doesn't have to miss out altogether."

"Oh, okay." Travis nodded his acceptance of her answer.

"I also thought I'd start looking around for a job for myself. I can't stay here forever."

Matt stared at her across the table, and then dropped his head back down when Travis looked his way.

"You could stay here," Travis said slowly.

Understanding that he meant she could stay if she

married him, Courtney shook her head. "No. Sooner or later someone will discover that there is no aunt and that the mail-order thing was just a ruse. I think if I move into town, I can convince people that my aunt's illness forced her to return home and to leave me here. That should pass as acceptable."

"And what about the wedding they expect?" Travis persisted.

Courtney shrugged. "They'll forget after a while or assume that it all fell through."

Travis tried another ploy. "What about Peter? He'll be hurt if you leave."

"Peter will get by," Matt interjected.

"You stay the hell out of this." Leaping to his feet, Travis spun on him. "If it wasn't for you, determined to hate all women, Courtney might feel more welcome."

Courtney stepped between the brothers and held up her hand. "Travis. This is something I have to do for myself. Not for Peter or you or Matt." His name seemed to stick to the roof of her mouth. He bowed his head, and she noted the way the hair waved back behind his ears. If her plan succeeded she'd probably never see him again. It seemed important that she be able to remember him, to envision him at will. She sensed that memories would be all she would have. Maybe someday she would forget, maybe someday she'd fall in love with someone else. Right now that didn't seem probable. The deep ache in her chest was only for Matthew Ward. His constant presence was a thorn in her heart and she was smart enough to admit it, to realize that she had to get away from him before she self-destructed.

"I won't deliver any letter," Travis declared.

As Courtney sat down at the table and smoothed

the paper on the wood surface, Matt gave Travis a hard, determined look. "I will."

For a moment, Courtney's pen poised over the ink bottle. She closed her eyes. It hurt, the way he appeared so anxious to see her gone. She drew a calming breath and turned her attention to the letter she needed to compose. Matt had just agreed with her, she reminded herself. That was all. He saw the situation in the same light as she did. She should be happy that he concurred.

She dipped the nib of the pen in the ink, and then wiped it on the side of the glass jar. This wasn't the way she wanted it, this was just the way it had to be. The pen scratched across the paper as she started to write.

She kept the message brief, just a note saying that her aunt's health had grown worse and she thought it might be necessary to send her home. She asked if Mary could recommend a place where she herself might stay. She said that she was more than willing to accept household duties, or any other chores, in exchange for her room and board. In fact, she would like to secure a position for permanent employment if anything was available. Mary would no doubt read between those lines and see this request as the demise of the marriage situation, as Courtney intended.

She preferred that Travis deliver the letter. That too was part of her plan. Perhaps if she could get Mary and Travis together, Mary would be able to make him forget his misdirected marriage proposal. As for Matt, well, there didn't seem to be any hope in that direction. He was too set in his ways and those ways didn't include a wife.

Courtney waved the paper in the air to dry the ink. Carefully, she folded the missive in thirds. She slid it across the table until it rested before Matt. His tapered fingers hesitated over the strips of harness leather. He didn't look at her. Slowly he reached for the letter.

Travis leaned over and snatched the paper up. It crumpled in his clenched fist. "I'll deliver it," he muttered. He folded it in three again and stuffed it into his vest pocket.

Courtney stepped around the table and laid her hand on Travis's arm. "Thank you."

He just huffed under his breath and refused to look at her.

"I know it's not what you wanted, but I think it's best. For all of us."

Travis looked up then, his pale blue eyes direct, his lips compressed into a thin line. He looked at her for a long time before he finally spoke, and then his voice was laced with resignation. "No. This isn't best for all of us. Peter needs a mother. I want a wife. And you need a husband, not a job. The only one that this is best for is Matt. He just wants things to stay the way they are forever. But no matter what happens, things always change. You can't keep them the same."

Matt's chair scraped against the floor as he pushed it back and rose. He headed for the back door. "I'm going to help Peter with the stock," he said as he pushed the door open. It banged shut behind him.

Both Courtney and Travis watched him go in silence.

Courtney hadn't realized how much she had hoped this move would make him ask her to stay. Had she really believed she could force his feelings by leaving? She pressed the back of her hand against her mouth and swallowed against the hot lump in her throat. This was just another confirmation that what she was doing was the right thing. She sighed and turned toward the basin and the dishes. It was only a matter of time. She felt confident that Mary would find something for her; after all, the woman had her own reasons for helping Courtney off this ranch. She'd only have to stay a bit longer, Courtney thought. Mary would act quickly, and no doubt get back to her within a few weeks. Courtney was convinced of it.

Travis stepped between her and the counter.

"You don't have to go. I'm not like Matt. I'll do anything that will persuade you to stay. Marry me. It will solve everything."

Courtney looked at the sprinkling of freckles on his tanned cheeks, at the way the lock of sandy hair dropped across his brow. He was solid and reliable, a good man. But she couldn't envision spending nights with him, sleeping in his bed. The thought left her cold. She wasn't willing to compromise. She couldn't condemn him or herself to a marriage that wasn't based on compelling feelings and desire. There had to be more than convenient need and brotherly respect.

It wasn't Travis Ward's hands that she imagined running over her bare skin, or his body that she visualized poised over her own in the dark of night. Instead she saw brooding eyes and dark wavy hair. She felt calloused hands and lean-muscled thighs, strong arms and insistent lips. She longed for the rampant desire she had felt in the barn during Matt's kiss. There was no substitute for that. There never would be.

It was time to move on. She'd documented all she could remember of the day when she had spun through time. She'd tried several more times to recreate the atmosphere. Even using the braided sweetgrass, nothing worked. It was time she faced facts. She was here and there was no going back. She had to get on with her life, make the most of the situation.

"I'm sorry, Travis. I just don't love you. I wish I did. It would make things so much simpler. A marriage without love would just be doomed from the start. You'd resent me for not being able to love you, and I'd resent you for trying to make me. There's no future in that."

Travis stared past her shoulder. "Love's no guarantee either. It couldn't save Kathleen or Grace or even Zach. We lost them all, love or not." He turned and looked at her with pained eyes. "I'll deliver your letter."

"Thanks." Courtney looked away to hide her own pain. Travis headed for the door, and she found herself alone. Turning, she braced her hands on the counter and gazed out the window, across windswept hills to the distant purple shadows of the Rockies. A couple more weeks and she could turn the last page in this chapter of her life. She should be looking forward to discovery and adventure, but instead she just felt hollow and alone, more than she ever had before. No sooner had she discovered a place where she felt she belonged than she was forced to forge ahead and leave it behind her. And she suspected that a piece of her heart would stay here always.

Matt found himself watching the road again. It had only been three days since Travis took Courtney's letter to town, yet Matt felt compelled to keep his lonely vigil. He was only slightly surprised, then, when a lone rider trotted into view near mid-afternoon.

Matt intercepted the man before he could reach the house. Riding down a small slope, he recognized Harding Lanbert, and hailed him just south of the yard. He had expected a reply to Courtney's letter, but he felt instinctively that this was something else. His heart sank down into his stomach. Harding worked at the blacksmith shop, but he also ran errands for old Jim Mattersby at the telegraph office. That could be the only reason for Lanbert's visit.

His worry was confirmed as Harding reached into his shirt pocket and withdrew a small piece of paper. The look on the man's face spoke volumes. Matt didn't need to read the telegram to guess what it said. There was only one reason anyone would send him a telegram.

He stared at the paper as it rustled in the breeze, for a moment almost believing that if he didn't read it, he wouldn't have to hear the news.

"Grace?" His voice came out in a whisper and he cleared his throat quickly. But Harding didn't seem to have noticed. The man nodded and handed Matt the message.

Matt took a minute to peel off his gloves and tuck them in his back pocket before he slowly unfolded the telegram. The message was brief. *Grace passed away peacefully June 14. Burial Sunday. Letter to follow. Please accept condolences.* It was signed Marvin Wesson. Matt recalled Peter speaking of the man, a friend of Grace.

"I'm sorry, Matt. It'll be tough on the boy."

Matt nodded. Telling Peter was going to be hard. He was checking fences with Travis today, so Matt had a few hours to try to decide how to broach the subject, some time to look for the best way to break it to him.

Harding mutter something about getting back,

and Matt nodded absently as the man wheeled his horse and rode off. Matt headed Red in the direction of the barn. He'd busy himself in there until Peter returned.

Courtney stood in the doorway, watching through the screen. Across the yard, beyond her hearing, Matt and Peter stood facing each other. Matt held a folded piece of paper. He pushed his hat back slightly on his head and then bent toward the boy. As he spoke, he ran the crease of the paper back and forth between his thumb and forefinger. Courtney felt a pang of alarm. Matt looked entirely too serious. He stopped speaking and laid his hand on Peter's shoulder, and then she knew. This was about the boy's mother. The paper was a telegram and the news wasn't good. She waited for the slump of Peter's back, her own hands clenched tightly into fists at her side as she imagined the boy's pain. She'd lost her own parents when she'd been even younger than Peter, and could guess at how he was feeling.

But the only sign of emotion from the boy was a slight stiffening of his shoulders. He nodded to Matt and then turned and walked away. For an instant, Matt extended his arm. But he didn't call after Peter and after a brief pause, he swallowed and slowly lowered his hand back to his side. He looked lost and uncertain. Indecision was something she had never seen from Matt before.

As Peter disappeared around the side of the barn, Courtney stepped out onto the porch. Matt gave her a despairing look. She nodded her understanding as she stepped down, crossing the yard to him.

"His mother?"

He merely nodded, his jaw clamped tightly, his

eyes straying to the spot where Peter had disappeared.

"Do you want me to talk to him?"

"I don't know. I don't know what to do."

Courtney put her hand on his forearm. "It'll be all right, Matt."

He just shrugged.

"I'll go talk to him."

Peter stood at the top of Anderson's Ridge, facing into the wind, his tousled blond curls swirling around his face. He didn't move or speak as Courtney stopped beside him. For a moment she too stared out across the open expanse of rolling hills. She moved closer, reaching out to smooth his hair from his face, letting her hand come to rest on his shoulder. He took a small step closer to her, his arm brushing against her skirt.

She took a deep breath to push down the burgeoning emotion that seemed to swell in her chest, to avert the sting of shared pain. This was beyond words. Sometimes there just wasn't anything to say.

For long minutes they just stood there, her hand resting on his shoulder, Peter gradually leaning more and more into her. And finally he spoke, his voice strained.

"I didn't think it would hurt this much." He looked up at her with pained blue eyes that brimmed with unshed tears. He rubbed his hand across his cheek and cleared his throat. "I knew it was going to happen. I thought I was ready."

"Oh, Peter." She choked on her own words. "Losing a parent is the greatest anguish of all. I know. Even though I was young when I lost mine, I still remember the hurt."

"You lost your parents, too?"

Courtney nodded.

"What happened?" He seemed grateful to change the subject, to make himself concentrate on something other than his own loss.

"An accident. When they were driving home one night."

He nodded sagely. "Wagon overturned?"

"Something like that." It still hurt to recall the overheard conversation about icy roads, no control, the car flipping, bursting into flames. Peter wouldn't be able to relate to any of those things, so she kept them to herself.

"I feel so alone," he confided.

She hugged him to her side. "But you're not. You've got Matt and Travis and me and we all love you."

He put a slender arm around her waist, nodding in silent acknowledgment.

"I miss her. Having you here helps, but I still miss her."

"I know."

"I feel like I need to do something. For her. To say good-bye."

"You could say a prayer," she suggested.

He considered for a minute, shifting under her arm.

"Tonight, when you're alone, before bed," Courtney added.

He nodded, and she felt him relax against her again.

They stood in silence for a while, lost in their own thoughts, comforted by each other's presence, until finally Peter stepped away.

"I'd better go do my chores." He slipped away before Courtney could say anything.

Her skin felt cold now where he had been. From

somewhere deep down inside her, pain welled up. Peter had said he felt alone. She could relate to that. Alone and lost, trapped in another time, in an alien place. And she had no one. Tears burned the back of her eyes. Slowly, she slid to the ground, her skirt pooling out around her. She buried her face in her hands and wept, for Peter, for Grace, for her parents, for herself.

Matt was doubly confused now as he stood at the brink of the rise. Peter seemed to have taken the news in stride, but now here was Courtney crying her eyes out. He'd never understand women.

He slowly moved toward her, pausing at her side. He placed a hand on her shoulder, and she instinctively reached out and pressed her own over it, seemingly drawing comfort from just the touch. He held his hand out for her and she took it and pulled herself to her feet, wiping at her eyes without looking at him. Matt patted her shoulder awkwardly. She stirred him to do more, but he was afraid to take her in his arms, afraid his body might betray the effect she had on him, afraid he wouldn't want to ever let her go.

She seemed to sense the distance he put between them. Without a word, she turned and walked away, down the hill.

As he realized where he was, Matt quickly did likewise, angling away toward the barn. His concern over Courtney had momentarily overshadowed the other painful memories. He forced himself to keep his thoughts trained on her, refusing to let the old visions return.

Her jeans felt tight and constraining after the loose freedom of a skirt. Courtney settled gingerly into the saddle and accepted the reins from Peter. He was teaching her how to ride. They'd had some spare time in the past few afternoons since the news of Grace's passing, and Courtney had decided that since riding a horse was a necessary skill in her new life, she had to learn sometime and teaching her would occupy Peter. He had eagerly complied with her request.

He adjusted the stirrup length for her longer legs and grinned up at her. She still felt uncomfortable and nervous. She shifted in the saddle and urged Patch into a walk with a nudge of one boot heel. She rocked in the saddle as she made a circuit of the northern corral. Daisy raised her head and watched the proceedings while she chewed.

"Why don't you try trotting," Pete called.

Courtney wasn't sure that was such a good idea. But if she expected to fit into this century, she had to get used to it sooner or later.

"Squeeze your legs tighter," Peter instructed as she passed by the spot where he was perched on the fence railing, legs dangling.

Courtney tried it. The pinto responded immediately and broke into a bumpy gait. She bounced up and down in the saddle. "How's this?" she called.

"Awful." Matt's deep voice from the door of the barn startled her. She sawed on the reins and pulled Patch to a halt.

"What are you doing here?"

He leaned back against the corner of the door and extracted a folded piece of paper from his shirt pocket. "Mary sent a message. Good thing I intercepted Ray before he got to the house or this whole ruse might have been uncovered. No telling what would have happened then."

Courtney slid to the ground as Peter came running

over and took Patch's reins. She eyed the paper warily. This was it. Matt stepped out of the shade and extended the letter to her with a gloved hand. She took it and stared at it, almost afraid to open it and read the words.

Matt laid an arm across Peter's shoulders and drew the boy aside. "Let's go up to the house for a minute," he suggested to Peter. He gave Courtney an unreadable look.

"But," Peter protested, "what's in the letter?"

"Private stuff," Matt said. "Let's leave Miss James alone." He took Patch's reins and looped them over the saddle. Then he steered Peter through the gate and around the corner of the barn.

This was it. Courtney ran her thumb over the paper's fold. It had taken Mary less than a week to reply. Courtney wasn't sure if that was a good indication or not. Stepping into the shade of the barn, she leaned against the wall. As she unfolded the paper, she slid down to a seated position.

Mary Emmery's writing swirled across the page in large hooped letters. She began by expressing her sympathies for Courtney's aunt, and followed with a notification that Widow Barnes, who ran a local boardinghouse, was in need of assistance. The woman agreed to provide Courtney with lodging in exchange for help with the household tasks, namely laundry, cooking and cleaning. Mary also suggested that Courtney might make a small wage by offering mending services to other local residents. She encouraged a reply or, better yet, Courtney's arrival as soon as possible.

Courtney slowly refolded the letter and rested it on her knee. She'd always prized her self-sufficiency. The job wasn't Compucorp, and it didn't come with a level-six salary, but it was a start. She'd have to break it to Peter somehow. He wouldn't like it and she'd miss him. She stared blankly out across the corral. She should be happy. Going to town was her idea. A shuffling noise in the barn drew her attention.

"Peter?"

The boy stepped out of the shadowy interior. Looking dejected, he held his felt hat before him in both hands. Courtney patted the ground beside her and waited while he sat.

She wanted to wrap an arm around his shoulder and draw him to her, but she reminded herself that he was twelve and didn't much like being fussed over, at least not that way. Instead, she picked up the letter and slid the paper back and forth between her fingers.

"I have to go to town for a while, Peter."

He stared at the hat on his knee and said nothing.

"It isn't right for me to be staying here, being a single woman. There are a lot of people who wouldn't approve. You know that, don't you?"

Peter looked up. "Matt says you want to leave because you aren't happy here."

Courtney had no reply for that.

"I'm sorry for what I did, Miss Courtney."

She jerked her head up. "You didn't do anything, Peter. This isn't your fault."

He shook his head. "I should have thought about it when I wished you here. You probably have people back where you came from. You must miss them."

He didn't add "like I miss my mother," but Courtney heard the words anyway in his tone.

"Is it your family you miss?"

"I don't have any family." At least she hadn't until she'd come here.

"But there must be someone, some friends. I know

what it's like. I'm sad when I miss people."

Courtney gazed across the corral. There really wasn't anyone, not anyone she could call her own. They were all borrowed friends, someone else's loved ones and family.

Peter stumbled to his feet. "Wait here." He dashed back inside the barn, and she could hear him race through the building and out the other side. She propped her elbows on her knees and her chin in her hands. The paper crinkled in her lap.

When Peter returned he held the twisted stalk of sweetgrass. He thrust it out to her. "Here."

She took it from him. She'd never told him that she had found it. Since it hadn't helped her to return to her own time, she had seen no point in making an issue out of it.

"I hid it," he confessed. "I found it up on the ridge but I didn't want you to go back. I don't want you to be sad. We can send you back. I'll chant and do the circles like you had me do before. You can go back to your friends and be happy."

Courtney ran the braid through her hands. "It doesn't work, Peter. I found it under your mattress. It doesn't work. I can't go back."

He absorbed the words, and his small hand came to rest on her arm. "I'm sorry."

Courtney shrugged. "I wasn't that happy back there anyway. I've been given a new chance, thanks to you and your wish."

That seemed to cheer him up a bit. "I want you to go to town then, if it's what you want."

"I think it's the best thing to do right now." She handed him back the sweetgrass. "You keep this for me, okay?"

"Okay. I'll put it back under the mattress," he said.

Matt spoke from the barn door. "Why don't you do

that now. I need to speak to Miss James for a minute."

Peter checked with her and she indicated with a nod that it was okay. He ran off through the barn.

Clutching the letter, Courtney pushed herself to her feet and brushed the grass from the seat of her jeans. Matt stood, hat in hand, just inside the barn door, the same spot where he had stood the day he had touched her hair and sparked a fire that refused to die within her.

"I'm sorry you don't have any family to go back to," he said, confirming her suspicion that he had heard the majority of her conversation with Peter.

"I'll be all right."

He nodded, and his gaze strayed to her lips for just a fraction of a second before he jerked his head up and peered off over her shoulder.

He stepped back into the barn. "I'm sure Travis won't mind taking you to town in the morning. You can pack your things tonight. If that's enough time."

She felt stiff, her limbs weighted and wooden. All feeling had drained from her body. "That should be plenty of time."

He nodded and turned away. Courtney watched him stride back through the barn. Frantically, she tried to memorize the way he moved, the long easy strides, the way his denims fit his long legs, the material folding at the knees and bunching over his boots; the way the sunlight caught his hair as he emerged from the shadows; the way the shirt fabric stretched across his shoulders as he brushed the waves back, settled his Stetson in place and reached to untie Red's reins from the railing of the front corral; the way his thigh muscles bunched as he mounted; the way his hands gripped the reins. She watched him ride out of the yard with a sinking feeling of loss. Tears burned the back of her eyes, but she blinked them away. It was better this way, she reminded herself. She pressed her hand to the spot on the wall and remembered how his very touch incited her rebellious body. It was better this way.

Courtney wrapped her hands around her first cup of coffee as dawn lightened the horizon. Matt was gone already, slipping out the door just as she emerged from the bedroom. She wasn't sure she would have known what to say to him anyway, even though she'd lain awake half the night thinking about it. What words were there to say, without admitting she was sorry she loved him when he didn't love her back? What words could effectively hide her inner turmoil?

As Peter helped Travis carry her parcel of belongings out to the wagon, Courtney looked around her. There was evidence of her presence here now. The dust-free surfaces shone, the new eyelet curtains brightened the windows, the starched white doilies were centered on the couch back and arms. The baking she'd done yesterday lined the counter beneath several new cotton tea towels. How had this ranch house become home in just a matter of a few short months? She stood, overcome by the desire to wander around the room and touch every item that attracted her eye, but just then Peter and Travis came back into the house. She sat back down and sipped the coffee, contenting herself with letting her gaze settle on the items instead, committing the room to memory.

"Well, I guess we're all set then," Travis said.

Courtney set down her cup, stood and smoothed her skirt. Peter rushed across the room. He wrapped his arms around her and hugged her with a desperate grip. Courtney ran her hand over his tousled blond curls and closed her eyes against the sting of emotion. When he pulled away she managed to mask her emotions.

"I'll come to town every time we need supplies. I promise I'll always stop and see you. And I'll keep the sweetgrass. Someday it might work." He ducked his head. "I'll miss you."

"I'll miss you, too," Courtney managed around the lump in her throat. "I'll hold you to that promise to visit. I don't want you growing up so fast I won't recognize you."

He smiled and puffed out his chest. "Matt says I can be a regular hand next spring at the roundup. Says I got responsible."

"Yes, you have," Courtney agreed. She picked up her small beaded purse, a purchase on Travis's recent trip to town. "Well, I guess I'm ready then."

Travis held the door for her. She gave Peter one last quick hug on the way by. She didn't trust herself to speak. Without a parting glance, she hurried out the door and down the steps. Travis gave her a hand up into the wagon seat and she stared straight ahead, down the road. He climbed aboard and snapped the reins. Relief mingled with sadness. A quick clean break was the best. Don't look back. Don't let the hurt show. Be strong, no matter what.

Matt sat astride Red on top of the same hill from which he had watched Travis escort Miss Courtney James to town the first time. It seemed a long time ago. Things were changing again. Just as he'd gotten used to having Peter around, he'd grown accustomed to Courtney's presence. But things were too complicated. She was right about going to town. She shouldn't have been here, unmarried and all. But it had been easier to allow her to stay, especially after she got sick from being out in the rain that day. How could he have justified turning out a sick woman?

Oh, yeah, his conscience replied. As if that was the real reason you didn't want her to leave. Quit kidding yourself, Matthew Ward. She drew you like a fire draws moths. And you had to keep getting closer until you got your wings scorched. You of all people should know better than to get too close, to love. Look at Kathleen, Zach, Katie and Jeanette. All your love ever got them was dead. You know it was right not to let yourself love her. Nothing good could ever have come of that.

The wagon topped the rise. Soon it would disappear, leaving only a cloud of dust drifting into the air, swept eastward by the breeze. Peter came out of the house and stood on the porch, looking after the wagon for long after it had vanished. He sat down on the steps, planted his elbows on his knees and rested his head in his hands. Even from here, Matt could see his bowed shoulders shaking. He clenched his jaw and turned Red in the opposite direction. The sorrel gelding leapt to a gallop as Matt tightened his legs on the horse's sides. He knew he couldn't outrun this ache, but he meant to try anyway, needed the rush of air past his face to blow away his regrets. No sense in having them now. He couldn't change things, not without a compromise he wasn't prepared to make. Courtney was right. It was better this way.

Travis pulled the wagon to a halt in front of a neatly fenced, pale yellow house at the far end of town. He helped Courtney down from the wagon, and then stared down at his hands as though afraid to look at her. Or perhaps he was trying to decide what to say.

Courtney spared him the trouble. She laid her hand on his sleeve. "Good-bye, Travis."

He looked up, sadness creasing his brow. "I don't know what to say. I'm sorry things worked out this way. You could still change your mind." For a moment his eyes brightened hopefully.

Courtney shook her head.

Travis nodded, once again looking down.

"I'll see you when you come to town for supplies," Courtney offered as a concession.

When he met her gaze, his expression seemed stricken rather than appeased, as though he hadn't considered the fact that although she would no longer be at the ranch, she would still be near. Courtney had a good idea of the emotions that must be inside him. They were the same feelings she got whenever she thought about Matt, so temptingly, torturously near, and yet so out of reach.

"I appreciate everything. I don't know what I would have done if you hadn't found me on that hill and taken me in. I'll always be grateful for that."

Travis straightened, seeming to compose himself. "It was the least we could do. I'm glad I met you, Courtney. You brought something back to the ranch. The place won't be the same without you."

"I'll miss you all," Courtney whispered as she blinked back the threat of tears.

Courtney heard the boardinghouse door open and footsteps on the porch behind her. It saved her from further conversation.

"Here's Sarah," Travis said unnecessarily.

He reached into the back of the wagon and lifted out the carryall bag that Peter had lent her. Courtney took it from him and turned to greet Sarah.

She vaguely recalled meeting Sarah Barnes at the dance. Sarah was a petite young woman, with fiery red hair that looked untamable as erratic strands constantly escaped from a loose knot at the base of her neck. Courtney wondered why Sarah's mother would need help. Surely her daughter could do the things she had planned for Courtney to do.

"Sarah," Courtney said in greeting with a nod and a smile. "Is your mother in?"

"My mother?" Sarah frowned.

"Yes, the Widow Barnes."

Sarah smiled, bright blue eyes sparkling. "I'm the Widow Barnes."

Courtney didn't know what to say. Things were looking up already. There was a hint of humor and a promise of close friendship in Sarah's warm smile.

The wagon spring creaked as Travis climbed back into the seat. Courtney forced herself to turn and put on a smile.

Travis waved, then slapped the reins over ol' Blue and they moved off.

"I'm sure you'll feel right at home here," Sarah promised, a slight Irish lilt warming her words. "It will be so nice to have someone around to talk with. I hope we can be friends instead of employee and employer."

"I'd like that very much," Courtney said sincerely.

"Let's get you settled. I'll show you to your room," Sarah said as she tucked her arm through Courtney's and led her up the steps and into the house.

"It's this way," Sarah said. She paused to pick up a vase of fresh flowers from a buffet cabinet in the entrance, and then headed toward a flight of stairs just to her left. "You can take the rest of the day to get settled in."

Courtney followed her up the painted wood steps,

careful not to step on the trailing hem of Sarah's gingham skirt. Sarah stopped to gather fresh linens from a closet on the second-floor landing.

"We have four boarders," Sarah explained as she handed Courtney the vase of flowers and scooped up the lavender-scented linens. "They each have a room on this floor."

Her skirt flared as she turned and flitted down the hall. Courtney hurried after her, balancing the flowers against her bag as she lifted her skirts to follow Sarah up the stairs at the end of the hall. Sarah's voice carried back down the narrow stairwell.

"Your room is up here."

Courtney stepped out into a renovated attic. The room ran half the length of the house. The walls, papered in a pattern of tiny roses, slanted inward halfway up, following the pitch of the roof. A single, lace-curtained window was set into a gabled alcove at the end of the room. Sunlight spilled across navy and pink braided rag rugs that lay in scattered ovals on the wood floor.

The room's furnishings consisted of a writing table, dresser and matching four-poster bed that sat against the back wall. A small nightstand held a ceramic pitcher and basin hand-painted with pale pink roses.

"It's lovely," Courtney said, thinking how much in vogue this style was in her own time. She moved forward, setting her bag on the unmade mattress, running her hand over the curves in the bedposts and then the folded crocheted coverlet on the foot of the bed.

"This is beautiful." She let her fingers follow the pattern in the spread.

"I'll give you the pattern," Sarah offered as she took the flowers and set them on the dresser.

"Oh, I couldn't make anything like this," Courtney protested. "I'm all thumbs when it comes to needle-work."

"Nonsense." Sarah's hand fluttered in the air. "It's easy. I can teach you in a few hours."

Courtney looked back at the spread doubtfully.

"Anyway," Sarah continued unabated as she laid the fresh linens on the bed, "I'll let you get unpacked and freshened up. There's water in the barrel on the second floor. Supper's at seven." She gave Courtney a warm smile. "It'll be nice to have an extra pair of hands around here. I hope you'll be happy with us."

"Thank you. I'm sure I will be."

Sarah nodded and left, darting off with a swish of skirts and pulling the door closed behind her.

Courtney moved around the room, touching the dresser top, fingering the lace curtains, opening the shallow closet recessed into a corner by the window and each of the dresser drawers. They were paper-lined and smelled faintly of roses. In the bottom drawer, she found the source of the smell, several gathered-lace sachets filled with rose petals and lavender blossoms.

She made up the bed and then unpacked, taking care with each item in her limited wardrobe, hanging her extra skirt and blouse on the padded hangers in the closet, folding her jeans and sweater and her underthings into the drawers, laying her few toiletry articles on the dresser top. She tucked the borrowed bag into the foot of the closet, making a mental note to remember to return it to Peter the next time she saw him.

She moved to the window. It faced north, down the street, but Courtney's gaze moved beyond the town, drawn to the hills. What were Peter and Matt and Travis doing at this minute? Did they miss her?

Or were their lives finally restored to normal? She pushed away the hollowness that threatened to expand in her chest. Then she checked her watch. Just after four-thirty. What she needed was something to do, something to take her mind off the ranch and the Ward brothers. It only took her a few seconds to make up her mind. Determined, she headed for the stairs. It was never too soon to start helping out. Surely Sarah could use a hand with supper.

The second floor was quiet. The boarders must all be out, probably at work. Courtney made note of the covered water barrel near the head of the stairs.

On the main floor she took a minute to study the layout of rooms, the living room to her left in the front of the house, the dining room to her right leading back into the kitchen. Sarah's rooms probably backed the living room. The bisecting hallway led straight through to a screened porch in back. She made her way to the kitchen. Sarah was already busy there, rolling pie crust on a floured side counter.

"Can I do anything to help?" Courtney asked as she stepped into the room. Heat radiated from the stove and the smell of roast beef and onions wafted in the air.

"Sure," Sarah replied as she brushed a stray strand of hair from her forehead with the back of her hand. "There are potatoes in the sink. Knives in that drawer." She pointed to the second drawer beneath the counter to Courtney's right.

Sarah's kitchen was equipped with a hand pump, and Courtney found a stopper on the side of the sink. She pumped water onto the potatoes, found a knife and started to peel.

"Mary Emmery said you're from up north," Sarah said, making conversation as she molded the crust into pie plates.

"Yes. Which pot do you use for potatoes?" Courtney asked, steering the conversation in a different direction as she looked at the array of pots on a shelf under the counter.

"Bottom one, right hand side," Sarah answered without looking.

Courtney retrieved it, filled it with water and set it beside the sink, cutting the first of the peeled potatoes into it.

"So you're going to marry one of the Ward brothers," Sarah continued as she wiped her hands on her apron, lifted a towel from a batch of rising bread and carried the loaves to the stove. She pulled a dish towel to use as a pot holder from a hook beside the stove, opened the door, moved the roaster to one side and slid the bread in.

Courtney concentrated on her task. "Actually, that might not work out."

"Oh, I'm sorry to hear that. I've been saying they need a woman out there ever since I first met them."

Courtney gave Sarah a quick appraising look. Was Sarah implying that she would like to be that woman, just as Mary Emmery wanted to be that woman?

Sarah chatted on, unaware of Courtney's perusal. "I always thought Mary would turn Travis's head. She's always all aflutter whenever he's around."

Courtney could read nothing possessive in Sarah's tone.

"But you know men," Sarah continued as she wiped flour from the counter with swift efficient strokes. "They have to be hit on the head before they can figure out a woman's interested in them."

"How about you, Sarah? Do you have a man you're interested in?"

Sarah laughed, a light tinkling sound. "I don't have

time for another man. I've already got four to look after."

"I didn't mean a boarder."

Sarah's smile faded.

Courtney shook her head at her own stupidity. Sarah was widowed, she reminded herself.

"Do you miss him a lot?"

Sarah chewed on her lower lip and a look of sadness passed over her face. She turned away quickly. "Yes." She reached for a stoneware bowl on the back of the counter.

"I'm sorry. I didn't mean to upset you." Courtney's hands stilled.

Sarah busied herself with the apple slices in the bowl. "That's all right. It was a long time ago. I just prefer not to talk about it." She filled the pie shells, covering the apple with sugar and a sprinkle of cinnamon and then the top crust.

Courtney turned back to her task, sorry she had cast a pall over the easy camaraderie that had been forming.

From the corner of her eye, she saw Sarah shake her head, stiffen her shoulders and turn back toward her, a smile carefully in place on her lips.

"I think you'll like the boarders. Joshua Wells is an assayer with the silver mines. Bryant Smith works for the railway, a freight agent. Samuel Mortby, he's only here off and on. He's a traveling salesman so he stays when he's in this area selling his ranching supplies. Landry Culvertson's not permanent either. He's through every month or so."

"What does he do?"

"He's a circuit court judge."

"Doesn't that affect your income, having boarders who are only part-time?"

Sarah shrugged. "It's not too bad. Landry pays me

as though he was here all the time, so I hold his room. And there's almost always someone in town who needs a place to stay for a few days here and there while Sam's away. I manage."

"I hope I'm going to be a help and not an imposition."

"Summer's here. There's gardening that will need doing and then canning in the fall. I plan on working you like a slave," Sarah teased, her easy smile back, the past forgotten.

"Good," Courtney said as she finished the potatoes and dried her hands on a towel on the counter. "It's just what I need." And I've found a friend, she thought to herself. I needed one of them, too.

# *Chapter Eleven*

The boarders returned at different times, banging in the door, calling a hello to Sarah and then stomping up the stairs to their respective rooms. At seven o'clock they began arriving in the dining room. Sarah made the introductions as she and Courtney carried steaming dishes of food to the table.

Joshua Wells, the mine assayer, nodded politely to Courtney. He was a thin man, thirtyish and a few inches shorter than Courtney. He regarded her briefly, his brown eyes magnified by the round lenses of his wire-rimmed glasses. His pin-striped three-piece suit showed signs of the day's wear with a fine layer of dust on the shoulders and around the pants cuffs. His light brown hair was neatly parted in the center and slicked down to each side. He ducked his head, extracted a gold watch from his pocket in a smooth exacting motion and clicked open the cover with a flick of a finger. The time determined, he wound the stem a few brisk turns and then dropped the watch back into the small vest pocket. His actions made Courtney give her own wristwatch a quick glance. Seven o'clock precisely. She suspected that Mr. Wells was a very precise person, as his assaying job probably required.

He bent forward.

"That's a very unique timepiece, Miss James." He motioned toward her wrist. Courtney's first instinct was to cover the watch. She stilled her right hand halfway to her wrist.

"Yes, it's foreign," she answered, reaching to center a bowl of peas in hopes of distracting his attention.

Her statement seemed to have just the opposite effect.

"Really?" He moved around the table. "May I?" He extended a hand.

Courtney had no choice. She allowed him to turn her wrist so he might better scrutinize the black lacquered face of the sport watch. He studied the digital numbers with a puzzled frown.

"How does it work?"

"I'm afraid I don't know precisely," Courtney said as she gently pulled her hand from his grip.

"A very interesting concept," he muttered, almost to himself, as Sarah returned with two platters of meat and, balanced on her forearm, a linen-lined basket filled with fresh sliced bread. Two of the other boarders entered the room just then, too.

Without missing a step, Sarah ran through a quick introduction. "Courtney James, this is Samuel Mortby. Samuel, Courtney."

Courtney welcomed the interruption, using it as an excuse to extract herself from Joshua Wells's side. She extended a hand to the elderly man before her.

He appeared to be around sixty, his hair grayed to almost white, his watery blue eyes tucked beneath thick sweeping eyebrows, his face lined by time and weather. After a second's hesitation, he shook her hand, his grip restrained, the handshake brief. His hesitation made Courtney wonder if handshaking between men and women was a twentieth-century custom. She'd have to remember to take note of the way men and women greeted each other and be sure she stayed with the bounds of propriety.

"And Bryant Smith."

The second man gave Courtney a curt nod. His thin black hair was brushed straight back. It shone blue-black beneath a liberal application of hair cream. Courtney averted her attention from his direct brown eyes. Middle-aged, he was dressed in a worn blue cotton shirt and a pair of black pants held in place on his thin frame by both a belt and a pair of suspenders. He hitched his thumbs under the suspenders and rested his hands on his chest as he watched Courtney help Sarah with the plates she was juggling in the crook of her arm.

Sarah chattered on as she darted around the table, repositioning bowls and platters. "Samuel's only with us for the rest of the week. He's all over the county selling ranch supplies. And Bryant is our local railway agent," she said to Courtney before turning to Samuel and Bryant. "Courtney will be staying here and helping me out around the house."

She stepped back and surveyed the table.

"Well, I think that's everything. Gentlemen, please sit down." She glanced toward the door expectantly as the three men found their places, settling in with the scraping sound of chair legs on the wood floor. "Is Mr. Culvertson back?"

"Don't think so," Bryant Smith volunteered.

"All right," Sarah said as she directed Courtney to a seat with a light touch on her arm. "We'll start without him."

Courtney thought she detected an undercurrent of disappointment in Sarah's voice. She gave her host a quick look, but Sarah had already moved away toward her own seat at the end of the table. The three men stood back up, only reseating themselves after Courtney and Sarah had both taken their seats. Sarah accepted the courtesy with little regard while Courtney felt a smile tugging at her lips. It stayed there through grace and the chorus of muttered amens.

The formalities out of the way, the meal began, an orderly procession of food passed clockwise around the table. Conversation was minimal, the sound of cutlery on porcelain and glass filling the air instead.

Courtney watched them all. Sarah conversed casually with Joshua Wells concerning his day, her gaze occasionally flitting to the empty chair on her right. Bryant Smith sat across the table, dividing his attention between his plate and Courtney, and Samuel Mortby was seated at the end of the table and to Courtney's right, eating quietly, his head bowed over his food. Courtney looked around the room, finding herself still awed at being in this era.

Dark paneling covered the bottom half of all four walls, and a burgundy wallpaper covered the top. The table, chairs, cabinet and sideboard were all carved of dark wood. Lanterns, one in the middle of the table and one on the sideboard, added to the light that came in through the single front window, and the glare reflected in the glassware and on the Wedgwood china in the cabinet on the far wall.

The sounds around her seemed to fade into the distance as Courtney felt the room begin to close in around her. What was she doing here? She didn't know the first thing about living in this time. Anxiety formed a tight knot in the pit of her stomach. How was she to survive? She felt as if her fate had been taken out of her command, as if she was on a roller coaster out of control and all she could do was hold on for dear life.

It was Samuel Mortby's touch on her arm that brought her back to the moment.

"Are you all right, Miss James?"

All eyes were on her, the men's curious, Sarah's concerned.

Courtney gave her head a shake to clear it. "Yes. I'm okay," she quickly reassured everyone. But her hand shook as she lifted her waterglass and sipped to wet her dry throat. Her appetite had vanished.

Sarah was on her feet, the three men hastening to rise as she came to Courtney's side and pulled her to her feet.

"You're exhausted. All this work after that long trip. It's just too much. You need to lie down." She herded Courtney out the door despite her reluctance to admit how weak she felt.

"But I should help you with the dishes," Courtney protested.

"Nonsense. I've been doing them myself for the last four years. One more night won't kill me." Sarah's hand was firm on her elbow. "Upstairs with you and get some sleep. You look positively drained."

Sarah's compassion touched Courtney's heart. She felt emotion burn the back of her throat. "Thank you," she choked out.

Sarah nodded and smiled. "You'll feel better after a good night's sleep." She stood at the bottom of the stairs until Courtney was at the top. "Good night."

Courtney turned, looked down at the petite

woman, red hair illuminated by the wash of light from the hall, and knew she had found a friend. "Good night, Sarah," she whispered as Sarah stepped back out of sight.

In her room, she didn't even bother with the lantern. She undressed in the dim light from the gable window. She found Matt's shirt in the drawer and slipped it on, letting the coarse fabric caress her skin, trying to no avail to ignore the rush of images provoked by the sight of the borrowed garment. As she crawled into bed and pulled the handmade coverlet up beneath her chin, she was certain those memories would keep her awake. But a few seconds later, she was asleep.

Courtney woke in the middle of the night, alarmed at first in her half-awake state by the unfamiliar surroundings. Gradually awareness came as she sat up and scrutinized the dark shadows that were her dresser and the wardrobe. Moonlight filtered in through the window, laying a blue swath of color on the floor planks.

She slipped from the bed, scooping up the knit afghan that lay across the foot and wrapping it around her shoulders to ward off the night's chill. Barefoot, she padded across the room. For the longest time, she stood at the window, staring out beyond the town to the hills that hid the ranch from view.

She wondered if Matt had moved back into his own bedroom, if he lay in the soft hollow of the mattress, if the bedsprings squeaked when he moved, if he missed her, even just a little. No man had ever made her feel this way before, had ever caused this dull ache just beneath her ribs. She wrapped her arms around herself to try to dispel the hollow feeling in the pit of her stomach. She tried to convince herself that it was only because she hadn't eaten, but her heart knew better. This hunger was in her heart and nowhere else. It couldn't be appeased by food or dulled by distance. Not now. Not now that she had started to fall in love. Not now that she had fallen for Matthew Ward. Gruff, uncooperative, unresponsive Matthew Ward. She sure knew how to pick 'em.

Matt looked around the table as he sat down. Silence filled the room. Both Peter and Travis kept their heads bowed over their plates, Travis eating without his usual intensity, slowly, mechanically maneuvering food from his plate to his mouth. Peter didn't eat, just pushed his meat around his plate.

Matt ran his fingers through his hair in frustration and let out an audible breath. Nothing had been the same after she came, and now, though she was gone, nothing would ever be the same again. Already in the last few days, dust had formed a fine layer over the room's surfaces: counters and tables and floors.

His gaze came to rest on the cookbook sandwiched between two jars on the sideboard. He'd bought it for Courtney at Peter's request, but instead of taking it with her, she'd spent an hour diligently copying the recipes. What good was the damn book to him, except as another reminder of her?

He turned his attention to his plate, savagely stabbing up a piece of beef, chewing without looking up, spearing a potato, eating it without tasting it. The food filled the emptiness in his stomach but nowhere else. Damn it! He missed her.

He heard Peter's muttered request to be excused and looked up, flinching inwardly at the silent accusation he read in the boy's blue eyes.

"May I be excused?" Peter repeated, a little louder but with no more enthusiasm.

Matt nodded, watching the boy as the chair

scraped back and he rose to his feet. Shoulders slumped, feet dragging, Peter made his way out the back door.

Matt pushed away his half-empty plate, his own appetite gone. Travis studied him from across the table.

"What?" Matt snapped.

"Nothing," Travis said hastily as he turned his attention back to his plate.

"I'll be outside." Matt pushed back from the table and stomped out the front door.

Darkness had settled over the yard, but the moon lent enough light once Matt's eyes adjusted. He massaged the back of his neck and crossed to the corral. He stood there for a long time, his foot resting on the bottom rail, his arms draped over the top one, feeling the solidness of the wood across his chest, staring off into the night, wondering for the thousandth time why he felt so damn mean.

He tensed as he heard footsteps behind him. They stopped. A match flared.

"Smoke?" Travis offered as he came alongside and took up a stance mirroring Matt's own.

Matt shook his head, wishing his brother would, for once, just go away and leave him alone. He wasn't fit company for anyone right now, not the way he felt.

The ember of Travis's cigarette glowed as he took a deep puff. He spat a piece of tobacco off the end of his tongue before he spoke.

"I've been doin' a lot of thinking lately," he said, his gaze fixed on a spot of darkness beyond the corral. "I've lived on this ranch all my life. I've stayed here because it was the easiest thing to do, the safest thing, the trail with the least burrs. But I always felt the ranch was yours, Matt. That it belonged to you.

Like I was just passing through somehow."

He paused and took another drag. Smoke curled up into the still air, and the red glow lit the planes of his face.

"When Courtney came," Travis continued, "I saw something I wanted and I went after it. And I'm sorry I didn't get what I set out after. But I'm not sorry I tried. I think it made me stop and think about my life, about what I've done with it so far, about where I'm going, or more to the point, not going."

He pulled back from the fence and dropped the cigarette butt, grinding it into the ground with the toe of his boot.

"I've decided to leave, Matt. I've always wanted to see more of the country. I hear there's gold up in Alaska just waiting for a man to pick it up."

Darkness hid the look in his eyes, but Matt could tell by the set of his chin that there would be no dissuading him. Travis could be stubborn as a mule once he had made up his mind about something.

"You don't have to go." Matt knew it was a feeble attempt, but he said it anyway. "A few more days and things will settle back to normal around here. Give it some time."

"Pretty soon I'll be all out of time. This thing with Courtney isn't the reason I'm leaving. It's just the thing that made me sit up and realize that I need to go after my dreams, that I need to do something that matters to me before it's too late, before I can't do anything but look back at my life and wish for all the might-have-beens."

"When will you go?" Matt spoke low, his voice resigned.

"Tomorrow."

Matt looked away, almost afraid to speak for fear

that his voice would crack, that the emotion would come pouring out.

Travis turned back toward the house, but Matt stilled him with a hand on his sleeve.

"I'll always be here. So will the ranch. You've got a home here anytime you need it, anytime you want to come back. I want you to remember that."

"The land's not in my blood like it is in yours." Travis brushed the lock of hair from his forehead. When Matt made no reply, he began to walk back to the house, but he stopped after a few steps and turned back to his brother.

"Don't be a fool, Matt," he said in a hushed voice. "Go after what matters. Go after her. Admit what it will take to make you happy."

"And you think that's some runaway whore?" Matt growled.

With a shrug, Travis ignored Matt's response. "I just know what I see, Matt. And that's the way the two of you look at each other when you think the other one isn't looking. If I had some woman looking at me like that . . ." He shrugged and left the sentence hanging. "But no one ever could make you do anything you didn't want to do. I hope things work out. You do what you have to, but me, I wouldn't want to think I grew old alone when I didn't have to."

"Maybe alone is safer."

"Maybe everything that's worth having in this life starts with taking a risk."

Matt stared silently across the yard at his brother. Travis started to walk away, but stopped again.

"By the way, Courtney knows about Katie and Jeanette," he called across the open ground between them.

Matt stiffened, finally speaking when Travis seemed to be waiting for a response. "Then I guess I don't have to worry about her having any further interest in me."

Travis let out an exasperated snort and shook his head. "You're the only one who ever believed any of that was your fault, Matt. Even Courtney said you couldn't be to blame."

Matt spun away, refusing to continue this conversation, feeling the stab of betrayal at knowing his brother had told Courtney about the events in his past, about his failings. He didn't want to face Courtney James and if she was smart, she'd stay as far away from him as she could get.

Another restless night, Courtney thought as she secured her long black hair at her nape and gave herself one last quick perusal in the mirror on the inside door of the wardrobe. Dark circles underscored her gray eyes. How much longer could this go on? When would she finally admit that she was wishing for something that just wasn't going to happen? Matthew Ward could manage on the ranch just fine without her. Hadn't they been managing out there for years? Had she really expected one of the Ward brothers to arrive in town with a plea for her to return, with an admission that she was indispensable? No one was ever indispensable.

She closed the closet door firmly. It was early, but Sarah was probably up. Courtney had yet to arrive in the kitchen when Sarah wasn't already there, with coffee made and bread rising. The woman must get up before the sun. The early bird gets the worm, Courtney thought, smiling as she descended the first flight of stairs. She drew up sharply as she emerged onto the second floor.

A half-dressed man stood at the end of the hall with his back toward her. Courtney immediately realized that he wasn't one of the three boarders she had met so far. And since Mr. Mortby, the only boarder whose room Sarah let when he wasn't there, had been at supper last night, she had to assume that Sarah hadn't taken in any strangers. No, this must be the elusive Landry Culvertson. The muscles along his broad shoulders flexed, drawing her eyes away from the tumble of unruly black hair that fell to his shoulders, down along his back, past a narrow waist, to slender hips and long legs clad in black pants. A pair of gray suspenders dangled from his waistband and looped loosely against his legs.

The man turned just as she stepped from the stairwell. He took several steps before his head came up. Dark jet-black eyes locked with hers as they both froze. He had hawkish features: a slightly hooked nose, a sharp angular jawline and prominent cheekbones, though his mouth was wide and full-lipped. Eyes narrowing, he raised the pitcher in front of his bare chest as though to ward off an attacker.

He dipped his head in acknowledgment, his eyes never once leaving her.

"Excuse my improper attire, ma'am." He had a strong voice, steady, deep, full of authority and propriety. "I wasn't aware Miss Sarah had let the attic room."

And to a woman, his eyes said, though he didn't voice that observation.

Courtney stepped forward, extending her hand. "You must be Mr. Culvertson."

He stiffened, but didn't take her hand. He gestured toward the open door just ahead to his right. "Excuse me for just one minute." He moved toward his room, turning back at the last moment. "Wait right there. I'll just be a minute," he added before disappearing into the room.

Courtney remained rooted to the spot. She heard the sound of movement, footsteps, the thunk of the heavy pitcher as he set it down, the rustle of clothing, and then he was back, filling the doorway as he secured his shirt cuffs with silver cuff links. His long fingers moved efficiently, deftly twisting the metal clasps into place while his eyes remained on Courtney.

He was a handsome man, but there was a hardness in this man's eyes that set her on edge, no hint of the compassion that Matthew Ward worked hard to hide but that Courtney knew was there all the same.

"Landry Culvertson," he said, taking a step forward, hand extended as he introduced himself. Courtney accepted his proffered hand, shaking it quickly, enduring the contact just long enough to note the sure, firm grasp. "And you are?" he prompted.

"Courtney James. I'm here to help Sarah out."

"Ah. You're employed here then."

"Yes."

"Sarah could use the help."

Courtney nodded, still rooted to the spot.

"Well, don't let me hold you up," Culvertson said as he stepped aside, clearing the way to the stairs.

Courtney stepped past him, her skirt hem brushing across the top of his bare toes.

"I'm sure we'll have a chance to get better acquainted during the day," he said to her back, his voice carrying just a hint of suspicion, insinuating that he intended to learn all there was to know about her.

Courtney looked back over her shoulder and gave him a forced smile. "I'll look forward to it," she replied with a politeness she didn't feel. She could feel his eyes on her back, but she forced herself to move calmly down the steps. She didn't heave a sigh of relief, however, until she entered the sunny kitchen, where Sarah was humming to herself as she covered several pans of shaped bread dough.

"You're in high spirits," Courtney commented.

Sarah just smiled. "It's a wonderful day, isn't it."

Courtney crossed to the ice box and pulled out a slab of bacon. "I just met your Mr. Culvertson."

Sarah ducked her head, fussing with the edge of the cloth covering the bread. "Yes. I believe he got in late last night."

Courtney detected a hint of blush on the half-hidden curve of Sarah's cheek. So that was how it was. Sarah had a thing for the judicious Mr. Culvertson.

"Serious kind of fellow, isn't he?" Courtney commented.

Sarah immediately came to his defense. "He's a circuit court judge. It's a dangerous job but an important one. He takes his responsibilities very seriously. Once you get to know him a bit you'll see that he's really very amiable."

Courtney wondered how well Sarah knew the good Mr. Culvertson, but she valued Sarah's friendship too much to ask. "I'm sure he is," she agreed instead, as she sliced bacon into a cold skillet. Sarah checked the stove and poured them each a cup of coffee.

Courtney had no intention of getting to know Culvertson too well. She had too many secrets that needed to remain hidden. Her past for starters. How was she going to avoid questions about her background and her family? She had best steer clear of Judge Culvertson if at all possible. He might not be so easily put off with her stock "I'm from the north" answer. He didn't strike her as the type to accept an evasive answer like that and let it lie. Courtney guessed he wouldn't be as trusting as Sarah Barnes or as concerned about seeming to pry as the other boarders and the majority of the townsfolk.

Later, as they all settled around the table for breakfast, she held her breath in anticipation. Thankfully, the conversation remained fairly general, centering on Landry's cases of the past few weeks. More than once Courtney felt his eyes upon her, but she purposely refrained from meeting his look. Instead she watched Sarah, noting the quick sideways glances cast in Culvertson's direction. There was something in Sarah's expression that intrigued Courtney, something more than interest. She told herself that it was none of her business.

With breakfast finally finished, Courtney volunteered to pick up Sarah's groceries at the mercantile. That would get her out of the house for an hour or so if she dallied a bit over the shelves of material and yard goods. She picked up the list from the kitchen table and escaped as soon as the dishes were finished, leaving by the back door to avoid running into anyone on her way out.

The crisp morning air rejuvenated Courtney's spirits.

"Welcome to Dodge City," she mumbled to herself as she approached the main street with its hitching rails, its merchants and the usual morning traffic of horses and wagons. Though she was starting to grow accustomed to the sight, it never failed to seem alien and unreal, as if she'd just stepped onto a movie set.

She lifted her skirts and stepped up onto the boardwalk leading to the mercantile. A wagon was parked in front of the store, a wagon startlingly similar to the one owned by the Wards.

The past days at Sarah Barnes's boardinghouse

had passed in a blur of instruction: the proper way to do laundry, the best techniques for removing stains from clothing and table linens, tips on cooking and needlepoint. As a further distraction, everyone in town had stopped by on one occasion or another to make her acquaintance or to reintroduce themselves if she had met them during the dance earlier in the summer. During the day, Courtney had managed to put thoughts of the Ward brothers from her mind, most of the time. It was at night, in the solitude of her room, when she couldn't keep the memories from invading her thoughts. Or maybe she didn't want to. She purposefully strove to remember every detail, from the ranch house and its contents to the particulars of Travis's proposal, Peter's goodbye hug and, of course, Matt's kiss. Sometimes she wondered why she tortured herself that way, but she was powerless to stop. Seeing the wagon brought all those memories surging to the fore, and she had to force them back, remind herself that every farmer and rancher in the county probably had a similar buckboard.

She picked her way around a stack of nail kegs that occupied one side of the walkway, and almost collided with the man coming out of the mercantile. She knew he was Matthew Ward before she even looked up into his face. The boots, the stance, the aura of power enveloping him were all too familiar.

As she looked up at him, her heart accelerated until its beats boomed inside her head. Surely he could hear them, too. She clenched her hands together to still the trembling that afflicted them all of a sudden, crumpling Sarah's grocery list in the process.

"Matt." She nodded her head in greeting and wet her dry lips. She wanted to smooth her hair, but was afraid to release the death grip she had on her hands.

247

She swallowed and tried to sound normal. "How are you?" Her hands shook uncontrollably.

"I'm fine. And you?"

"Fine." This was ridiculous. She couldn't even carry on a decent conversation. If only he hadn't surprised her like this. If only she'd had a minute or two to think about what she should say. All she could think about was that kiss and how much she missed him. Lord knows that wouldn't make for proper conversation.

"How's Peter? And Travis?"

"They're good."

She nodded and fell silent. Her eyes took in every aspect of him: the worn blue shirt, the tanned triangle at his throat, the curls of hair at his collar, his dark whisker-shadowed jaw. He swallowed, opened his mouth and then shut it and sucked in one corner of his lip.

Something inside her chest was tightening up, restricting her breathing, forcing the air from her lungs, closing up the back of her throat, clutching her heart.

"Peter misses you," he said.

She smiled slightly. "I miss him, too. Is he with you?"

He nodded. "He went over to the school to get some books from Miss Emmery."

"I see."

He shifted the sack in his arms.

Courtney stepped back. "I'll let you get back to what you were doing then. I'll go over to the school to say hi to Peter."

"Sure."

She hesitated halfway into the turn. "It was nice seeing you again, Matt."

"Yeah, you too."

She lifted her hem and went down the mercantile steps on shaky legs. Their conversation left her feeling as if she had just been walking on eggs. She was surprised she hadn't just blurted out that she loved him and made a complete fool out of herself. Maybe seeing Peter would loosen the tight constriction that wrapped her chest. She held her hands out in front of her and noted how they shook. Meeting Matt was almost as unbearable as wanting to meet him. She wished for an instant that she could be invisible, that she could turn around in the middle of the street and drink in the sight of him. But of course that wasn't possible.

"Miss James." Peter's call snapped her from her reverie.

"Peter." She hurried to greet him, and tousled his hair when he halted just short of a hug. He transferred his books to one arm and held out his hand for a formal handshake. She shook his hand, then turned him around. "Let me look at you. I swear, you've grown a whole inch since I saw you last."

He scratched his sunburned nose. "Naw."

"What happened?" She pointed to the sunburn.

"I told Matt it was from spending too much time hoeing the garden, but it's really from fishing."

She nodded with a conspiratorial smile. "How's everyone? I ran into Matt at the store."

"We're okay. Things are mostly back to the way they were before you came."

She nodded. Life went on. She half wished that their lives hadn't converted back so easily.

"It was better when you were there."

"I miss you, too," she said as she tugged a book from his arms to distract him from seeing the true extent of her feelings in her expression. "What did Miss Emmery give you to study?" Her voice quivered just a bit, only enough that she noticed it.

"Reading, mostly. And some arithmetic. I used to be pretty good at arithmetic back in Boston."

He waved, and she almost turned. It would be Matt who had attracted his attention.

"I suppose you'll be heading back right away? I'm glad I got to see you. I'm making a lot of new friends here, but no one who's able to teach me to ride and fish and explore the way you did."

Peter grinned. "We did have a lot of fun, didn't we?"

"We did."

"I could walk you back home, if that's where you were going. Or we could give you a ride if it's very far."

"No. That's all right. I need to get some things at the store. And I live at the boardinghouse, so it's not terribly far."

Matt stepped up beside her. She started. She hadn't even heard him approaching.

"Are you ready to go, Peter?"

The boy nodded. "See you next time," he said as he raced off toward the wagon.

"See you," Courtney whispered after him.

Matt stood, shuffling his feet and staring at the hem of her skirt. He cleared his throat, but didn't look at her as he spoke. "I talked to Jake over at the livery. There's a horse there for you any time you want."

Courtney frowned, puzzled at this strange offer.

"In case you want to ride out sometime. You know, to see Peter. Or if you need anything."

Courtney knew she would never avail herself of the mount he had put at her disposal. Returning to the ranch only meant having to endure leaving all over again. She didn't think she could bear that.

"You didn't have to do that."

"It's no trouble." He shifted uncomfortably. "Uh, I better go."

He started to extend his hand, and then thought better of it and let it drop to his side. "Good-bye."

As he walked away, Courtney watched him go without a reply. She clamped her jaws tight together and blinked away the burn of tears. Her arms ached with emptiness. She folded them across her chest, but the action did little to ease the hollowness inside her.

# Chapter Twelve

Reining Red in as he topped the rise, Matt looked back with a measure of surprise. His mind had been so preoccupied that he didn't even remember checking the last few miles of fence. He couldn't believe he was up by the creek already. He used to joke that he could check fences with his eyes closed. It appeared he could also check them with his mind closed. Or with his thoughts miles away, at least.

Travis was gone. He'd always suspected that his brother felt restless on the ranch. Now he was gone, headed north to seek his fortune and adventure in the Alaskan gold fields. Travis had explained his leaving to Peter with a lot of talk about wanting to see the country and being tired of ranching. He'd even suggested that, now that Peter was here, Matt didn't really need him to run the place. He'd offered every excuse, every reason except the one that Matt believed to be true. Travis didn't want to stay here without Courtney.

Matt knew how Travis felt, though he'd be damned if he'd admit it aloud. Now, when he came home at night, he expected to see her there in the kitchen, bent over the stove or setting places at the table. He'd grown accustomed to the smell of soap and polish. No matter how much time he spent after Peter had gone to bed, Matt couldn't recreate the atmosphere that Courtney seemed to have evoked so easily.

Sure, he missed her, but they'd survive. The sense of loss would only have been greater the longer she stayed. Her leaving was a good thing.

He checked the sky. The sun was almost directly overhead. He'd fill his canteen, then start back toward the ranch.

Ahead, an outcropping of rock jutted from the ground like a misplaced piece of the distant mountains. The shallow creek twisted along its base. He nudged Red forward.

Sometimes cows and their calves came here to drink. The shrub brush was thick along the creek's edge. While he was here, he'd make a quick check to see that no calves were tangled in the intertwined branches.

Red's shoes clicked over the ledge of rock at the base of the jutting granite formation. Matt scanned the area, but all was quiet. Too quiet maybe. He stiffened in the saddle and tilted his head to listen. The only sound was the murmur of the water. The stillness was unnatural. Red let out a snort and shifted uneasily.

Then Matt heard it, the low throaty rumble coming from the top of the rocks. He turned in the saddle just as the big cat hurled itself from the rocky ledge.

Matt didn't need to kick Red into motion. But the sorrel's reaction wasn't quick enough. The mountain lion's claws raked the horse's flanks. Caught in the process of jerking the rifle from its scabbard, Matt grabbed for purchase as Red kicked, then reared. His glove closed on air as Red bolted away from the cat's attack. The mountain lion's high-pitched growl echoed off the rocky ledge as Matt plunged sideways out of the saddle.

He hit the ground with a hard thud that jarred his shoulder and sent the rifle clattering across the rocky ground. He ducked and rolled as Red kicked out at the cat. The mountain lion bared sharp incisors and hissed angrily. With blood oozing from the deep cuts on his haunches, Red reared again and then spun and thundered off.

Matt scrambled for the gun, but his movement drew the cat's attention. The sleek animal leapt forward, clawing through the denim that clad Matt's legs. The animal's weight drove Matt to the ground. He reached for the rifle, driven by the sharp pain inflicted by the cat's claws. His hand closed on the stock. With a grunt of agony, he struck the cat with the full length of the rifle. It rolled away from him, emitting a snarl of rage. He pulled his gun closer and his finger slipped over the trigger guard.

The barrel jerked as he fired. The rifle's report startled the big cat and it jerked back for a moment, growling. On adrenaline alone, Matt pulled himself upright and turned to look into the cat's glittering gold eyes. His blood stained the animal's fur. He cocked the gun.

The muscles gathered on the cat's haunches and bunched in its front legs as it drew itself in and prepared to pounce.

Matt's arms felt leaden. The rifle seemed to swing

toward the cat with agonizing slowness. He could hear the sound of his heart beating and the ragged gasps of his own breath with startling clarity.

With a sharp growl, the cat sprang. Its shadow blocked the sun as Matt brought the rifle completely around. The gunshot reverberated in the still air. For an instant, the cat seemed to hang suspended in the sky, before landing on Matt's chest. The weight and impact forced all the air from Matt's lungs and drove him back to the ground. Gasping for air, he fought back, beating the animal's sides for frantic seconds before he realized that the cat wasn't moving. He felt a sticky warmth on his chest as he pushed the cat's lifeless body aside and stared down at the deep red that stained his shirt. Amazingly enough, there was no pain in his chest. Urgently, he felt his ribs and abdomen before realizing that the blood wasn't his.

Knives of pain shot through his legs. Already his blood had plastered his pants to the gashes in his legs. He looked southward, but Red had vanished from sight. Tearing strips off the bottom of his shirt, Matt tied them together and wrapped improvised bandages around each thigh. Pushing himself to his feet, he staggered down the incline. More than once he had to use the rifle butt as a crutch to keep himself from falling headfirst down the rise. The ranch lay six or seven miles to the southwest. Matt hoped he could get there before he passed out from the loss of blood.

Seated in a straight-backed chair, Courtney stared out the parlor window of the boardinghouse. A shirt to be mended rested idly on her knee. She'd been here one month as of yesterday. Knowing Matt's makeshift schedule, she guessed that there should be a trip to town this week. She'd been watching the street since Monday. Three whole days. Every time a wagon rolled into town her heart surged into her throat.

The clock in the hallway chimed the hour. It was three o'clock, too late for them to be coming today.

Her anticipation was ridiculous. What exactly did she expect anyway? That Matthew Ward would ride right down the street to her door? She wasn't certain she would be able to garner the nerve to approach him on her own. What would she say? He didn't want to hear how much she missed him, missed them all. He'd never hidden his belief that a woman wasn't needed on the ranch. He was probably glad she was gone.

The street bustled with the usual activity as people went about their daily lives. Looking out this window was like watching an old Western on television. She remembered the first few days when she had found herself actually waiting for Festus or Marshal Dillon to step into the street. Even now, that occurrence wouldn't have surprised her.

The sound of the blacksmith's hammer clanged in the hot summer air. Somewhere beyond her range of vision, children called as they played. Their laughter filtered back to her. She was still alone, still lonely, definitely no better off than she had been in her own time. So much for the old Indian's intervention. Even traveling through time hadn't been enough to fix the solitary nature of her existence.

A pinto and its rider trotted into sight from the opposite end of main street. Courtney watched him for a second. Then she jumped to her feet and pressed her hand to the window frame.

"Peter," she whispered as the boy pulled the horse to a halt near the barbershop and dismounted. Without even hesitating to look around, Peter rushed up the stairs along the shop's western wall. Courtney's pulse began to pound. Those stairs led to Doc MacIntyre's office.

She dropped the shirt she was mending onto the seat of the chair and grabbed a handful of her skirts as she hurried from the room. Something was wrong. She slammed out the door and rushed down the street. At the foot of the doctor's stairs, she paused to catch her breath and to calm herself. It wouldn't do for her to rush in there all hysterical. She took several slow inhalations to calm her harsh breathing and slow her accelerated heartbeat. She gripped the wooden stair railing just as Peter came out of the upstairs door. Doc MacIntyre followed close behind, pulling on his jacket as he emerged into the bright sunlight.

"Miss Courtney," Peter said as he spotted her. He hurried down the stairs, his eyes wide with worry.

"What's happened?"

"Mountain lion got Matt."

Her breath escaped in a rush. Adrenaline surged through her veins. "How bad is he?"

Peter just shrugged and bit his lower lip. "Doc's coming out. Maybe you should come, too."

Doc MacIntyre straightened his jacket collar with his free hand. "I'll bring the buggy around as soon as Jake gets the horse hitched." His look implied that he could take her if she wanted.

"You'd better come, Miss Courtney," Peter said. "Matt's all alone."

"Can you meet me at the boardinghouse?" Courtney asked the doctor.

He nodded, then hurried off in the direction of the stables.

"Where's Travis?"

"He's gone."

"Gone where? Checking cattle?"

Peter shook his head. "No. He left a week ago. Said he was going to Great Falls, then north to Alaska to seek his fortune in the gold fields."

"What? Why would he leave? I thought he owned a part of the ranch."

"Said the ranch was Matt's now." Peter gave her a glance from beneath the tumble of hair falling over his forehead. "I think he didn't like it at the ranch anymore after you left. Always seemed like he was looking for something and then he'd get mad when he couldn't find it."

This kid was too observant for his own good, Courtney thought. Travis had acted the same way she felt, as if something was missing. Travis was missing her, while she was missing Matt. Strange how things always seemed to work out that way. She swallowed against a surge of guilt. If she had never come, maybe he wouldn't have left.

Peter seemed to read her thoughts. "Travis said he always wanted to go. He never belonged to the ranch the way Matt does. It wasn't your fault."

Courtney stared down at her hands. "How's Matt going to run the ranch now with Travis gone?" she wondered aloud.

"I can ride the fences and keep an eye on the cattle. There's not all that much work this time of year. Matt can tell me what to do." He looked at Courtney expectantly. "But we really need you now."

Peter was right. They did need her, with Travis gone and Peter only a boy. Matt needed her. Someone had to look after the house and the garden and him. He wouldn't like it. The townspeople wouldn't think it was appropriate behavior, but suddenly she didn't care. What else was there for her here? What was the point of protecting her reputation if it just meant sitting alone in a house full of strangers? The ranch was where she felt she belonged, and they honestly needed her.

"Peter, you ride back and tell Matt we're on our way."

"Okay." A grin split Peter's face as he hefted himself into the saddle and swung Patch toward the outskirts of town. "I'm glad you're coming home, Miss Courtney," he called as he rode away.

Sarah was standing on the veranda as Courtney hurried back to the boardinghouse.

"What's happened?"

"Peter said a mountain lion attacked Matt."

"Is he okay?" Concern creased Sarah's brow.

"I don't know." Courtney pressed her fingers to her forehead. "This is all my fault."

"Well, I don't see how," Sarah said as she took Courtney's arm.

"If I hadn't showed up and turned their lives upside down, Travis wouldn't have run off and Matt probably wouldn't have been out there alone." She squeezed her eyes shut and shook her head. "I just feel like I've split their family up. And now Matt's hurt. I'm not sure what I should do. I have to go to him." She looked at Sarah for confirmation.

"Where's Travis?"

"Peter said he's headed for Alaska. Can you believe that? Alaska. Doesn't he know how dangerous that is?"

"Don't worry about Travis," Sarah said. "You go look after Matt. He's the one who needs you right now."

Doc MacIntyre's buggy rattled up in front of the house.

Sarah gave Courtney a hug. "Go. He needs you."

Courtney closed her eyes against a rush of tangled

emotions. But there were things to worry about now besides her feelings. With a wave to Sarah, she hurried toward the buggy.

Oh, for a car, Courtney thought for the thousandth time as the buggy clattered toward the ranch. They could have been there inside of twenty minutes instead of riding for hours. Thank goodness the buggy and Doc's horse were quicker than a wagon. She stiffened in her seat as they topped the last rise and the ranch house came into view. She wanted to jump out of the buggy and race for the house, but she forced herself to remain seated, to display some measure of restraint. Matt would be all right. He had to be.

Peter opened the door and came out to stand on the stoop as they rolled into the yard. Despite her intention to remain calm, Courtney jumped out of the buggy almost before it came to a halt. She definitely didn't wait for anyone to give her a hand down. She just hoisted up her skirts and bailed out. Ignoring the doctor, she followed Peter inside.

The house appeared the same as when she had left.

Matt was in her bedroom. No, she reminded herself. Since she had left, it was his bedroom again. His eyes were closed. Dried blood was smeared across his cheek and into his tousled hair. She stumbled to a halt a few feet back from the edge of the bed. What if he was dead? He shifted uneasily in his sleep. The bed frame creaked.

Courtney felt a hand on her back. The doctor turned her and steered her out the door. "Let me take a look at him. You can boil some water and find me some clean dry strips of cloth. I'll call you when I'm finished." With that he pushed her out of the room and closed the door firmly behind her.

Courtney shook her head to try to clear it of the cobwebs that seemed to be dulling her thoughts. She concentrated on the doctor's instructions, and hurried into the kitchen to fire the stove and put on a kettle of water. Peter fidgeted by the table, and Courtney couldn't deal with the imploring look in his eyes. Just as the doctor had found something for her to do to occupy her thoughts, she did the same for Peter. When she asked him to get some more wood, he hurried to do her bidding.

She found a worn cotton tablecloth in the bottom drawer of the china cupboard. The sight of it brought a hesitant smile to her lips. Trying to picture this family with a cloth-covered table just didn't work. With a muttered apology to Grace, who must have been the owner of the tablecloth, Courtney began to tear it into strips. She rolled each strip and placed it on the table as she listened for any sound from the bedroom. Doc's low-pitched voice rumbled from beyond the closed door. There was a gravelly reply. Courtney's shoulders slumped with relief. At least Matt could talk.

She got up and checked the fire and the kettle. She emptied out the washbasin and set it near the stove in preparation for the boiling water. She assumed the boiling water was to be used to clean Matt's wounds. She looked up sharply as the bedroom door opened and the doctor slipped out. He had removed his coat and rolled his sleeves to the elbows.

Peter stepped inside, alerted by the opening door as well. Doc MacIntyre nodded at them both as he crossed into the kitchen. "He'll be fine. I'll clean the cuts and stitch up the worst ones. He's lucky that cat didn't sever an artery. He's lost a lot of blood and he'll need to rest and let everything heal."

Peter stepped to Courtney's side, and she wrapped

her arm around his shoulders. She gave him a quick hug as the tension eased from her stiff muscles. As the doctor washed his hands and rinsed the basin with the boiling water before emptying it and refilling it, Courtney dropped into a nearby chair. Suddenly her legs felt like rubber. MacIntyre dropped a couple of strips of cloth into the steaming basin, and gathered the rest against his midsection. "This shouldn't take too long."

"Do you need some help?" Courtney offered.

He gave her a surprised look before he shook his head.

Courtney realized the reason for the doctor's startled look. Of course, unattached women could not see men unclothed in this era. She silently cursed propriety as the doctor went back to tend to Matt.

"Will you stay now, Miss Courtney?" Peter implored as he took a seat beside her and looked up at her with big blue eyes. How could she refuse such a look? Besides, this was her chance to make Matthew Ward need her so much that he'd never want her to leave.

"You'll have to go to town and get my things."

Peter let out a shout of joy as he leapt to his feet. Courtney reached out and restrained him with a hand on his shoulder.

"Tomorrow is soon enough," she said.

Doc MacIntyre slipped out of the bedroom and closed the door. Courtney rose and went to stand in front of him as he closed his medical bag and began to button his coat.

"I've given him a sedative and attended to his cuts. They were deep, but they should heal. They need to be kept clean to prevent any infection."

He looked at Peter, then back to Courtney.

"Is Travis around? Perhaps I should be telling him what's required."

"I'll see that Matt follows your instructions," Courtney answered.

"You're staying here?" There was a trace of disapproval in his tone.

Courtney stiffened her shoulders. "Travis isn't around. Peter will have to look after the ranching operations for a while. I don't see any other choice."

"Yes, well, all right." He cleared his throat. "I'll stop by in a few days to see how he's mending."

"Is there anything I should put on his wounds?"

"A bit of iodine or some medicated ointment will do."

"What about for the pain?"

"A shot of whiskey if necessary. Matt's tough. He'll bear it out. The hardest thing will probably be keeping him from getting up. He should stay in bed at least a week."

Courtney nodded her understanding, and the doctor headed for the door. He opened it, and then stopped and turned back to her.

"I could send someone out, maybe the Widow Ramford, if you like," he suggested.

"Thank you, but I think we'll be able to manage," Courtney assured him.

He gave her one last curt nod, then went out, shutting the door behind him.

Courtney stood in the middle of the room, uncertain what to do, torn between going into Matt's room and remaining within the bounds of propriety of which Doc MacIntyre had just subtly reminded her.

"I'm going to go out and check on Red," Peter said, drawing her attention. "You check on Matt. Womenfolk sometimes know more than doctors about nursing sick people."

263

It was probably another of Peter's manipulations to force the two of them together, but right now Courtney didn't care. She'd use Peter's reasoning to justify her urge to go to Matt, at the same time pushing her emotions down deep inside herself. Now was not the time to be distracted by her feelings.

The back door banged shut behind Peter. Courtney hesitated at Matt's door, her hand on the latch. Finally she took a deep breath and pushed the door open. As she crossed to the bed, her gaze never strayed from Matt's face, pale beneath a growth of dark stubble. His eyelids flickered, but remained closed.

She pulled the chair up close to the side of the bed and sat, one hand resting on the bedcovers, the other clenched in her lap. It never ceased to amaze her when she stopped to analyze her feelings for this man. She had never expected love to hurt so much. Just looking at him made her heart ache. He mumbled something in his sleep, and she used his restlessness as an excuse to reach for his hand. His fingers tightened automatically around her own, his skin warm, the contact sending shivers of sensation up her arm, wrapping tendrils of longing around her heart.

She didn't turn though she heard the door open behind her. Peter came and stood beside her without speaking. He laid his hand on her shoulder, and moved close as though by joining strengths they could will Matt to be better, as though her presence reassured him.

"I'll do my best to see that he gets better," she whispered, finally turning to look at Peter.

Peter nodded, his expression suddenly too mature, too understanding. "I know."

*　*　*

From her bed in the other room, Courtney listened for the sound of movement, but the sedative Doc MacIntyre had given Matt seemed to be working. All was still. She should be able to sleep now, knowing that the doctor believed that Matt just needed rest and his wounds to be kept clean. But Matt's proximity affected her even more strongly now than it had before. It was almost as though her being away had heightened her perceptions, made her achingly aware of the man on the other side of the plastered wall. Memories of his kiss intruded into her thoughts. She shifted in the bed and wrapped her arms around herself in an attempt to ease the sharp pang of longing that tightened her chest. She wanted to be in his arms with a desire that was alien to her. Never had she felt this compelling urge to get close to a man. She longed to feel the firmness of his chest against her bare breasts; to feel his rough calloused hands caressing her skin; to run her fingers through his hair and pull his mouth to hers.

Courtney folded back the quilt and slid her legs out of the bed. She needed a drink of water to quench the sudden dryness in her throat. She tiptoed out of the room, carefully easing the door open to prevent it from squeaking. The plank flooring cooled her bare feet. At the water barrel, she dipped out a cup of water and drank. The liquid left a chilly path down her throat. Wide awake, she stared out at the moon-washed landscape for a few minutes before turning back to the living room.

She paused outside her bedroom door, then turned to Matt's instead. She left Matt's door ajar behind her, and quietly settled into the chair at the side of his bed. Tucking her feet up and wrapping her arms around her raised knees, Courtney straightened the hem of her nightshirt to cover her toes. She rested her chin on her knees, and in the swath of moonlight that shone into the room, watched Matt sleep. His chest rose and fell with rhythmic consistency. In sleep, his face lost some of its roughness. Long dark lashes swept his cheeks and his mouth relaxed into a softer line. Courtney imagined kissing his lips as they were now, unresisting in sleep. She pressed one hand to her own mouth and felt the soft fullness as she closed her eyes against the fierce ache that made her chest seem hollow and empty. She concentrated on the sound of Matt's breathing, and gradually, with the passage of time, the ache eased.

Matt slowly opened his eyes. They felt as if they had been glued shut. The lids felt thick and heavy. His whole body felt heavy, he realized as his vision cleared. His heart skipped a beat as his gaze came to rest on the woman perched in the chair beside his bed. Her long dark hair spilled over the arms she had wrapped around her legs. Her head tilted to rest on her knees. She was back! He felt the urge to jump up and down with joy. He frowned at his overemotional reaction, and squelched it with logic. Peter had probably gone for help and she had come with the doctor. He didn't need her. He was glad to see her, but he didn't need her.

The pink of the morning sunrise gave her features a rosy glow. Or maybe it was the chill in the room. She had to be cold wearing only that thin cotton shirt. She had rolled up the too-long sleeves, but pulled the shirttails down and tucked the cloth around her feet.

She had to be uncomfortable sleeping upright on the hard wooden chair. The fact that she had stayed with him during the night touched something deep inside. He expelled the feeling with a shake of his head. Carefully, he moved his legs. He clamped his jaw tight to keep from groaning aloud. Shafts of pain pierced the dull throbbing ache that had been present before. He used his elbows to ease himself up, but a wave of dizziness made his stomach churn. He lay back down and conceded that he might indeed need Courtney's help. At least until he was back on his feet. He was confident that wouldn't be too long.

She shivered as he looked at her.

"Courtney," he whispered. His voice came out in a grating rasp, but it was enough to wake her.

She straightened stiffly, and then seemed to jolt awake. "Are you all right?" she asked as she sprang from the chair. Her quick motion gave him an intriguing flash of long pale legs. She didn't seem to be aware or concerned about her half-dressed state as she bent over him and laid a cool hand on his forehead.

"Does it hurt? Can I get you some water or something? I'll make breakfast right away." She fussed and straightened the blankets once she determined that he wasn't feverish. Matt let the soothing lilt of her voice wash over him. It filled the air like music, and the scent of her was perfume to his senses.

"Aren't you cold?" he asked with a nod in the direction of her bare legs.

She hesitated, clearly taken aback at his concern for her well-being when he was the one who was injured. "Well, yes." She glanced down, then back up. A blush warmed her cheeks as he studied the exposed limbs. "Oh," she muttered as if just realizing what she was wearing. "I . . . I . . ." she stammered. "I'll get breakfast as soon as I get . . . Right away." She pulled the hem of the shirt down and hurried from the room.

Matt would have smiled if the sight of those long legs hadn't urged a more primitive response from his body. Try as he might, he couldn't prevent the image of those legs wrapping around his hips from invading his mind. His blood stirred. There was just no cure for her. Relief would only come in one of two ways, and that was either to bed Miss Courtney James, or to get as far away from her as possible. Unfortunately, neither option was feasible at the moment. He would just have to suffer with this affliction, in addition to the wounds inflicted by the mountain lion. He wondered which would be more difficult to endure.

He lay staring at the ceiling, listening to the sounds of Courtney in the kitchen. There was the clang of the stove door and the dull thunk of wood shifting in the bin. Then the snap of a match. The sounds all seemed right, as if they had been missing before and only now was he realizing that they had been absent. The room grew brighter as daylight seeped in around the open ruffled white curtains that she had made before she left. She was here even when she was gone, remembered in pieces of cloth, in special smells and images.

Peter stuck his head around the door.

"How you feeling?" the boy asked as he tucked his shirt into the waist of his pants.

"Like the cat won."

Peter smiled.

"How's Red?"

Peter's look grew more serious, and Matt realized just how much the boy had grown up in the past few months. The boyish attitude was gone, replaced with the very air of responsibility that Grace had asked him to instill. He wasn't sure if he had taught it to Peter or if the ranch had just brought out what had always been there. He suspected it was the latter.

"I cleaned the cuts and put some salve on them. Should I have done anything else?"

Matt shrugged. "Not much else a person can do. Are they very deep?"

"Not so bad. He doesn't seem to be too bothered by them."

"Then I'm sure he'll be fine."

Peter nodded and turned to go.

"Peter?"

The boy stopped and half turned.

"You did good."

Peter gave a slight tilt of his head. "I better see to the stock before breakfast," he said as he slipped out of the room.

Matt could hear Peter and Courtney conversing quietly in the kitchen. Then the screen door banged as Peter went outside. A few minutes later, the smell of bacon began to permeate the air. Matt's stomach reminded him that he hadn't eaten since yesterday morning. He started to get up, but nausea and dizziness forced him back down again.

The minutes crept by as the smell of food tantalized him. Finally, Courtney appeared in the doorway holding a plate. She set it on the night table while she arranged the pillows so he could sit comfortably.

"I'm not an invalid," he said, but when he reached for the plate, his hands shook from the exertion of pulling himself upright. She leaned forward to help, but he moved the plate away, holding it against his chest with one hand while he gripped the fork with the other.

"I can manage to eat by myself. You go have your breakfast. I'll call if I need anything."

She reluctantly agreed as he turned his attention

to the food before him. But Matt couldn't finish the meal. As he lowered the half-empty plate to his lap and wiped the dampness caused by the exertion from his brow, he was forced to concede that he was as weak as a new calf. Leaning back against the headboard, he closed his eyes.

Courtney returned a few minutes later and took the plate away. She made no comment about how little he had eaten. When she returned, she was carrying a basin of steaming water and a bundle of cloth strips. Matt realized her intentions just as she set the basin on the night table and reached for the quilt.

Hastily he pressed his arms down, anchoring the blanket to the bed. "What are you doing?" he demanded.

"I'm going to clean your cuts." She pulled a bottle of iodine from her apron pocket and plunked it down on the table beside the basin.

Actually, Doc MacIntyre had told Courtney that he would return in a few days to care for Matt's legs, but she wanted to see the damage herself, in part to assure herself that he really was going to be okay. In these days, there was no telling what doctors believed to be acceptable medical practices. The ambulance training she had taken as part of her volunteer services might just prove useful in this situation.

She gave Matt a stern look and reached for the edge of the blanket. For an instant, he held fast, then finally let go, though he modestly clutched a section of cloth across his midsection while she turned up the edge that covered his legs.

The bandages were still dry, showing no blood. She lifted the edge of one, and Matt twitched as it stuck in the fine hair that covered his calf.

"Sorry." She eased the cloth aside and examined the cut. It showed no sign of infection, and was held closed with several dark stitches. The skin was stained with iodine, but other than looking painful, the cuts looked as if they would heal. She gently folded the bandage back into place, and then replaced the quilt. Standing, she picked up the basin.

"I think they're all right for now," she said as she stepped back, determined that Matt not see the flush that crept up her neck. He had well-muscled legs and pale feet. She had an overwhelming desire to run her fingers over the smooth arch of his foot and across the rough-textured skin of his leg. She refused to let her imagination climb higher. Suddenly flushed, she peeked out from beneath the fall of her hair and wondered what kind of response she would evoke from Matt if he knew her thoughts. Too bad women weren't allowed to be demonstrative in these times. Maybe, once he was better, she'd act out her fantasies and convention be damned.

"Try to rest," she said as she slipped from the room.

# Chapter Thirteen

Courtney heard the bed creak and Matt's muttered curse as she edged the bedroom door open with her shoulder while juggling the bowl of chicken soup and the mug of hot coffee.

Matt, with the quilt wrapped around himself, was halfway out of the bed, gripping the foot rail while he gingerly lowered his legs to the floor.

"What do you think you're doing?" Courtney demanded as she rushed over. She set the soup and coffee on the night table and stood before him with her hands planted on her hips.

"I'm getting up, damn it. I can't stand this laying around." He eased himself to a seated position on the edge of the mattress.

"Doc MacIntyre said you were to stay in this bed."

"No. Doc said I was to rest."

"He meant in bed."

Matt pushed forward. Sweat dampened his brow

and a grimace of pain contorted his face. "I can rest in the parlor just as well." He started to rise, pushing himself upright with the help of the footboard.

Obviously, he wasn't about to be deterred. And Courtney couldn't say that she blamed him. He'd been in bed for three days. Did all males make such restless patients? She knew from experience that the men at the senior citizens home had been almost unbearable if confined to their beds. Matt was no exception. Courtney shook her head as she eased herself under his right arm and offered her support. "You're stubborn as a damn mule, Matthew Ward."

"What kind of language is that for a woman?" he grunted as the exertion began to take its toll.

"Language that's appropriate to this situation," Courtney answered sternly.

He gave her a shaky grin, draped his arm over her shoulder and leaned heavily on her. The strain of his movements were evident on his flushed face. Courtney allowed him to take his time as he eased each foot into an unsteady step. His breathing grew labored.

"I can get the chair if you need to rest for a minute," she suggested. "You don't need to do this all in one stretch."

"I'll do it," Matt grunted as he took another faltering step.

It took forever to reach the couch in the parlor. Courtney bit her lip as Matt fumbled for the arm and used it for support as he lowered himself onto the cushion.

"I . . . made . . . it," he declared between audible gasps.

Courtney dragged the footstool over and lifted his feet onto it. She reached for the edge of the quilt, intent on checking to make sure none of the cuts had opened up or were bleeding.

Matt's tanned hand came down over her own, stilling her movements.

"I'm fine."

"Then you won't mind me checking." Courtney could feel the warm pressure of his hand. The contact sent shivers up her arm. He acquiesced, finally withdrawing his hand.

Courtney lifted the quilt and examined his legs, determined to ignore the sensations created by the sight of thick calf muscles, concentrating instead on the wounds. Everything appeared to have withstood Matt's excursion without damage. She folded the blanket back down.

"Did I pass inspection?"

"For now," she said as she rose and went to retrieve his dinner.

While he ate, she used the opportunity to strip his bed.

There wasn't much to occupy him in the living room, but Matt appeared happy to just sit and whittle. He asked her to fetch the ledgers for him, which she did before heating water and washing the bedding.

And so a pattern began to emerge. Each day, she would help him to the living room, where he could sit and watch her work. Sometimes they would talk, about the ranch or Peter or Travis. Courtney skirted the issues that concerned her own background, answering vaguely but with as much truth as possible. Her parents were dead. She had been raised by her grandmother, who had since passed away. She lived up north. Mentally, she added that she had no future.

Doc MacIntyre came by. After a brief examination, he pronounced Matt on the mend. He advised limited exercise to start to build up Matt's strength. The cuts would leave scars, but no permanent damage.

Matt began to rely less and less on Courtney for his daily forays into the parlor. He started dressing himself and making trips to the barn, usually in the evenings. Courtney suspected that he missed spending time with his horse.

With the return of his health came the old independence, the determination not to need anyone, especially her. He refused her ministrations, bathing his wounds himself, even cooking when she was occupied with other chores.

Courtney had to face it. Matt was healing. He didn't want her. He didn't need her, as he was quick to point out. Peter was rapidly outgrowing his boyhood. The added responsibilities the boy had shouldered during Matt's convalescence had matured him much beyond his years.

Courtney started, drawn back from her musings, as the potatoes on the stove boiled over. Instinctively, she grabbed for the pot. The handle seared across her palm. Uttering a twentieth-century expletive, she dropped the offending pot back onto the hot stove and then snatched up a dish towel to shove the potatoes back, away from the hottest part of the cast-iron surface.

As she stared down at the red welt across her palm, another hand came into view. Matt took her hand and examined the burn.

"We're going to have to do something about your language," he suggested quietly as he turned, still holding her palm, and rummaged through one of the kitchen drawers until he found a tin of salve. Somehow holding her hand between his thumb and forefinger, he managed to hold the tin with the same hand and open it with the other.

Courtney's heart beat an erratic staccato in her ears. All she could think of was the way his touch sent a blaze of warmth surging up her arm. The sting of the burn dulled in comparison to the ache that filled her chest as she gazed at the top of his bowed head and knew that she would never accomplish the one thing that had suddenly come to be all-important in her existence. She wanted Matthew Ward as she had never wanted a man before. Sadness billowed inside her chest like building storm clouds. The urge to weep pushed upward from her bosom, drying her throat as it came, burning against the backs of her eyes. She closed them, hoping that obliterating the sight of him would ease the ache. But divested of vision, she became more aware of his touch, of the way her nerve endings tingled in electric reaction to his nearness. She drew a deep breath, but even that failed to still her frantic heartbeat.

Courtney's eyes snapped open as he applied the salve to the burn. His action seemed anything but clinical. A shiver of sensitivity chased across her hand in the wake of his touch. It crept up her arm, evolving into desire as it went.

This was her last chance, her final opportunity to try to express her feelings. He looked up, his dark eyes catching her stare and freezing there for what seemed like forever. Courtney ran her tongue over her dry lips as she let her gaze travel down to his mouth. His lips were pressed in an uncompromising line. She exhaled, and her breath sighed past her open lips.

He was standing too close. She could feel the warmth of his legs through the folds of her skirt and the heat of his chest against her arm and shoulder.

Her desire blazed like dry tinder at his nearness. She leaned closer, needing the contact this one last time. And she knew it would be the last time. Already she had decided that she could not stay here without a reciprocation of her feelings. Even now Matt was stiff and unyielding.

She didn't want to be like Jeanette. Travis had said that Matt needed to do things his own way and in his own time. She shouldn't push him. But there was so little time left. How long would it take for him to make a move? Would he ever make one? Could she leave without trying, just once more? And live with the knowledge that she hadn't tried? She didn't think so.

He offered no resistance when she slid her injured hand from his. Turning slightly, she let her fingers trace a path up his chest, flattening her uninjured hand as it came to rest over his rigid chest muscles. She could feel the heavy thudding of his heart in the tips of her fingers. Her chest was so tight, she could hardly breathe.

How could she go back to that lonely room in that lonely boardinghouse without at least one more memory, without again tasting his lips or feeling the hard length of his body pressed against her? How could she endure those long lonely nights without ever having tried, just once more, to get him to respond as she dreamed and wished? One more try, she thought as she swayed against him and his hand came up to her waist to steady her.

How could he not see how she felt? It seemed as though love radiated in palpable beams of light all around her. Surely it glowed in her eyes and colored her cheeks. She could feel the heat of it, even now, flushing her skin. She eased her hand higher, running her sensitized fingers along the rough line of his jaw and over the faint cleft in his chin. Like a blind person, she committed that feel to memory, converting the ridges and valleys of his face into a mental picture that she could see with her eyes closed, memorizing the textures as well as the shapes and lines.

From beneath half-closed lids, she studied the indentation at the base of his throat and the steady pulse that pounded there. She shifted against him, slipping her arms around the back of his neck, sifting her fingers through the dark curls of hair that spilled over her hand, pressing her breasts into the hard planes of his chest.

Still, he did not move. He remained frozen, motionless. Even his breath seemed to be suspended as though he feared the act of inhalation would diminish the slight space between them. She could sense his desire and his fear.

Matt knew he was afraid. Afraid that the slightest movement on his part would release the tight dam of control that he fought to maintain. He wanted her. God, how he wanted her. He wanted to bury his hands in her hair and kiss her mouth until her lips were swollen from his passion. He wanted to taste the sweetness of her breath, drawing it deep into his lungs until it burned an imprint there. He wanted to wrap his arms around her so tightly that they ached with the intensity of his embrace. He wanted to bury himself in her so deep that he would never find his way back. He wanted her as he had never wanted a woman in his entire life. And it scared the hell out of him. One wrong move, one false step, one slip of his resolve and he knew he would take her. Right here, right now, on the kitchen table or floor like an animal in heat, like a man possessed.

Like a brand, her touch and heat seared through the layers of his constraint, drawing perilously near the limits of his tolerance.

He wanted to kiss her. Her lips glistened where she had licked them. Red lips, full and inviting. They were parted just a little, just enough to hint at the sweet cavity beyond. He pressed his tongue to the top of his mouth and swallowed. He kept his arms stiff at his side. But while he could command his limbs, other responses were beyond his control. He couldn't suppress the tightening in his lower body.

She shifted. One lithe leg brushed him there. He screamed silently inside his head to keep from moaning aloud. Through passion-glazed eyes, he watched her slowly raise her head. One kiss and it would be over. One kiss and he would not be able to hold himself in check. He knew that as surely as he knew his own name. Her eyes began to drift shut. Her breath was a wisp of minty sweetness in the scant space between them as she tilted her head, aligning her lips with his own. Another instant and it would be too late.

Panic erupted inside Matt as his resolve began to crumble. His arms snapped up, his fingers tightened on Courtney's upper arms as he pushed her away from him. Her eyes flew open, silver pools filled with longing and desire, quicksilver shimmering with pain. But this time he couldn't assuage her anguish. This time he was the cause, not the cure. If he didn't get away from her, there was no telling the damage he would do.

He dropped his hands and stepped back, focusing his eyes on the hem of her skirt.

"Matt?"

It was more than his name. It was a question that hung in the air. A question that he couldn't answer.

At least not right now, not while his feelings were stripped this raw, not while his control was ebbing away entirely.

Without answering, he turned, crossed the kitchen and stepped out onto the porch. He didn't draw a breath until he heard the screen door slam shut behind him. Head down, he shuffled across the yard toward the barn.

Courtney pressed the back of her hand to her lips and squeezed her eyes shut. Her tattered emotions twisted inside her, ribbons of pain converging in the middle of her chest. She'd thrown herself at him in a blatant exhibition, and his response had disclosed more than she had bargained for. She was only fooling herself if she thought she could ever be part of his life. She had thought she sensed something, but like that time in the barn, she was mistaken. He had shown not the slightest hint of desire. Her advances had left him stiff and unyielding. Silently, she vowed never to make such a fool of herself again.

The surge of cattle, the dust, the noise, all were like the spring roundup with one sharp exception. Courtney watched Matt's stiff posture as he and Red cut toward the milling herd. He wasn't riding with the smooth ease that had marked him early in the year. But despite his injuries and the fact that he obviously wasn't yet completely healed, he'd insisted on saddling up and taking a major part in cutting out the cattle to be herded to Helena for sale.

Courtney settled back against the trunk of the poplar, her eyes following him even as he faded in and out of the rising dust. Instinctively, she seemed to know which rider was Matt, seemed able to pick him out even in mere silhouette. Occasionally his voice would rise above the lowing of the cattle as he shouted to one of the hired hands.

Thank goodness she'd been able to persuade him that others were capable of driving the herd once the animals had been selected. Even Peter had agreed with her, with reminders that Matt himself had always commented on the honesty of Mr. Janby, who was in charge of cattle purchases. Matt had finally conceded after his first full day in the saddle. He'd been too tired that night to even eat. He'd stumbled into the house, made it to the washbasin, tossed water over his face and then plodded off to bed. When Courtney had taken him a dinner tray a short while later, he was sprawled across the bed, still fully clothed and sound asleep. Exhaustion had won out over hunger.

But Matt wasn't one to ever admit defeat. This morning he'd been up before Courtney, ready for another day of hard labor. It started at sunup, and would last all day until sundown, with only a few brief pauses for a handful of hardtack or jerky from the mess wagon.

He swayed in the saddle. Courtney sat up straighter, her eyes glued to his movements. He shifted, gripping the saddle horn with both gloved hands until he regained his balance, and then he reached up and wiped his brow with the back of one glove. Even from here, Courtney could see the pale color of his face.

She pushed to her feet. Enough was enough.

Dust stirred from around her skirt hem as she stamped across the meadow toward the perimeter of the enclosure that contained the cattle and the men on horseback. Peter noticed her first, and when she pointed at Matt, the boy rode over to his stepbrother. Courtney couldn't hear above the cattle's lowing and the shrill whistles of the cutters. Matt looked in her direction, and she gestured for him to come over. He shouted a few commands and pointed out several cattle before wheeling Red and trotting over to the edge of the fence, his expression a mix of suspicion and concern.

Courtney stepped up onto the bottom rail of the log fencing.

"Which of these men would be most capable of selecting cattle if you weren't here?" she asked.

Matt's eyes narrowed slightly. "Why? You planning on starting your own ranching business."

Courtney narrowed her eyes right back at him. "A hostile takeover, maybe."

He frowned, confused.

She climbed another rail and reached out. Before Matt could react, she freed the reins that he had draped loosely over the saddle horn and wrapped the ends around her hand.

"Pick someone," she ordered. "You're through for the day."

The protests followed in swift order. "I am not. I can do this. I'm fine."

"You're practically falling off this horse. Last night you didn't even have the strength to eat. Now pick someone to take over."

He tried to back Red away from her so she'd have to let go of the reins, but she held firm.

"Don't make me wrestle you for it," she threatened. "Because right now we both know that I'm stronger than you are. The men might get a real laugh if I physically dragged you off this horse and back to the house."

A stricken look paled Matt's face even further, but he quickly transformed his expression into a dark one of warning. "You won't."

Courtney gathered a handful of her skirt in her free hand, lifted the fabric to her knees and climbed up another rail on the fence. She braced the hand holding the reins on the top pole and started to swing her leg over.

A sharp wolf whistle cut the air. As she looked up, she noticed that all the cowhands had stopped what they were doing and their attention was riveted on her and Matt. Even the cattle seemed to have quieted, though surely that wasn't possible.

"Put your skirt down," Matt growled under his breath.

Courtney shook her head. "I'm coming over this fence and they're all going to get an eyeful if you don't agree to come back to the house with me right now."

He looked at her for a minute, gauging her seriousness.

She lifted her skirt again to help convince him that she meant what she said.

"Okay, okay," he quickly acquiesced at the sight of the pale skin being revealed. "Carl," he shouted, turning back to the staring men, "you take over for a while." He looked around at the unmoving group. "And the rest of you get back to work."

They hesitated another second. Courtney let her skirt drop back to cover her ankles.

"Now!" Matt shouted angrily, and that seemed to jerk everyone back into line. The men returned to their duties, but not without remaining where they could see what was about to play out between their boss and the woman across the fence.

Courtney dropped to the ground. Without releasing Red's reins, she started along the fence toward the gate at the corner. Unless he wanted to rudely jerk the reins from her hand, Matt was forced to allow himself to be led.

"I can do this on my own," he informed her, his tone stilted, "if you'll give me back those reins."

Courtney shook her head. "I don't trust you. You're stubborn and pigheaded and too obstinate to admit that what I'm doing is for your own good."

"I said I would go to the house. You don't need to make a fool out of me in front of the men."

Courtney looked around Red toward the corral. Sure enough, all the hands were watching intently, some with big grins.

One called out, "Remember, Matt, the meaner they are the more they care."

Several of the other men burst out laughing at the fellow's comment.

Courtney felt the heat rising up her neck and into her cheeks. Her eyes shifted from the corral to Matt. He was watching her intently, his back stiff, his obvious discomfort over the situation fading as his dark eyes caught her gaze and froze there for an instant. It was a look that reminded her of the way he had looked at her in the barn, a look that sent chills of desire shivering along her skin, a look that broke her heart.

She swallowed down the emotion building in the back of her throat and, tossing the reins at him, spun on her heel and stomped in the direction of the rise.

Damn you, she thought. Go ahead and kill yourself then. Why should I care? But she did care. That was the whole problem. She cared way too much.

Matt gathered up the reins and considered his options. A minute ago he wouldn't have dared to defy Courtney for fear of what she might do, but now the situation had taken a sudden turn. Still, he thought as he listened to the barely muffled laughter at his back, Courtney's silence seemed preferable right now to facing the men's taunts.

It was dangerous to be near her now, though, with her face flushed, her quicksilver eyes flashing. For no matter how he tried to reason with himself, no matter how often he realized the danger, something drew him. And not just the sight of those pale ankles either. It was her inner fire, her compassion. He ached to take her in his arms, to soothe away her hurts, but at the same time he knew that he couldn't do that and stay detached. He didn't have the willpower it would take to hold her and not to kiss her. Even now his body was responding to her silent call. He pulled off his hat and ran his fingers through his hair in distress. What was he going to do about Miss Courtney James? What was he going to do about these feelings that she stirred in him?

A dull, tired ache was settling in his lower back and down his legs. He had been overdoing it. Who was he fooling? Even if he wanted to, he was in no shape to manhandle any woman, never mind one as vigorous as Courtney. He took a deep breath and stiffened his shoulders, prepared himself for another burst of laughter, then nudged Red into a walk to follow Courtney back to the house.

Stars studded the navy velvet of the sky as Courtney stood in the doorway and looked toward the barn. A lantern glowed within, casting a rectangle of light into the yard. Peter had turned in. Hours in the saddle meant an early night. That meant Matt was in the barn. Courtney hesitated at confronting him in a place where the memories of his kiss were too real, but she had made a decision. It was time to go. Staying here was breaking her heart. She ached for the slightest show of need or emotion, but could detect none. Matt had always professed his independence. It was time she acknowledged it.

She took a deep breath to bolster her resolve, and then went down the steps and across the yard. Butch raised his head from where he lay outside the barn door, then satisfied that he didn't need to sound an alarm, went back to sleep.

Courtney paused at the barn door. Red turned his head in her direction. Matt stood with one arm draped across the top rail of Red's stall, but his attention didn't seem to be on the horse. He stared into the lantern light. The yellow glow glinted in the dark strands of his hair. His shirt stretched in folds across his broad shoulders. Red tossed his head and Matt started.

Courtney stepped inside. Her movements drew Matt's gaze. Neither spoke. She walked to Red's stall and offered her hand, letting the horse command her attention, delaying in order to allow herself time to find the words for what she knew she had to say. The sorrel blew softly into her palm. She patted his neck before turning her full attention to Matt.

He watched her with unfathomable eyes. She looked away, fearing he would read too much in her expression. She wet her dry lips while she fingered a sliver of wood that protruded from the top plank of the railing.

Get it over with, she prodded herself. She took a deep breath and looked up, meeting Matt's look directly. She refused to let herself look away. "First, I want to apologize," she said.

His eyes narrowed and his forehead creased into a hint of a frown.

Courtney forged ahead. "I'm sorry that Travis left. I know it was because of me. And maybe you wouldn't have been hurt if I hadn't interfered with the workings of the ranch. I didn't come here on purpose. But I feel I owe you an apology for any trouble that I may have caused."

She couldn't hold his gaze. His dark eyes seemed to bore right through to her very soul. She wanted something she could never have. She wanted this man. She wanted love and a home and a family. She looked down, diverting her thoughts by picking at her work-worn finger nails.

In the periphery of her vision she could see Matt's legs and boots. He didn't move. Suddenly, he seemed too close. She needed to put some distance between them. She gripped her hands together to still their trembling as she stepped away and walked over to the tack shelf, where she stopped and turned back toward him.

He seemed to sense that this was only the start of what she intended to say. He didn't reply, just stood watching her with those dark eyes.

Courtney squared her shoulders.

"I guess what I really wanted to tell you is goodbye." It sounded so final now that she had finally said it. It seemed to hang in the dusty air. "I think it would be better if I left now. You're well enough to look after yourself. Peter doesn't need a mother. Not that I ever thought I could be one to him." She swallowed against the hot lump that had welled up into her throat and brought the burning sting of tears with it. She blinked them away. "I . . . It's just too hard for me to stay here. The way I feel. . . ."

She spun away from him, bowing her head and staring through blurring vision down at the tack shelf. She braced her hands on the rough wood. Quit, she told herself. Quit talking before you say something that neither of you want to hear said aloud.

She heard him move. She tensed as he came to stand behind her, afraid he would touch her, afraid of her own desperate response if he did. He made no move other than to stand there. She realized that this had been where she had secretly expected him to beg her to stay. How could she have entertained such a foolish belief? The knowledge reinforced the realization that she needed to leave.

"It wasn't your fault that Travis left," he said, his voice low, washing over her in a caress that she committed to memory. One more thing to take away with her, to relive and treasure. "It was mine."

She looked up and caught his reflection in the small window over the jumble of harness and tools. He met her gaze there, holding it for indeterminable seconds.

"I guess it doesn't really matter who was at fault," she whispered. "It's done now."

"I was planning on riding herd tomorrow."

She started to protest, to ask if he thought he was well enough, then remembered that it wasn't her place any longer. It had never been her place.

"I could take you to town instead," he offered. "If that's what you want."

Her heart thudded against her rib cage where tight bands of emotion choked off her ability to draw a deep breath. She shook her head. "I'd rather Peter took me if it's all right with you."

She didn't want to admit that she didn't think she could endure the long ride with her thigh pressed against his, knowing he was so near yet so unreachable.

"I'd like a chance to explain everything to him," she said. That excuse was halfway true, at least. She did want to say good-bye to Peter. With his new maturity, she was certain he would understand.

Matt stepped away from her.

"Sure."

Courtney's heart constricted as he walked to the barn door. This was it then. Good-bye. So simple, yet so difficult. Things never turned out as she wished they would. She gripped the wooden shelf as his footsteps faded. She opened her mouth to gasp in air, but still couldn't seem to catch her breath. Her heart ached, physically ached, a painful wound in her chest. She swept the harness aside and dropped her head, pressing a damp cheek to the cool surface of the wood, staring at the back wall. She refused to sob out loud, though that was just what she felt like doing. She sniffed, dashing away the escaped tears with the back of her hand. There wasn't any use feeling sorry for herself. This just wasn't meant to be. The sooner she accepted it and decided what she was going to do with the rest of her life, the better.

She straightened, fumbling with the scattered bits of leather, horse brushes and tools, absentmindedly aligning the harness. A pouch decorated with flattened porcupine quills peeked from the pile. Courtney went dead still, staring at the familiar Indian artifact. She slid her hand across the bench surface until her fingers touched the softened leather. It was real, not just a figment of her imagination. Her fingers tightened on the pouch. She gathered it up, lifting it in front of her. The way home, she realized. The timely discovery awed her. She had just come to the conclusion that she must leave, and the pouch had appeared. Almost as if it had been waiting for this moment. She had been given the way back.

"Oh, God," she moaned as she pressed it against her chest.

"I found it on the ridge."

Matt's voice startled her out of her dismay. He

stood just outside the door. How long he'd been there, she didn't want to guess.

"I gather it's yours."

She turned her face away as she nodded.

"Then I'm glad you found it before you left," he said.

Out of the corner of her eye, she saw him turn and walk away. She smiled a sad, ironic smile. If only he knew how the two things related, her leaving and this pouch. They were dependent, one upon the other. She wouldn't need a ride to town in the morning. She knew it as surely as she knew that she had somehow traveled here through time to a place where she had been needed. Now the need was fulfilled. The Wards no longer required her assistance. It was time to go home, though she knew she would never be the same again. A piece of her heart would always stay on this sprawling ranch at the base of the mountains in Montana.

She reached for the lantern. It was time to make plans. Tomorrow was going to be a very eventful day.

Matt eased his door open a sliver. He knew every creak of this house, every whisper of wind, every settling of timbers. He had detected Courtney's movements despite her attempts to move silently. Moonlight spilled in through the windows and illuminated her form where she bent, pen in hand, over a piece of paper at the kitchen counter. She hadn't bothered to light a lantern. He watched her intently scratching words onto the paper. She would have plenty of opportunity to bid Peter good-bye on the trip to town. So Matt assumed that the message must be for him rather than the boy.

Or perhaps she was leaving right now, sneaking off into the night. His eyes narrowed as he took in

her attire. Fully clothed, she wore neither of the outfits he had purchased for her, but the same sweater,
denims and rawhide jacket in which she had arrived.
Her unbound hair swayed over her shoulder in thick
waves that brushed her arm as she wrote. The moonlight colored her black hair with blue light.

He stood absolutely still as she straightened. Folding the note, she placed it in the center of the table
and picked up three items that Matt had not noticed
before. One he recognized as the pouch she had re-
claimed last night in the barn. The second appeared
to be a thick braid of straw or grass. And the third.
. . . His pulse quickened, and he had to stifle a quick
indrawn breath as she caressed the fabric of the
white cotton shirt she had borrowed from him that
first night. She stood for a while, one item held in
each hand and the shirt clutched to her chest as she
surveyed the inside of the ranch house. A final look,
Matt realized when she turned and slipped out the
back door.

She really was leaving.

Panic gripped him. He hadn't acknowledged the
actuality of her going until this very moment. He
stepped back and grabbed his pants and shirt from
the back of the chair. He pulled the Levi's on as he
hopped across the living room. Snatching up the
note from the table, he followed Courtney out the
back door. Looking around, he spotted her approaching the east corral. He frowned. Where was
she going? Not to the barn as he had originally expected. Obviously she was not sneaking off alone.
She must be meeting someone.

While he waited for her progress to put the corral
railings between them so he could follow unseen,
Matt shoved his arms into his shirt sleeves and then

unfolded the note, tilting the paper so the light struck the words. As he read, his breathing slowed.

*Matt.*

*I guess this is good-bye. I wish it didn't have to be. I know about your mother and Katie and Jeanette, and I sense that you blame yourself for them leaving you, that you feel it was your fault. It wasn't, none of it. Those are just things that life throws at us, things that make us who we are, that make us stronger or weaker, as we choose. My leaving is your fault, though. You wouldn't respond though I tried to show you how I felt. I did everything but say the words. Somehow, I think you were afraid I would say them. So was I. I was afraid they wouldn't matter to you as much as they mattered to me. But I need to say them now. I can't leave without being sure you know. I love you, Matt, in a way I have never loved anyone else, in a way that takes my breath away and makes me ache inside. But knowing you can't return that love hurts too much. So I have to go. I have been given the way back. I don't think we'll ever see each other again. But you will always be in my thoughts. I hope you will think of me sometimes, too. Give Peter my love.*

*With love and regret, Courtney.*

Matt swallowed against the tightness in his throat. She loved him. He squeezed his eyes closed as joy and pain collided in his chest. This was love, this ache that filled his insides. He couldn't let her go. With sudden clarity, he knew that would be the biggest mistake of his life. He looked across the yard, but she had vanished around the corner of the corral.

She loved him, but was leaving because he didn't

love her. She thought he didn't care. The truth was he cared too much. He cared so much that he was afraid admitting it would ruin everything. But everything was ruined. Maybe if he found out where she was going, he could think about this sudden revelation of his feelings, could contemplate the realization that he didn't want to live without Courtney James. The acknowledgment of his desire for her filled his chest to the point of bursting. He could plan out what he should say, could try to think of a way to persuade her to come back, to convince her that here was where she belonged. Damn, he'd been a bloody fool. She'd tried to give him a chance to show his feelings, and he'd pushed her away instead. How else could he expect her to interpret his actions if not as rejection?

Matt carefully refolded the paper and tucked it into his shirt pocket, then padded barefoot across the step. Butch stretched from sleep and looked at him inquiringly.

"Stay," Matt whispered. The dog obeyed, dropping back down but regarding him with curious eyes.

He slipped across the yard. In the moonlight, he glimpsed Courtney trudging up Anderson's Ridge. Fitting, he thought. That was where they had first found her. Somehow, it made a sort of fatalistic sense that she would leave from there. He circled around, working his way to the hill from the far side of the yard, where his approach would be half hidden by the shrubs and poplars that lined the creek. This way was steeper, but his presence should be undetectable. He cursed softly under his breath as the stream's gravel cut into his bare feet. His legs began to throb before he climbed even halfway up the steep incline, but he pushed himself onward.

He paused to catch his breath just as he reached

the peak of the hill. Any minute now he would see that tree, remember Katie and Jeanette, feel the anger and pain cloud out all other thought. But he had no choice. To refuse to climb to the top would mean the end of whatever might have existed between Courtney and himself.

He took a deep breath. Knowing the mountain backdrop behind him would conceal his presence from her, he looked over the crest. Without leaves the tree's limbs seemed skeletal, stark fingers of death. He waited momentarily for the onslaught of the dark memories. They flashed before his eyes. He shook them off. Courtney was right. What had happened here was not entirely his fault. Somehow she had the ability to dispel his demons, to make the world seem right and good. The sight of Courtney huddled alone on the hilltop drove his self-recriminations to the back of his mind. He'd been wrong in thinking she was meeting someone. He watched with curiosity, wondering why she had come up here.

She sat with her back to him, resting cross-legged in about the spot where he had first seen her, the spot where the stones made a mound on the hill's top. The grass had been cleared away around the rocks to reveal a distinct pattern. He narrowed his eyes in thought. Why hadn't he recognized it before? Those stones were arranged in the same pattern as the one cut into the face of the black stone in the pouch.

She pulled something from her pocket. He couldn't quite make it out. Behind her, the sky in the east glowed with a hint of pink, making it difficult for him to perceive her actions.

A match flared. She bent and touched it to the steepled pile of kindling resting in a cavity in the stone circle. The resulting light lit her features with an eerie reddish glow. She added bits of wood from a pile beside her. When the fire was burning freely, she rolled his shirt and tucked it inside her jacket, buttoning the coat to hold the other garment against her chest. Then, cupping her hands, she captured the spire of rising smoke, drawing it over her face and hair in a smooth washing motion. She whispered something into the wind, but Matt couldn't catch the words. He edged closer, staying low, searching the horizon again for accomplices. But they were alone, touched only by the subtle nuances of the night, the whisper of wind, the rustling of leaves, the faint scent of smoke.

Courtney was humming now. Chanting was probably more accurate. She picked up a braid of grass and touched it to the fire. The sweetgrass aroma carried to him. Following the direction of Courtney's gaze, he watched the plume of smoke trail upward. She reached for the decorated pouch that he had found here the same night she'd appeared.

All sound vanished. As her fingers came in contact with the decorated leather of the pouch, everything went completely still. Matt cocked his head. Somewhere in the distance he thought he heard the faint reverberation of drums, Indian drums. The light began to fade. He shifted his attention back to the far horizon. Clouds amassed there, shutting out the hints of dawn and darkening the sky. Across the pasture below him, he saw the wind come. Actually saw it. He blinked twice, unable to believe his eyes. The tall grass bent in its passage, swaying and tossing in the turbulence. Wind pushed the clouds, bunching them in a thick mass that swirled in from all directions and congregated over the peak of the hill.

Movement drew his attention back to Courtney. She had risen from her seated position so that she now stood facing into the wind. The gusts lifted her raven-colored hair. Like dark wings, it whipped across her face, then eddied out on the currents of wind. Sound returned, growing until it rumbled from overhead, a combination of wind and thunder and . . . Matt listened again. Yes, he could hear chanting and drums.

All around him, the air seemed charged with energy. Staring at Courtney, he caught his breath. Tiny sparkling fragments of light glimmered all around her, like sparks of frost caught in a beam of sunshine. Only there was no sunshine, only darkness, darkness everywhere except for a single beam of light that illuminated her from above. His vision flickered. For a second, Courtney seemed to fade, her body shattering into particles that allowed him to see right through her.

He blinked hard. No, she was solid. The vision had just been a figment of his imagination. His heart pounded in his chest. Not caring if she saw him or not, he pushed to his feet. He took a few steps in her direction, but the wind screamed out of the east, battering him, impeding his progress. He put his head down and pushed into it.

She turned then, silver eyes glowing with some internal fire that Matt couldn't understand. The sparks of light were growing brighter, coalescing in a whirlwind around her.

He saw her mouth his name as she extended her hand. But even then she was fading from his sight.

*The light brought her. The light brought her.* Peter's words echoed inside his head. The light was about to take her away. Realization crashed down upon him. There would be no return. From this moment forward, she would be gone, forever unreachable.

"Courtney," he yelled, but the wind forced the word back down his throat.

As he started to run, the sudden bolt of light blinded him. Later he would compare it to lightning, though it had not been accompanied by any sound other than the feverish howl of the wind. He stumbled, tripping on a ridge of grass at the hill's lip. Then he fell, rolling down the steep incline, crashing to a bone-jarring halt against the rough trunk of a thick cottonwood. Every muscle in his body protested, but he stumbled to his feet, groping around blindly, calling to her. It took a few seconds for his vision to clear. When it did, the night was pitch black, the light gone.

# *Chapter Fourteen*

Frantically, Matt clawed his way back up the hill. The sound of his ragged breathing shattered the silence of the night. His bare feet slipped on the damp grass. He jarred his knees into the packed ground, but struggled on despite his discomfort.

Clouds blotted out the sky overhead and left the landscape dark and shadowy. As he pulled himself over the lip of the hill, he cast around urgently for some sign of Courtney. Only the mound of stones rose above the slope of the hill. Matt collapsed to the ground with a moan of disbelief. The sound echoed back to him. It took a second before he realized that the sound wasn't an echo of his voice, but had come from what he had thought was the pile of stones. The bump shifted. He scrambled to his feet, running even before he had completely found his balance.

\* \* \*

Courtney came to in stages. She shifted through layers of fog, struggling to find the surface of the dark depths that imprisoned her. All she knew was that she felt safe, warm and safe. As consciousness returned, she realized that a strong pair of arms were wrapped tightly around her, crushing her into a solid wall of chest muscle. She tried to pull away, but the arms wouldn't let her go. As she persisted, finally raising her hands to press her palms against the warm skin that brushed her cheek, the grip eased enough that she could pull back.

She swept the loose tangled mass of hair from her face and looked up into dark eyes that watched her with suspicion and something akin to fear.

"Courtney?" Matt's voice was a harsh whisper. "Are you all right?"

She turned slightly. To her left, the ranch spread beyond the base of the hill, sweeping out then up into the rolling foothills. The mountains loomed dark against the horizon.

"Why did you come?" she asked.

He lifted his hand to turn her head back toward him. She studied his face: square, uncompromising features, strong chin and nose, dark fathomless eyes that gave her no indication of his thoughts. She'd have to do it all over again. He'd stopped it somehow. How was she to find the strength to go through that again? She had almost been swept up, almost succeeded. The terror had been just as real the second time. She had felt herself being pulled apart in the seconds before everything went black.

"We should get you back to the house," Matt said as he rose and, still holding her, lifted her to her feet.

Courtney swayed against him. "Maybe I should sit down for a minute?" she said. Her knees felt like disintegrating rubber. As much as she hated to be released from Matt's embrace, she recognized that if she didn't sit down she was going to fall.

He helped her to the ground, settling himself beside her so that his leg rested alongside her own, barely touching. The hint of contact was almost more that Courtney could bear.

"Are you sure you're all right?" he asked.

She nodded. "I just need a minute."

"Maybe we should talk," Matt suggested.

"Talk? About what?"

"About you. About who you are and where you come from." He studied her in the faint light. "There are things I need to know."

Courtney pulled her knees up and wrapped her arms around them. Why not? The next chance she got, she'd try the ceremony again. And the next time she would succeed.

Meanwhile, she needed to distract Matt.

"What do you want to know?"

"Everything."

She rested her chin on her raised knees while she stared off toward the mountains and tried to decide where to start, what to say.

Matt edged closer, wrapping an arm around her shoulder. She almost resisted, but it felt so right. Just this one last time. Another memory for her to cherish.

"I'm Courtney Anne James. I lived north of here, in Canada. But I have no family there any more."

"What's your home like?"

"Just a small apartment."

His fingers twisted in the strands of hair that trailed down her back.

"And why did you come here?"

She closed her eyes, intent on concentrating on the

feel of his touch. "Because I wanted to be needed," she whispered.

His hand stilled. When she opened her eyes, his face was mere inches from her own. His gaze fixed on her mouth as he slowly lowered his lips to hers. She held her breath as his mouth brushed across her own. Flames of passion began to smolder, stealing through her veins, pooling in liquid heat in her abdomen. His hands chased a shiver down her arms as he leaned forward, pressing her back to the ground with the weight of his body.

He gathered her to him, holding her to his chest.

"I need you, Courtney James. I don't want to. But I can't seem to help myself."

His lips found the smooth hollow at the base of her throat as his breath warmed her skin, sending shivers of desire along her limbs. The smooth sure stroke of his hand over her rib cage and up to just beneath her breast stilled the breath in her throat. Her body went from languid to tense in a heartbeat. Her nipples hardened at the thought of his touch, but still his hand remained poised just far enough away to make her body cry out for contact. She shifted, closing her eyes and trying to urge his fingers to that taut aching part of her anatomy that they rested so tantalizingly near. He moved with her, his fingers warm against her stomach but no nearer to her breasts.

Courtney covered his hands with her own, moving them upward until they rested, palms hard, against the rigid peaks. A moan filtered from deep in her throat as she tilted her head back. Desire snaked from her chest in liquid ribbons. Of its own accord, her body arched upward, seeking. Matt remained absolutely still.

Courtney refused to be denied. His nearness had

pushed her too far. The feelings she had tried valiantly to suppress surfaced and demanded release. She wrapped her arms around his neck and pulled him closer, pressing herself to the length of him.

"Love me, Matt," she whispered. "Love me once before I go."

Matt didn't respond immediately, and when he did, it wasn't the response she wanted. Stiffly, he pushed away from her, and she slumped back against the hard ground. Now she'd disgusted him for sure. He'd never believed her to be anything but wanton, a prostitute. She'd proved it now with her own words.

"I don't want you to go."

She pushed upright, resting on her elbows and stared off into the night.

His hands came to rest on her shoulders, and he turned her so she looked at him. "Did you hear me?"

"What?"

He smiled. "I don't want you to go."

When she continued to stare at him, speechless, he added, "Ever."

"Ever?" It took a minute for the meaning of his words to penetrate her mind. "What made you change your mind?" She squelched the first faint glimmer of hope that flared in her chest.

"This." He held out a folded piece of paper that was clutched in his fist. Courtney recognized her note. The look on his face told her that he had read it. He unfolded the paper and read one line out loud. " 'I love you, Matt, in a way I have never loved anyone else.' "

He looked into her eyes. "I always thought that admitting love was like admitting need. I never wanted to need anyone. But I need you Courtney, like I've never needed anyone, like I need food. It's like a hunger in my heart."

"But what about my questionable morals?" she persisted, repeating the words he had once used, determined to have all the obstacles in the open.

"You've a heart of gold, Courtney. I've never seen you hurt anyone. You go out of your way not to. You're kind, generous to a fault, hardworking beyond belief. I'm the last person on earth who can question your morals."

"You don't know what I've been thinking. Just looking at you, Matt . . ."

"That's the one thing I couldn't resist, Courtney, the way you looked at me." He lifted her chin upward.

"I love you, Matthew Ward," she whispered. "Hold me."

"I don't know if I can and still control myself."

She ran her hands down his chest, pausing only when her fingers touched the rim of his waistband. "Maybe I don't want you to control yourself."

"You are wanton, you know that?" he growled into her hair.

Much to her surprise, he released her, pushed to his feet and extended a hand to help her up.

"I'll have Peter get the wagon ready."

She gave him a startled look.

"Unless you'd rather ride into town on horseback." He seemed to consider that alternative for a moment. "It would be faster," he mused.

"To town? What for? I thought you said you wanted me to stay."

Matt took her hand in his and dropped to one knee. "I want to get you to a preacher, Courtney James. If you'll marry me?"

Stunned, Courtney stared into his dark eyes. What

she saw there was a reflection of her own desperate love. She dropped into his arms, covering his face with kisses as she wrapped her arms around his neck.

"Shall I take that as a yes?" he asked.

"Oh, yes," she whispered as her lips found his. His gentle kiss grew hard, demanding.

"Courtney." He pushed her back slightly. "Stop or I won't be able to."

She snuggled closer. "Where I come from," she whispered, "engaged couples aren't so strictly ruled by convention. I don't think I can wait to go to town." She nibbled at the curl in his bottom lip.

His eyes filled with stubborn determination, but Courtney just smiled. Shifting, she shrugged out of her jacket and lowered her hands to the hem of her sweater. With one lithe movement, she pulled it over her head. Her bare skin shone pale in the darkness. Matt's jaw tightened. His hands closed into tight fists. He struggled to control the urges that were blatantly obvious in his eyes as his gaze traveled down to rest on the sheer white cups of her French lace undergarments.

Courtney let her hands slide down her stomach until she found the fastener at the waist of her jeans. The sound of the snap popping free seemed as loud as a shot. The noise was followed closely by the sharp inhalation of Matt's breath. His gaze shifted lower as she eased the denim material over her hips. He got a shocking display of cleavage when she bent and pushed the jeans all the way down her long legs.

Straightening, she stepped out of the pants. She waited, standing motionless before him. He rose to his feet. His fingers twitched, his hands clenching and unclenching. He started to reach out, but jerked his hand back like a child afraid of being burned.

Courtney could wait no longer. She stepped forward and found his hands with her own. She laid them on her bare waist.

"Love is like fire," she whispered. "But it burns so sweet. I need you Matthew Ward. Touch me."

He looked deeply into her eyes as his hands began to move, tentative in their exploration. His warm touch on her cool skin sent a shiver of desire up her spine. She pushed his shirt aside, needing to touch him, skin to skin, flesh to flesh, heat to heat. She gasped as his hands slid up to cover the semitransparent lace of her bra. She felt her nipples tighten against his hard palms. She closed her eyes and allowed a small moan of pleasure to rumble in the back of her throat as the pad of his thumbs brushed across the sensitive nubs.

He lowered his head, drawing the tips of her breasts into his mouth, silky lace and all. Knees weak, she folded against him, relishing the damp heat of his mouth. His quickened breaths heightened her own awareness and desire. She felt the evidence of his passion, hard and pulsing through the stiff denim against her abdomen. Her hand strayed there of its own accord, cupping him. He drew a great breath that washed her breast with a rush of cold indrawn air.

His arms tightened around her, one hand coming up to hold the back of her head as he found her mouth. He drove his tongue deep inside and she relished the intrusion, urging him further still, sparring tongue to tongue, needing more.

She pushed his shirt down over his shoulders without taking her lips from his. He shrugged out of it as she dragged her nails down his chest. The muscles quivered beneath her fingertips. She found his waistband, pushing her fingers past the constricting material as far as they would go. It wasn't far enough.

"Take them off," she urged into his mouth.

His kiss moved down her jaw to the small hollow just below her ear. "Are you sure?"

"I've never been more sure of anything in my life," she assured him in a whisper.

He undressed without taking his mouth from her skin. Even as he shoved his pants aside, he trailed his warm breath down her breasts and stomach. His hands came back up, moving from her calves, up along the inside of her thighs, questing and finding the heart of her desire. She cried out at the tight ache of need evoked by his feather-light touch. He dropped to his knees, tasting her, pushing her further over the brink of desire. She wove her fingers into his hair, tilting back, opening herself, burning with passion.

He pulled her down to the ground, pressing her back into a pile of scattered clothes, raising himself above her, between her legs, holding poised. She arched upward, feeling his engorged manhood against her stomach.

"Love me, Matt."

Slowly, he slid into her. The passage was agony and ecstasy all rolled into one fiery bolt of sensation. She peaked, gasping aloud at the wonder of it, at the way her body responded to his, at the total abandon and trust she felt with this man. He moved, sliding into a smooth rhythm that rekindled the fire to a blaze with only a few strokes. She surged upward, meeting his thrusts, crying out at the unbelievable awe of the moment.

She wrapped her legs around his solid thighs, pressing to him, urging him toward release as her own body sought liberation. Hot tears spilled from Courtney's eyes. Never had she known such joy, such utter elation. This was where she belonged, in the arms of this man, warmed by his heat, fed by his passion, clothed in his love. She knew. She had come here to be needed and had found a greater need within herself. A need that could only be assuaged by this man in her arms. Her heart swelled until it felt large enough to burst.

"I love you, Matthew Ward."

He looked at her with dark eyes. "And I love you." He kissed her, a gentle kiss, a kiss full of awe and wonder. His fingers brushed her face, his touch light until she felt him begin to move again inside her.

He kissed her with mounting hunger as she met his thrusts. The passion of the moment obscured all other thoughts as they strove for release, carried higher and higher on the shimmering sensations of intense emotion until they reached the summit. His hands slid beneath her buttocks, lifting her to him, sealing them closer together as he cried out. Joined in love, they found release together. He buried his face in her hair, his breath hot against her neck as they drifted slowly back to earth.

"I think that preacher can wait until later," he said in a low, husky voice. "I want to love you properly," he added as he pulled back. "In a bed, in my house, in our house."

Courtney slipped back into her clothes. When she was dressed, he helped her to her feet and led her down the hill.

On the stoop, he pulled her back into his arms and kissed her with an insatiable hunger. They barely made it to the bedroom.

Courtney lifted her face to the mid-morning sun as the wagon rocked over the uneven ground. She was aware of the pressure of Matt's leg alongside her own. The touch made her feel oddly reassured.

She openly studied the cut of his jaw, the dark eyes, the sweep of thick auburn hair. She felt a thrill of pride as she admired the span of his shoulders, the flat stomach, his narrow waist and muscled thighs. He belonged to her and she to him.

"You'd better stop looking at me like that or we'll never get to town," he warned.

She just smiled and laid a hand possessively on his thigh.

He looked at her, and then reached up and pulled her close for a kiss. "I can't seem to get enough of you."

"That's good."

He wrapped an arm around her shoulder and they rode in silence for a while, each content with the other's company.

"I saw a magician do a disappearing act once," Matt said casually.

"Mmmhm." Courtney's thoughts were a million miles away, still fragmented by the response of her body to his touch and looking forward to more of the same at the earliest opportunity.

"Well," Matt continued. "I was just thinking that with that act of yours, you could probably go on the stage."

Courtney's attention shifted back to the present. "Did I actually disappear?"

He shrugged. "More like faded."

She thought about that for a moment. The pouch and the rock it contained had been the catalyst necessary to send her back to the future. She looked down. The rawhide strap was still suspended around her neck, and the pouch dangled on it.

She pulled the throng over her head, lifted her hair free and handed the pouch to Matt.

He gave her a questioning look.

"I can't do the trick without this stone. I want you to keep it. It's my way of promising that I'll never leave."

"How did you do that anyway? What exactly happened right before that flash of light?" he asked.

Courtney took a deep breath, then expelled it slowly. "Do you promise not to have Peter hide the cutlery again?"

He gave her a questioning look, eyebrows raised.

"Somehow I traveled back through time. It must be a combination of the ceremony and the medicine wheel and the sweetgrass and that stone. Together they open a lane from one era to another. I think both Peter and I were in the medicine circles. He wished for a woman at the same time as I wished to be needed. What he told you about the light was the truth. It did bring me."

"And it almost took you back."

He touched her face gently in a gesture of affection, then tucked the rawhide bag into his pocket. He fished in his shirt pocket and then extended his hand to her. The carved silver band caught the sun's rays and flashed in the light.

"This was my mother's," Matt explained. "If you would, I'd like you to wear it now."

When she nodded, her throat too constricted to speak, he picked up her hand and slid the ring onto her finger. The metal was warm from his grip. His eyes said more than words ever could have, and her own must have complied.

Courtney laced her fingers with his as he urged Blue to a quicker pace.

Peter had galloped off ahead with the news of their intentions, so by the time Matt and Courtney reached town their wedding plans were common knowledge. It seemed only a prairie fire could spread faster than gossip in a small town.

A crowd gathered as Matt pulled the wagon to a halt in front of the church. Courtney overheard one man insisting that he had said all along that Matthew was the one who had sent for a bride. Another answered that he had been sure Travis seemed more likely to do something like that. He claimed Matthew Ward had never seemed particularly interested in women, at least not until now. Courtney just smiled a secretive smile. When she glanced at Matt, his own lips twitched with a measure of amusement that told her he too had overheard the men's conversation.

"Matt," Courtney said, suddenly reminded of his black eye. "If people say things about me, you aren't going to go around punching them out anymore, are you?"

"Nobody's going to say anything." There was a glint of stubbornness in his eyes.

"I don't want any violence."

"I'll try, Courtney, but I can't promise to change who I am. I can only promise to love you."

Sarah pushed through the group of people, and waited impatiently while Matt helped Courtney down from the wagon.

"I'm so happy for you," she said as she wrapped Courtney in a hug. "We all are." She turned and gestured to someone behind her.

Travis stepped forward.

"I sent Landry after him," Sarah confessed in a whisper. "Then I gave him a good talking to."

Travis looked sheepish, and then he reached out and shook hands with Matt.

"Congratulations."

"No hard feelings?" Matt asked.

"No," Travis assured him as Mary Emmery moved to stand beside him. As Travis looked down at her, the teacher gave him a shy smile.

"I hear Travis took Mary to see a particular spot over on Calhoun's Creek," Sarah whispered as she pulled Courtney aside.

Courtney hugged her friend again. "Everything's working out, isn't it?"

"You look so happy, Courtney."

"I am."

Sarah touched her lightly, as though contact would make Courtney's happiness contagious. Courtney smiled at her friend, knowing the growing friendship would be something to treasure.

Peter stood on the church steps, his chest puffed out as if he was solely responsible for today's excitement. And then Matt was gone, rushed around the side of the building by a bunch of laughing men. Courtney knew the next time she saw him he would be inside, standing at the front of the church.

She looked down at the gray and blue plaid skirt and her white cotton blouse. Four months ago, if someone would have asked her what she envisioned her wedding would be like, she would have described herself in a long white satin gown trimmed with lace and seed pearls. She would have told of masses of flowers, flowing from lavish bouquets that edged the church altar and draped from satin ribbons at the end of each pew. She would have recited the titles of her favorite pieces of classical music to be played by an orchestra while she waltzed the night away. Yet despite her knowledge of the exact details of the ceremony, she would never have been able to put a face to the man waiting at the end of the aisle. Now that she could, the rest seemed utterly unimportant. It didn't matter what she wore or what music was played or if there were any flowers at all. All that mattered was being with Matt. She knew she'd gladly promise to be with him forever no matter where or how the ceremony was performed.

Courtney had imagined a bouquet of white lilies or orchids with faint rose or mauve centers, but when Sarah pressed a hand-picked cluster of flowers into her hands, she saw symbolic perfection in the tiny bluebells nestled in a cloud of white baby's breath. They matched the blue ribbon in her hair and the colors in her skirt.

"Something borrowed," Sarah said as she draped a white lace shawl around Courtney's shoulders.

The flowers constituted the something blue, and when Sarah asked about something old, Courtney showed her the silver ring. Something new, ironically enough, turned out to be a shiny copper penny from 1896. Courtney tucked it into her shoe.

Inside the church, someone struck the first faltering chords to the "Wedding March." Courtney felt herself propelled up the steps. She waited at the top with Peter while the others hurried inside to take their seats.

"Will you give away the bride, Peter?" she asked. "I mean, since I am sort of yours. It was *your* wish that brought me here."

Peter smiled up at her. "I guess Matt needed a woman most of all."

"And I needed him," Courtney confided.

"Did you tell Matt about the light?" Peter whispered.

Courtney nodded.

"Good." Peter took off his hat and smoothed his blond curls, and then offered her his arm.

"You'll be my sister-in-law now," he said. "And you'll never have to leave."

She gave him a quick hug as, together, they stepped into the church.

Courtney was only vaguely aware of her surroundings. Afterward she would have been hard-pressed to describe anything around her other than the tall, dark-haired man at the end of that aisle who drew her eyes like a magnet and caused awareness of everything else to fade into obscurity. Her surroundings were a blur, a fog of details that swirled around her while her eyes remained focused on only one person. Her heart pounded heavily in her chest. Somehow she managed, one step after the other, to traverse the gap between her and him. As Matt took her hand and folded it to his chest, she had to swallow against the rush of emotion that swelled inside her.

The music faded into the background. Matt's voice washed over her, gravelly yet clear as he repeated the minister's words. She hardly recognized her own voice. Emotions choked her words into a husky whisper.

The ceremony seemed to take both forever and only seconds. The meanings of the words she was saying escaped her, but she remained anchored by looking into a pair of dark eyes that said more than words ever could. As the minister declared them man and wife, Matt bent and kissed her, wrapping her in his arms and banishing all her trepidation. He was hers forever, and that was all that really mattered. She trusted in their commitment wholeheartedly. Only death would ever separate them.

A loud cheer interrupted her thoughts. Matt pulled away, quickly donning his Stetson to hide the flush of pleasure that brought color to his cheeks. Tucking her arm in the crook of his elbow, he led her out into the sunlight, accepting the people's congratulations, handshakes and hugs along the way.

"Peter can stay with me for a few days," Sarah offered with a conspiratorial smile. "Newlyweds should have at least a bit of a honeymoon."

Courtney let out a cry of surprise as Matt bent suddenly and scooped her up. She wrapped one arm around his neck as, with purposeful strides, he carried her over to the wagon.

"I'll take you up on that offer," he said to Sarah when Peter nodded.

"But what about the dance we've planned," Mary stuttered as Matt lowered Courtney into the seat and vaulted into the wagon beside her.

Matt slapped the reins on Blue's hind quarters. "We're going to skip that and go straight to the honeymoon," he called as they rolled away.

Laughter followed them out of town.

Courtney pushed herself up from the kitchen floor at the sound of boots on the veranda. As she heard a hat slap a leg, she tossed the knife onto the counter just before Matt came through the door. He made his usual production out of having to take off his boots before he came in. Courtney smiled and turned toward the stove, purposely letting the hem of her skirt brush away the small pile of wood shavings from around the leg of Matt's chair.

"You don't have to take your boots off if it's such a big deal."

"No big deal," he muttered.

She slid the knife back into the drawer. "Supper's almost ready."

Matt crossed the room, pulled out his chair and dropped into it. "Peter not back yet?" he asked as he eyed the two table settings.

Courtney carried bowls to the table. "He decided to stay in town one more night."

Matt nodded as he filled his plate. Supper was a subdued affair without Travis or Peter. Matt had never been much for conversation. But his verbal skills weren't what Courtney loved about him. When he finished eating, Courtney removed his empty plate and served him a piece of peach pie.

He gave her a nod as he chewed, a subtle indication meant to communicate his appreciation. When he finished, he pushed back his plate, grabbed a toothpick and began to lean back in his chair.

"You'll break that," Courtney warned.

He just narrowed his eyes, and Courtney could image what he was thinking. She fought back a smile as the sound of rending wood split the air. Matt's feet and arms flailed out. One foot cracked solidly on the underside of the table as he toppled over sideways, broken chair and all.

Her expression a mask of concern, Courtney dropped beside Matt's sprawled form. Her skirts pooled out around her as she pressed one hand on his chest and held him on the ground. "Are you okay?"

He growled something as he tried to rise.

She planted both hands firmly on his chest. "I think it's time you started listening to me and what I say. I told you not to lean on that chair."

"I don't need someone bossing me around. I don't have to do everything you say," Matt growled, but there was a spark of amusement in his eyes.

Courtney pushed the fragments of the chair aside and swung her leg over, effectively straddling him. She plopped herself down in his lap and bent close. She extended her arms, stretching out until her fingers were entwined with his, then pushed his arms up over his head. Her breasts rubbed suggestively over his heaving chest.

She lowered her mouth within inches of his lips.

"Kiss me, Matthew Ward," she whispered.

There was a glimmer of desire in his dark eyes, but he shook his head.

She stretched out full-length on top of him, molding her body against his, rubbing against his chest and hard-muscled thighs. "Kiss me."

She released his hands. While she stared into his eyes, she began to unbutton his shirt.

"Hold me," she whispered.

His breath feathered across her mouth. Slowly his arms came around her back, and then moved lower.

"Let me feel how much you want me," she said raggedly as her body shivered with the response that she had hoped to elicit from his. His eyes glittered. With a quick movement he flipped her over onto her back and pressed against her. Her body reacted with a flush of heat and moisture.

His fingers fumbled with the buttons of her blouse until he cursed, lowered his head to her breast and found her through the fabric, drawing her nipple to a taut peak with his mouth while his hands urgently bunched her skirt higher around her hips.

Matt drew in a ragged breath as need surged more urgently through him. She was naked under all that cloth, her thighs smooth, her legs spread, her body arching to rub suggestively against the hard evidence of his desire. He watched as she tossed her head back, eyes closed, lips parted, her breath coming in sharp little inhalations. He pulled the pins from her hair and let the silky strands fall through his fingers.

"Love me, Matt," she whispered breathlessly.

He smiled down at her. "Damn women always trying to tell me what to do."

"You didn't mind last night," she breathed as she pulled his head down.

His lips met hers. The small leather pouch he wore around his neck fell forward and brushed against her skin. She sensed the hum of the stone but the pounding in her head wasn't the echo of Indian drums. It was the heavy beating of her heart. A boy's wish may have transported her back through time, but it was this man's love that bound her here for eternity.

The Wards may have needed a woman's touch but they had won a woman's heart. And in return, Courtney had received more than she ever could have wished for. She'd found a love that could endure beyond the limits of time.

# THE TARNISHED LADY
## SANDRA HILL

**Sandra Hill's romances are "delicious, witty, and funny!"**
          *—Romantic Times*

Banished from polite society for bearing a child out of wedlock, Lady Eadyth of Hawks' Lair spends her days hidden under a voluminous veil, tending her bees. But when her son's detested father threatens to reveal the boy's true paternity and seize her beloved lands, Lady Eadyth seeks a husband who will claim the child as his own.

Notorious for loving—and leaving—the most beautiful damsels in the land, Eirik of Ravenshire is England's most virile bachelor. Yet when a mysterious beekeeper offers him a vow of chaste matrimony in exchange for revenge against his most hated enemy, Eirik can't refuse. But the lucky knight's plans go awry when he succumbs to the sweet sting of the tarnished lady's love.

_3834-X                                   $5.50 US/$7.50 CAN